BARELY A CRIME

BARELY A CRIME

A Novel by

Robert Ovies

IGNATIUS PRESS   SAN FRANCISCO

Cover images from iStockphoto

Cover design by John Herreid

© 2016 by Ignatius Press, San Francisco
All rights reserved
ISBN 978-1-62164-089-9
Library of Congress Control Number 2015939071
Printed in the United States of America ∞

PROLOGUE

Kieran Lynch was born in a pine bed in his parents' lower flat in West Belfast, Ireland, on a night that was, for the middle of summer, unusually cold.

His mother, Maureen, cried and laughed out loud when she saw her new son wailing in the Widow Shea's fat hands, free of his umbilical cord and his purple coloring, his hair already as black as pitch.

Kieran's father, who was called Thomas rather than Tom and who had stayed downstairs in the kitchen with Kieran's four-year-old sister, Colleen, let out a whoop at the sound of his firstborn son crying and his wife laughing. With little Colleen bouncing in his arms, he danced like the sailor he had been for more than ten of his forty-seven years, wheeling in tight little circles toward the stairs leading to the upstairs bedroom, where he knew that everything was surely better than fine.

A sharp knock at the back door interrupted his dance and his momentum; a knock at the back door meant friends or relatives, for sure.

Thomas hesitated, undecided about the moment's highest priority.

A second knock sounded as the Widow Shea rushed red-faced and beaming down the stairs and fairly shouted to the proud new father, "Well, for heaven's sake, you'd better come see your own handsome son, man!" She rushed to gather up Colleen as Thomas' wife called his name from upstairs and laughed out loud again, bright as a bell.

But the knock sounded again, this time more insistent than before, so Thomas exclaimed, "God's breath. This'd better be good!" and took four quick steps to open the door.

He recognized Brandy Shane instantly, although it had been nearly twelve years since he had seen him, and although he had heard that Brandy had died in prison, where he had been sentenced on the strength of Thomas' testimony for what they both thought at the time would be the rest of Brandy's natural life. The charge had been murder, after all, and the dead were Alice Faye Shanahan and her daughter, Faith. While Alice Faye was notorious and a criminal herself, as both Brandy and Thomas had been at the time, poor little Faith had barely turned five.

Thomas stopped smiling, but he did not move, even after Brandy's first shot passed through his stomach. With the second shot he staggered backward, aware of the widow's screaming in the background and even more desperately aware, in the flash of that single moment, that he had not yet held his only son.

He fell with the third shot, which passed through his heart.

Kieran Lynch had been less than four minutes old when his father died without holding him. Kieran spent much of his next twenty-two years trying to get those four minutes back.

I

It was one of the world's great feelings: lips as full and soft as bath towels breathing warm whispers against Kieran's ear.

Brenna Stack's long arms were wrapped around his shoulders from behind his chair as she pressed her cheek to the side of his head and used the nickname that only she used, "I know we can't forget what they say, Kiero, about things that sound too good to be true."

He moved his fingers lazily through the easy, red curls spilling past his shoulder and onto his chest. He nodded, but just slightly, as though not wanting to brush her lips away. "Right," he said. "They usually are."

"Mmm hmmm," Brenna murmured. Then, with a sudden smile brightening her voice, she added, "But the key word is 'usually'. Which means, you see, sometimes they're not."

Kieran raised his eyebrows and turned his head.

Her green eyes were smiling too. She said, "So I'm thinking this is going to be one of those times that it's not too good to be true. I can just feel it, honest to God."

"It could be."

"Wouldn't that be a treat for a rainy day?"

"We'll see," Kieran said. "I'm sure gonna see."

He was a lean and broad-shouldered twenty-two-year-old with deep black hair that he let Brenna cut short and then left largely untended. His eyebrows were set low on his brow, as if with a weight of their own, over darkly quiet eyes. He wore faded blue jeans, a gray T-shirt and black boots. Kieran Lynch was a young man who had stopped caring about clothes, and about a lot of other things, a long time ago.

He sat facing their kitchen window at the only table he and Brenna owned—a metal-legged card table with a permanently wrinkled green and white plastic tablecloth, which was pressed tightly to the wall of their small East Belfast upper flat, not far from Trident Port.

Softly, almost absentmindedly, he laid his left hand on Brenna's arm as his attention focused again on the open letter that lay in the middle of the green and white checks of their tablecloth. Its top fold was raised and facing him, as though it was studying him in return.

He could read the day's date and the words:

Mr. Lynch: I invite you to join me for what will be something less than one-quarter hour of light work fifteen nights from tonight, on March 18. I have also issued this invitation to your friend Mr. Crawl Connell. My guarantee to you both is that there will be no robbery, there will be no weapons involved, no one will be harmed in any way, your risk will be largely nonexistent.

He took another swig of his Guinness stout and opened the second fold with the little finger of his bottle hand.

The letter continued:

Your payment and your friend's payment upon completion of this single, perfectly planned operation will be fifty thousand pounds, which I will pay each of you in either cash or as a deposit in the account of your choice anywhere in the world one hour prior to your undertaking the task at hand.

If you are interested, we will meet at Mrs. Dougherty's Dining Room, with which you and Mr. Connell are both familiar, at nine o'clock tonight, Monday. You will both come alone, as will I. Mrs. Dougherty will leave as soon as I arrive, at five minutes to nine. She will stay away until ten o'clock in the evening, which gives me more than enough time to pay you handsomely for the time spent in our initial meeting, and for letting me detail my simple request.

Even the name was typed, not signed, by someone calling himself "Mr. Day".

Kieran released the fold of the letter. His hand drifted from Brenna's arm and his mind drifted again to the serious discomfort of being promised too much money for an unspecified job that would, regardless of promises about risk, weapons or safety, have him back in a place he had been working hard to avoid: the breaking of the law. Worse, the proposal had been hand delivered by a messenger he hadn't seen and so had no chance of questioning. And it had been delivered late in the day, practically too late for any clear thinking.

Brenna watched Kieran reread the letter, then kissed him lightly on the ear and eased upright. She stood five feet eight inches tall, four inches shorter than Kieran. Like him, she was athletically trim. Waves of scarlet hair hung over her faded yellow shirt, which was open to the third button. Her skin was milk white and her features sharp, although gently so. Her lips, deep red even without lipstick, offered a thoughtful smile. "Oh, that's a lovely, fat pile of money," she said, drifting into the chair on Kieran's right.

Kieran nudged the fold of the letter one more time, as if testing to make sure it wasn't alive. "It is if he's not just a deranged grocer or something. Somebody who figures he knows how to steal the Queen's jewels."

"He doesn't sound like a grocer," Brenna said. She leaned forward and picked up the letter in her right hand. She snapped it once, hard, to hold it open. "Grocers write on shopping bags or order slips. This is expensive paper, Kiero. This is an intelligent man, who's obviously put a lot of time and thought into something important to him."

"Could be a trap, like Crawl says."

"Crawl sees traps every day or two, from what I remember." She didn't take her eyes off the letter. "Very expensive person here," she mused, "this Mr. Day or whoever he is."

Kieran stared out the window on the opposite side of the table with narrowed eyes. He didn't respond to Brenna. He didn't move. He didn't blink.

Brenna noticed and grew silent. Kieran wore that far-away look she had seen in him more often than she liked. After more than a minute passed, she glanced at her black Timex and said quietly, "Pretty soon now, you should go."

She waited another fifteen seconds, then added, "When you come back, if it looks good, you can pick up something to party on. How's that sound?"

"Yeah," Kieran said softly. But he didn't turn to face her. And he didn't say anything more. He simply stared through a light-falling rain at the flat, four- and five-story buildings squeezed shoulder-to-shoulder on the opposite side of Glenreed Street.

All of them were old, with brightly colored trim and shutters; greens and reds and bright blues. All had struggling little shops or markets or pubs on the first floor and little flats for struggling people on the second, third and fourth floors. All had noise all day, every day, and well into every night. Most had their windows lighting up as the sun set behind Lagan Bridge by the docks and the evening clouds grew thick and aggressive.

A horn sounded in the street below and an angry man's voice shouted what sounded like, but wasn't, "The same sewing trailer you went!"

Kieran recognized the sadness that sometimes came back to him when it rained as it was raining then, especially when it was cold. It spread from the inside out and seemed to touch everything and everybody. He hated its coming, although he knew it would pass. It came without face or body or voice, yet he invariably found himself thinking of it as "the ghost." It wasn't just a feeling to him anymore; it was the ghost that rose up from places too deep to fathom, unidentified and unwanted, to cover his world like a shade. If he ever did see the ghost, he had long ago decided, it would have black hair matted down by a cold rain just like this one.

He flicked a glance at Brenna, winked without smiling, then looked out the window again. The wink had not been playful, more a gesture saying, bear with me, girl, but don't talk to me right now. Just give me these last few minutes to think, then I'll join you again and be just fine.

And so she did. But she was no longer smiling.

The flat they shared was rented on their combined hit-and-miss paychecks. It had just three rooms, the living and kitchen areas combined into one. The only art on the tan walls was an old movie poster taped above a gray couch: *Odd Man Out*, starring James Mason. The rug was an oriental imitation with no padding, four feet by five feet and worn badly. An eighteen-inch television set was the one costly thing they had purchased since they had moved into the hard streets of Belfast's east side three months earlier, in December, just two days before Christmas.

In an upstairs window across the street, Kieran saw a light go on between green shutters and a fat man in a brown shirt raise his shade, squint out at the rain and gathered darkness, and lower it again.

He circled his left fist around his bottle of stout. "Here's what happens," he said quietly, reaching for Brenna's arm with his right hand. "I go. And I listen to the man. Me and Crawl both. We listen is all."

"That's all you can do. Just listen." Brenna reached for his hand. "And keep an open mind."

10

"We listen," Kieran said again. "Then I come back and we talk over what the deal is. You and me."

"And we take it from there?"

"And we take it from there."

"Together?"

"I'll tell you the whole thing."

"You know I don't want you getting hurt or thrown in jail, for God's sake," she said. "I love you. But I just know how much it would mean to us, all that money."

"I know."

"And I do think this thing, whatever it is, is going to turn out to be golden. I just have that feeling."

"But he's not just going to ask me to poke through some old lady's dressers for him."

She grinned. "Maybe he is. Maybe she's the one with the money."

Kieran grinned lightly and rose from his chair. He started across the room toward his black leather jacket, which was thrown over the back of their couch, against the poster of *Odd Man Out*. "I'll find out why he wants us, too, me and Crawl. He doesn't know us."

"You can't know that." Brenna rose and walked toward him. "How do you know that?"

"He's going to pay us just to meet him, he says. Not just pay us, but pay us 'handsomely'. How's that for a word? Pay us 'handsomely'. If he knew us, he'd know he didn't have to pay us handsomely or any other way just to sit down and talk to us. Hell, he buys us a few stouts, we listen all night."

"He's heard good things about you. He knows about some things you're able to do. From the Force, probably."

"It's not smart to waste money on us just for a meeting, though. If he's not smart about that, maybe he's not smart about other things."

"He wants to make sure you come, is all. Maybe he has a plane to catch. See, you don't think like rich people think. To him, that doesn't mean anything."

"Well, we'll see, won't we?"

Brenna gripped the lapels of his coat and eased him close. She kissed him lightly. Her smile was back. "I swear to God," she said. Taking his cheeks in her hands, she lowered his face closer to her own and kissed him very softly, once on each eye. "If somebody put five gold bars in your pocket, you'd say, 'Oh, now I never have to worry again.' But then you'd do all that quiet thinking you do, and you'd say, 'Oh, but now if I fall off a bridge, I'll drown for sure.'"

Crawl Connell emptied his pint of Guinness, his third, and resumed his watch.

The noise in the Long Neck Pub was picking up, the music above all, a recording with a single fiddle under a man and a woman singing "The Baron of Brackley". Monday's crowd was not a big one, and his table was nestled against the front window with a clear view across Tanner Street to Mrs. Dougherty's Dining Room, where the meeting the letter talked about would take place in exactly twenty minutes, at nine o'clock.

That is, if Mr. Day, or whatever his real name was, was going to be on time.

Crawl had come early to sit by the window where he would be able to see the man go into Mrs. Dougherty's. See if he got dropped off and who was driving if he did. See if he was being followed by any friends. See how he dressed and carried himself and whether or not he looked over his shoulder. See if he looked like IRA or even old military, which was a slim chance, but possible. These were the possibilities on his mind when Kieran, the boyhood friend he still called his little brother, called him to ask if he had just gotten a letter dropped off by messenger, and then added, without waiting for an answer, "So what the hell you think is goin' on?"

"It could be IRA history coming back to haunt us," Crawl had said. "Could even be some ex–British military who joined them in the end. Settin' us up for payback, for things still unsettled, by makin' it sound too good for us to stay away." When Kieran scoffed and asked why they would care after all this time, Crawl let go of the idea with, "Not likely, but it could happen." Then he added, "Or maybe it's just some fool proposin' something that couldn't happen in a million years. We'll find out, but we'll watch our backs."

With fifty thousand pounds and promises too good to be true being tossed around, anything was possible.

He took another mouthful of warm stout and looked again at the light in Mrs. Dougherty's door, where the closed sign hung and the glass ran with the evening's light rain. He found himself remembering what it felt like to be trapped on a March night just like this one, trapped and afraid, hearing the terrible shouts of soldiers with his heart hammering in his chest and he just eleven years old, for God's sake. Hiding and soaking wet. Crawling his way under parked trucks as fast as the law could chase him, which was how he got his nickname, Crawl. Clutching so hard to the underbelly of a sixteen-wheeler, his hands went numb. Grasping the drive train with his legs so that the beam from the soldiers' torches skimmed under him back and forth. Hearing the soldiers cursing and yelling to one another, then shouting that the older members of the Ulster Volunteer Force had been taken, his father among them.

He blinked and took another long drink of his stout. Most memories, to Crawl, were hard things. But that one was the hardest of all, and it came back to him often.

"Nobody should have to die in prison," he had cried to his mother after it had happened. He had even complained to God, the last time he tried that connection, but even God couldn't fix it. His father was known to be a commander in the UVF, which had been formed in Belfast to take up arms against the IRA and other nationalists, and which continued across Northern Ireland as a vigilante group all the way into 2009, sixteen years after Crawl's father was convicted of armed robbery and assault with a deadly weapon, sentenced and sent to Maze Prison.

Sixteen days into his sentence, Crawl's father was stabbed and killed. The knife was twisted in his abdomen so that the blade would cut him badly; then the handle was broken off so that no one could pull out the blade. He died on the spot. Twenty days later, the man suspected of stabbing him was killed, his head nearly severed with piano wire.

The killings were reported in the press as "two minor incidents in the continuing shedding of Irish blood by Republican and loyalist militants". But his father's death was not a minor incident to Crawl, because he had been with him in the yard of the trucking company on the night when his father and the others had been caught and arrested, the night his father had enlisted Crawl's help as the group's lookout, even though he was just a boy.

Another drink from his pint, longer and deeper this time, nearly draining it.

Short-haired Molly Dolan slid a chair close to him and said with a smile and her hand on his arm, "Hey, Crawl, how about a kind word for Molly?"

He turned toward her with a light smile. "Later, darling," he said in a voice that was naturally melodic, a gift he had put to good use in what he chose to call his "art of profitable persuasion."

"I do like your sweater, though," he said. "I like red in a sweater, and I like you in a sweater. Or not in a sweater. Maybe just painted red."

Molly laughed.

"But," he said, turning to the window again, "I haven't time to enjoy the red life tonight, love. Some other time, now."

Molly dropped her gaze to the letter on the table in front of Crawl. She tilted her head but couldn't read it, so she shrugged, smiled again and said, "Right. Some other time." Then she leaned to squeeze his arm one more time, slid out of her chair and walked away, turning her head to study him.

Crawl was five feet eleven and wiry. In fact, he looked as though he could crawl as quickly as a snake if he had to, although he could no longer run, at least not at full speed and not without effort. A nationalist bomb had cut short both his right leg and his service in the Force; his leg by nearly an inch. He was left with such a pronounced limp that people who didn't know about his frantic escape from the trucking company wrongly assumed that the nickname "Crawl" had come about after his limp was delivered years later by the nationalist bomb.

His hair was dark brown and straight, nearly long enough to touch his shoulders. His nose was long and pointed, like his chin. Narrow, plotting eyes gave the impression, which was often accurate, that he was making plans no one else knew about. But his smile spread wide and showed itself easily and often. His reputation as a risk taker—first as a young volunteer in the Ulster Defence Association, where he began to learn about weaponry and the basics of military action, then as a member, with his father and brother, in the more violent Ulster Volunteer Force—had spread well into the neighborhoods. In the streets he now occupied, a dozen Molly Dolans in any three-block area would be quick on a rainy evening in March to approach the severe-looking twenty-seven-year-old at his place at the end of a bar, or in his chair pulled up to a window in the Long Neck Pub.

He had fatally shot only two men that he knew of, though, in all that time and with all that opportunity. Only the second bothered him in the least, and then, the bother was momentary. The man was a sad-eyed security guard uniform, who cried as he died. But everybody died, Crawl told himself. The crier only died sooner than he expected. Or sooner than his family expected. But the way time flew, what the hell difference did it make? If Crawl hadn't shot him, he might have gone through five years of hell dying with cancer in his throat or brain or something.

He drained his stout and slid the glass to the side. He was a man who dearly loved to drink, but this third pint in a half hour would be all for him tonight. Any more and he might start to dull an edge without realizing it.

That would be his worst case scenario for the night: the mysterious "Mr. Day" would turn out to be with some renegade or old nationalist soldier out to take revenge for something he had done to one of their friends while he was in the Force. Or that they thought he had done, even if he hadn't, he being out of the paramilitaries for so long now.

In fact, he had been largely, although not entirely, a law-abiding man since recovering from the bombing and leaving the UVF. He still broke-and-entered on a small scale, mostly alone in the few years since Kieran lost his taste for working with him, and always either in rich and vacant homes, petrol stations or little markets in far-out places. Nothing in or around Belfast. He thieved a little and conned a lot, had been pulled in and questioned by the law on four different occasions but never charged. Overall, he had worked legitimately for about five months of each year, taking odd jobs that involved talking fast and convincingly. He had been a car salesman, a door-to-door pest-control salesman and an insurance salesman, all with part-time rewards for part-time work. He had even worked as manager of a storefront salon offering a radio-frequency cure for arthritis, named Gonz-o-tron, which didn't last long and didn't make him much money because it didn't work.

Talk about people with sad eyes. Old, bent ladies and fat, middle-aged men would come in, twisted up from arthritis in their hands or someplace else. Then they would sit for forty-five minutes in thin-padded, straight-backed chairs waiting for radio waves to make their pain go away. Them thinking, "Is this working?" Crawl thinking, "How stupid can you be after all the time you've been around?"

He looked out the window, checking one more time to make sure that Day wasn't approaching their meeting place. Then he slid the letter closer, reviewing what he saw.

All type. Even his name on the envelope typed. Delivered by a kid who took off running before he could ask any questions, not mailed. Kid getting paid to do it that way. The man paid the kid, he paid for delivery, he paid for fancy paper. He sounded smart. The letter dated that same day, March 3. And he addressed Crawl as "Mr. Connell", which got his attention more than anything else. Not because it was cordial, but because it let him know he was already being worked on, just as he had worked on so many people over the last six or eight years to get them to part with their time, money or what little virginity there was left in Belfast.

In fact, Crawl couldn't remember anybody calling him Mister before. Not ever. Unless maybe phone-call salespeople trying to sell him crap he'd never be dumb enough to try to sell to anybody at all.

Jane Regan, the Jane they called Jellyroll, who had known Crawl for more than fifteen years, wandered up, smiling. She was red-nosed, red-faced, red-eyed, nearly fifty and nearly drunk.

"Mr. Crawl, my young hero," she sighed, rubbing a fat hand over his long hair, from the top of his head to his shoulder. "You have a hunted and lonely look tonight. But I can help."

She started to sit down, then stopped in mid-crouch to reach out suddenly and snatch away the letter with a fat hand. "Who is she?" she blurted out, laughing.

Crawl's right hand shot out, grabbed her thick wrist and twisted it hard into the table.

"Ow, God!" she squealed. She swung at him with her free fist, but the blow was weak and bounced off his shoulder.

Crawl held her there as he rose to his feet.

"Owww! Crawl!"

The bartender shouted, "Play nice, children! We'll have none o' that, Crawl."

Crawl slipped the letter from Jane's hand and released her wrist. "You mustn't ever do that, darlin'," he said without expression. Jane sniffed and rubbed her wrist. "You mustn't ever grab a man's personal mail. It's a highly dangerous thing to do." His voice was still quiet, but his eyes were not. "So go the hell away from me, now. I mean it."

Jane took a step backward. "You didn't have to do that," she whispered, glancing around to see how humiliated she had to feel.

Molly Dolan, the bartender and two men at the end of the bar were the only ones still bothering to watch. The rest of the sixteen patrons had gone back to their drinking and talking and humming along with the music, unconcerned in the dim light.

Jane waddled away to plead her case to a short man at the far end of the bar.

Crawl put the letter inside his jacket, in his shirt pocket, and leaned to the window, cupping his hand to block out the light.

The door of the restaurant was still shut. The shade was still drawn The crooked, red-lettered closed sign still hung at eye-level by a string.

If it isn't IRA or something like that, he thought, and the man really meant business, it would be some kind of corporate espionage Someone wanting to draw on what he and Kieran had learned as paramilitaries, although Kieran hadn't learned as much in his time with the Force as Crawl had. Kieran had a temper from hell, but deep down never liked violence; that was the way Crawl figured it. At least he didn't like violence when it got to the point of bloodshed. Crawl didn't mind because he understood Kieran. Others, like the older men in the Force, thought Kieran wasn't at home with violence. But just the opposite was true. Kieran was so at home with it, Crawl thought, that it scared the hell out of him. Kieran had things inside of him that scared him. Maybe hurting somebody would uncork a bottle inside, and he would pay hell trying to get it corked again.

Crawl hadn't seen Kieran much since the few times Kieran visited him after his leg got blown up. After Brenna moved in with Kieran, Crawl didn't see him at all.

This job didn't have any blood-letting, so Kieran would be fine with it, Crawl figured. From the way the letter sounded, all they would have to do is get in and take a few pictures of documents of some kind. That's the only thing that would make sense if what the letter said about no robbery and no weapons could be believed. Nothing would actually be taken out, but something would be copied; had to be that. Press a key into a mold and disappear, something like that. Copy directions, plans, corporate secrets.

His thinking time was just about over. It was ten minutes to nine. The man wanting secrets to be stolen would be there soon. Crawl leaned toward the window and looked up and down the street again. He realized his heart was beating faster and wondered why.

He looked more closely. No one in sight yet. Not Kieran. Not Day.

Unless that was Day, the tall man in the dark raincoat, up the street to the north, walking fast and straight as a lamppost, even in the rain, with an attaché case in his right hand. One arm barely swinging, the other, the one with the case, held tightly against his side.

He was still a full block away, but he was closing fast.

2

Crawl watched, giving the scene time to develop.

He noticed that the tall man didn't look around before he knocked and entered Mrs. Dougherty's place. He didn't look for friends of his own, and he didn't check to see if he was being watched.

Did that mean he was careless, or confident? Or could it mean he didn't care one way or the other?

Crawl looked for other activity in the area, anything that might be related to the man, near or far, up and down the street, but no one else seemed to have followed him. Cars and trucks went by, and people walked in the rain alone and in pairs to both his left and his right, but no one turned to look at the dining room.

The bartender asked if he wanted another pint. He told him no, not yet. The bartender asked if he was expecting somebody else. He said he was. He said there would be ten or twelve people, all of them wanting to get drunk tonight at the Long Neck. The bartender left him alone.

Kieran was coming up the street from Crawl's left.

Not good timing, though. As Kieran approached, Mrs. Dougherty came out, shutting the door behind her and looking to her right and her left. She paused to study Kieran, whom she had known for years in and around the neighborhood.

Kieran noticed her and turned away, but then he continued up the street with a normal stride.

He realized it's too late to hide, Crawl thought.

And it was. Mrs. Dougherty looked him over for several seconds before she turned and shuffled in the opposite direction without acknowledging him.

Crawl wondered if something important might have just happened. The first thing gone wrong.

He watched Kieran try the door, then knock. He saw the tall man open the door to let him in.

The man didn't smile or reach out to shake hands, which Crawl thought was good. Why pretend it was a reunion of old friends? But the man was dressed in a suit and tie, for God's sake. Nine o'clock at night, in a district like this, and he in a suit and tie. What did that say?

The closed sign swayed as the door closed hard behind Kieran.

Crawl's heart sped up again. He still didn't know what to think of it all.

He waited another five minutes to make sure no one else approached Mrs. Dougherty's, or posted themselves across the street, or drove by staring longer at her door than they should have. Then he swung slowly out of his chair and started for the door. The bartender yelled after him: Were his friends still coming? He shrugged and left the Long Neck to see what the tall man, who walked like a general and wore a suit and tie when he didn't have to, had in mind when he wrote the letter about Crawl and Kieran getting all that money for no risk, with nothing being stolen at all.

Mrs. Dougherty's Dining Room was no more than that: a single room.

Four lamps, two on each side of the room, stood like sentries along the walls, which were papered yellow with outlined flowers of pale green and orange, but just one of the lights had been turned on.

Kieran watched from a back table as the man who had written the letter opened the door for Crawl and said, "Mr. Connell, come in, sir," in a deep voice that definitely did not sound Irish.

Crawl nodded and slid past as the man stepped aside.

Kieran smirked. He wanted to ask Crawl how it felt to be called mister and sir at the same time, and by a man whose suit looked as if it cost him the price of a good car.

He waved as Crawl spotted him at the table farthest from the door, and said, "Hey." Then he dropped his hand, wondering why he bothered waving, and he smirked about that, too. What was he trying to do? Make sure Crawl didn't maybe look around and leave the place before he spotted the back table, with the whole place being no bigger than a minivan?

Crawl murmured, "I see you, little brother," and started across the room to join Kieran as the tall man in the dark suit closed and locked the front door, making the closed sign jiggle again.

Each of the room's six round dining tables had four chairs and a yellow plastic tablecloth. Each had a stand-up menu leaning against a white plastic vase with cloth flowers that were red, blue and yellow.

There was also music playing, a Celtic group singing from a radio in the kitchen. Kieran had assumed it was for distraction, just in case someone was upstairs listening. But he knew Mrs. Dougherty as well as she knew him, and taking the money and running would be the only thing in the old lady's mind. No one would be upstairs listening.

The so-called Mr. Day took a seat opposite Kieran and Crawl. He sat rigidly, with his forearms flat on the table and his hands joined.

Kieran studied him, then turned to Crawl and saw he was studying the man too, only taking longer to do it.

His attention went back to the man in the suit.

There was nothing friendly in the man's expression. Nothing nervous about him, either. He should be nervous, though, Kieran thought, with that much of his money at risk. He was older, probably over sixty-five, but healthy looking. His hair was mostly white and combed straight back without a part. Everything else about him was neat, too—like his pressed suit and polished shoes—so he probably took care of details. That was good.

He had sharp eyes. A hard expression. The most noticeable thing was a pale scar that ran jagged from his lip to his chin. Kieran wondered how a man could get that kind of scar. Not from a simple cut. More like a tear in a piece of cloth. A rip, with no more whiskers where the skin had torn.

Crawl broke the silence. "You can call me Crawl," he said. "I don't answer to Mr. Connell, tell you the truth. That was my father, and he died."

"Thank you. I will," the man said. "You can call me Mr. Day."

"I'll call you Mr. Daylight," Crawl said with the beginnings of a smile. "That name means a lot to me. My father's brother was called Mr. Daylight, and he was always a favorite. He slept till about noon every day, so they'd say, 'Wake Bryan up, it's daylight,' and the name stuck. Daylight. So, to you I give the honor." He nodded, smiled more broadly. "Mr. Daylight."

Kieran smiled too because he was watching the game begin.

Way back when Kieran was twelve or thirteen or so and Crawl and his older brother, Michael, moved in with Kieran and his mother after their own mother died, Crawl told Kieran that everything a man did was going to gain or lose him something with the next man. That was how he taught Kieran. Saying things like, "The game to see who ends up on top is always in play." Even when they were just little kids. Crawl called it "the game" even then.

"Even the smallest things," Crawl would say, the two of them hunched down on a curb or leaning against a brick and yellow plaster wall on Tenny Lane, smoking and watching life struggle by in dock worker's clothes. "Even the smallest things will leave you either closer to being on top of the next man or closer to being under his foot." And he would give an example or two: "If a man offers you a cup of tea, you tell him, 'I don't really like tea. I'll have a bottle of stout instead.' Or, if he offers you stout, the other way around. 'No stout for me,' you say. 'I'll have a cup of tea.' Or if the man wants to do a deal and the window's open, you say, 'I'd like you to close your window first.' Or, if it's closed, the other way around. You find something to make him give way, you see? Even small things count."

"But why?" Kieran asked him once. "What do I care if he opens the window or not?"

"It's not the window," Crawl told him, leaning close, as if they had secrets. "It's, you're the one makin' the rules. Don't you see? If they open the window instead of leaving it down, which is the way they wanted it to be or it wouldn't have been that way in the first place, then you've got them goin' in your direction. They've started giving you control. Don't you get it?"

Well, Kieran didn't get it, not for a long time. Then one day, he did.

It was one of the reasons he didn't really trust Crawl. He was still the closest thing to a brother Kieran would ever have, but to Crawl everything had strings attached, and they were usually hidden. Nothing was ever straight up with Crawl Connell.

And so Kieran watched, wondering. Would Day actually let Crawl call him a name Crawl just made up instead of saying the name the man wanted him to say, and the man being the one having all the money?

That would be worth an opened window and a cup of tea and a whole lot more.

But the tall man just smiled a thin smile, the top of his scar stretching slightly to the right, and said, "I don't answer to Daylight."

No apologies. No jokes. No follow-up.

Crawl returned the man's stare, then pulled the letter from his shirt pocket and dropped it, still folded, on the table. "I guess that's enough pleasantries," he said, smiling again, then letting the smile fade. "What are we here to talk about?"

Kieran shifted in his chair.

The man said, "You were referred to me by persons I trust." He spoke slowly, like a man with time to kill. "As I wrote in my letter, I am inviting you to join me in a single, specific operation for which you are well qualified and for which you will be well paid."

Kieran asked, "Who are these people you trust?"

Crawl added, "And what did they say that made us look like the well-qualified lads you're lookin' for?"

"I've decided that's not necessary information for you to have," the man said. "Neither is what I do for a living, or where I come from, or anything else about me. Neither are the specific what's, where's and why's of the operation. They're certainly not necessary for you yet. Certainly not here, tonight."

Kieran looked at Crawl. Who was setting the rules now?

Crawl leaned forward. "Well, see, we may differ on what's necessary information, Mr. Day. So can we start off being honest here? Because you're talking about things that don't really go together, like no risk and—"

"I said your risk will be largely nonexistent."

"Whatever. But no risk with all that money?"

"And no robbery?" Kieran added.

"And us with questions," Crawl said. "Here we are—and I'm not telling you anything you haven't thought out long and hard, I'm sure of that—but here we are walkin' in thinking: How do we know this Mr. Day isn't about to try and talk us into a scheme that's not thought out real well? Something that'll just end up with us staring into an illegal and very dangerous situation. How do we know he's smart enough to know what he's doing, in other words? What's he want us to do? Why'd he choose us? All kinds of questions. No surprise to you there. In fact, the only two things we know for certain, walking in that door, are: you're talking about throwing a lot of money at us, number one, and number two, whoever pointed you toward us did

23

not tell you Kieran and I are stupid. Which means, as much as we love the nice talk you're throwing around, we don't really think that 'Hey, Mr. Connell and Mr. Lynch, what I'm paying you for is none of your business' is a great answer to all the questions we have."

Kieran was watching for the man to blink, but he didn't do it. What he did was raise his attaché case to the table, snap it open and pull out two dark canvas packs, each about four by eight inches. He put the two packs side-by-side on the table, pulled out two letter-sized manila envelopes and placed them next to the packs. Then he closed his attaché case, put it back on the floor and laid his hands flat on the canvas packs.

"I am not throwing around nice talk, as you put it, Mr. Connell. That would be inadequate. In each of these two packs is five thousand pounds, cash. Small bills. These are yours this evening, if you care to do business with me."

Kieran shifted and sat back in his chair, glancing first at Crawl, then staring at the canvas packs. He was thinking about Brenna, how she would greet him if he came home with five thousand pounds.

Crawl was looking at the packs, too.

The man kept talking. "The envelopes contain detailed instructions for you both. There is nothing you have to know beyond what I tell you in these, and everything in them is clearly detailed."

Crawl reached for one of the canvas packs but the man kept his hands firmly in place on both of them.

"What I am doing," he said after Crawl eased back into his chair empty-handed, "is offering you each five thousand pounds before we leave this room, with the guarantee I will give you another forty-five thousand, either in cash or by electronic transfer, as my letter indicated, before we begin our operation. That willingness to pay up-front buys me some confidentiality, gentlemen."

Mister, sir and now gentlemen. Kieran almost smiled again.

"Five thousand here and now?" Crawl said. "And that's cash?"

"If we agree to work together."

"And another forty-five thousand each . . . ?"

"Before the operation."

"Before."

"Cash or transfer to your account, anywhere in the world."

Crawl rubbed his chin. "If we do this, we get the transfer early enough to settle in our accounts before the job is done. We get to check that. We don't have you tell us you're transferring it as we roll out the door with masks on our faces."

The man stared at Crawl. His expression didn't change. "Before we carry out the operation. Cash or transfer. I'm willing to go that far, which is a good distance out of the ordinary. You know it, I know it. It's that or we don't do business together."

Crawl hunched forward. "Ten minutes before the job or ten days before, what difference would it make to you? We could back out either way if that's what we wanted to do. What's to stop us?"

Kieran nodded. He leaned forward, too. "That's right," he said. "You must have thought about that. How do you know we won't just take this five thousand here and kiss you goodbye? Five thousand for doing nothing. Or how do you know, we wait for the whole fifty thousand, we won't just smash you on the head and go home?"

Crawl said with his eyes narrowed, "Like my friend says, you must've thought about that."

Again, there was no blinking, no raising of the man's voice. "I know how you got the name 'Crawl', Mr. Connell. You told me your father is dead, but I knew that too. I know who turned on him, who killed him in H-block of Maze Prison. And I know how the law got so close before your father noticed them."

Crawl's face paled. He eased his hand from the table and sat up straight, moving slowly, jaw set tight.

"I know why your mother died," the man continued, "and where and how she died. I know the date you and your brother went to live with Kieran and his mother and his sister, Colleen."

"Your point is what?" Kieran asked sharply.

Nothing about the man moved except his eyes, which shifted toward Kieran. "I also know about Willy Doyle," he said evenly. "I know about the gasoline and the fire."

Kieran's mouth opened. He didn't speak. He didn't move.

"And I know why you did it. I know about Colleen."

Kieran shot to his feet, tumbling his chair backward, his lips pulling in a furious scowl.

Crawl jumped, grabbed him by the arm. "If you know us so well, Mr. Day," he said loudly, "you know about this young man's temper, about places you'd better not go."

Kieran jerked his arm from Crawl's grasp and glared at Day.

"Easy." Crawl grabbed Kieran's shoulder and held tight. "Easy, little brother."

"Well, what the hell's all that about?" He was shouting at the man, not at Crawl.

"He's making a point," Crawl said evenly. He turned to the man, who hadn't moved. "Aren't you?" Then back to Kieran. "He's making a point, Kieran, and I'll tell you what it is."

He picked up Kieran's chair and pressed him back toward his seat.

"We said to him, 'What if we just take your money and tell you to shove it up your ass?' His point is: we shouldn't be thinking about doing that. The reason is, because he learned about us inside and out before he sent that letter, and we're right for the job, and if we say we'll take the job and then decide just to take the money and disappear, it won't work because he can find us again, and he will. That's what he's sayin'. Or he'll have someone else do it, more to the point. He's sayin' he knows what he's doing, so he's advising us not to try to steal his money."

"Say what you mean, mean what you say," Kieran said to the man with a hard stare. "But my family's not the subject here. I don't like that."

For the first time, the tall man leaned forward. "A fair request," he said calmly. "What I'm saying is this: if you do agree to help me in this few minutes of safe and simple work, you will each be fifty thousand pounds richer than you are right now. I swear that. But if you agree to help me and then betray me, I will spend a half-million pounds, if that's what it takes. But I will find you. And I will have your heads delivered to me in a box." He paused. "I said what I meant, I meant what I said."

Crawl nodded at Kieran. "See? That's the man's point."

The silence lasted nearly thirty seconds, Kieran and the man staring at one another, Crawl looking back and forth between the two.

"So," Crawl said, finally settling his gaze on the man and sounding relaxed again, "what are you going to tell us about the job here and now?"

"Only the information that's already in these packets and envelopes."

"And why is that? At least tell us why you won't spell it all out."

"Because you drink too much," the man said. He didn't hesitate and he didn't change his expression. "You both do. And when you're drunk, you talk too much. That's as honest as I can be."

The two men stared at the man with a scar and with so much information about them, and another silence settled in, this one lasting a full twenty seconds. From the kitchen, Connie Dover sang, "Laddie, lie near me." Outside a horn sounded, and the rain rapped harder against the front door and windows.

Kieran broke the silence. "So tell us what you're gonna tell us."

"You are each registered for a prepaid, two-week tour of Italy."

Kieran raised his eyebrows. "For what?"

"Two different, legitimate vacation tours. That's where you'll begin."

"The job's in Italy?"

"You, Mr. Lynch, leave in six days from Belfast. You, Mr. Connell, in seven days from Londonderry."

"That's quick," Crawl said.

Kieran asked, "Why Italy? And why so fast?"

"You each have active passports and no police records to complicate your travels. The calendar is important to me."

"And the job's in Italy?"

"You'll leave your tours to help me in this endeavor, then rejoin them fifty thousand pounds richer."

"And the job's in Italy?" Kieran repeated.

Crawl said, speaking quietly, "Italy has museums, and Italy has churches."

"Your respective tours both pass through Genoa, although on different days. Not long afterward, they pass through Milan on the same day."

Kieran stayed after it. "That's where we're doing the job then, in Genoa? Or is it Milan?" He paused, then added, "And why do I feel like I'm talking to a parked car?"

"When you are each in Genoa, on your different dates, you will offer your tour director an instructed amount as payment for a new service rendered. You will confide that you have, in whatever way you choose to phrase it, lost your heart to the love of your life. You will beg the tour director's understanding with a wink and money in his or her pocket, and you will instruct them to hold your place at the tour hotel in Milan, where both tours will spend the latter part of the same week. Your promise will be that you'll rejoin the tour there with another cash payment at that time for their understanding and cooperation. The individuals leading the tours have accepted payment for much more bizarre reasons in the past, and for less money than you'll be giving them. You'll have no problem."

Crawl tried again. "Those days between Genoa and Milan, that's when we do the job."

"You will be picked up in Genoa on your appointed day and time by a man in a white Fiat. He'll introduce himself as Mr. Day's friend Antonio."

"At a place you're not going to tell us about tonight." Crawl had leaned back in his chair. His smile had returned.

Kieran shook his head, then looked at Crawl and smiled. What the hell? Might as well enjoy it.

"Antonio will bring you to meet me."

"Milan's got a lot of museums," Crawl said, grinning and glancing back at Kieran.

He was in another game now, and Kieran knew it. He knew that the tall man knew it too, and watched him. He expected no direct response to Crawl's remarks and got what he expected.

"There are maps of Italy included in your tour packs."

"You look like a man with an eye for art," Crawl said, still with a smile.

"When we meet again, in Italy, we'll rehearse the operation for three days. We'll carry it out on the third night. You'll both be in Milan by sunrise of the following day ready to rejoin your individual tours, your hearts broken by your rudely shattered love lives but your spirits hopeful, nonetheless."

"Why not just fly straight home?" Crawl asked. "You said no risk. Nothing stolen."

"I'm thinking of your safety when I suggest you stay with the tours. Even minimal risk is worth covering your steps. For my part, it makes no difference. You'll never see me again in any event."

"And we're doing the job within a night's drive of Milan," Crawl said.

"Or train ride," Kieran said. "Or flight. How big is Italy?"

"At this point, we won't discuss geography. Instead, I propose to play a children's game with you."

Kieran looked at Crawl, eyebrows raised.

"It goes like this. I will give you sixty seconds to make up your minds, with no more questions. Then I'll count to three. If you have not picked up your five thousand pounds and your tour instructions by the time I say three, I'll take them with me and you'll never see or hear from me again. If you do take them before I say three, I will see you both in Italy in a very few days. I will have forty-five thousand pounds in small used, unmarked bills or be ready for a cash transfer in those amounts for each of you at that time. But this meeting is over."

He slid the packs and envelopes several inches closer to them and looked at his watch.

Kieran and Crawl looked at one another. They looked at the packs and the envelopes. They looked at one another again.

Kieran thought about Brenna and about the five thousand pounds, cash in hand.

But more than that, he thought about Italy and fifteen minutes of work and forty-five thousand pounds more.

After what seemed to Kieran like several minutes, the man said, "One."

Kieran looked at Crawl.

Crawl raised his shoulders in a slow shrug.

"Two."

Kieran nodded.

Crawl nodded back. A smile played again at the corners of his lips.

They reached for the packs and envelopes.

"Goodbye, gentlemen." The man rose to his full height and put on his coat. Retrieving his attaché case, he crossed the room and opened the door. "I will be walking to the north when I leave," he said to them in an even voice. "Do not follow me. And please don't disturb things for Mrs. Dougherty. That would not be kind."

He closed the door behind him.

Kieran and Crawl had the canvas packs opened and the money out by the time the closed sign in the door stopped quivering. There were five thousand pounds in each pack, all in small used bills, exactly as promised.

"Said what he meant," Crawl said with a grin, "meant what he said."

"Meant what he said," Kieran whispered.

Crawl held his grin. "I guess we're going to the land of Italy."

Kieran stared at the money for a long moment, then raised his gaze to meet Crawl's. "So. What have we got ourselves into?"

3

Kieran washed down a mouthful of cheese and sausage sandwich with a long drink of Guinness and said to Brenna and Crawl with narrowed eyes and a soft smile, "It seemed pretty clear, if there's no risk and no weapons and no possibility of anybody getting hurt, and if it's really about nothing getting stolen, why, hell, you think about it, it's barely a crime."

"Just take some pictures or make copies of something," Crawl said, nodding in agreement. "More like espionage."

A map of Italy was taped to the wall next to the kitchen window. It had circles around Genoa and Milan. Their green-and-white table-cloth was littered with biscuits, breads, cheeses, meats and six bottles of stout, two of them already empty, all bought with the money given to Kieran and Crawl. A dozen more bottles, still full, waited on the floor like soldiers on standby. The radio on the table near the couch was on. Classics in jazz, playing low. Outside, the night rain had stopped. It was 10:40.

"Barely a crime," Kieran said again, looking at Brenna.

Her chin rested on the lip of the just-opened bottle of stout she cradled with both hands. She gazed at Kieran, who had made the decision to do the job without talking it over with her, after all.

"So tell me what you're thinking, Bren," Kieran said. "I know you're thinking something, just staring at me. And I know it's not, 'Give the money back.'"

She raised her chin from the bottle and said in a lazy voice that was hard at the edges, "No, I'm glad for the money. I'm just thinking, I'll bet the job is in a museum or someplace like that. What do they have in Italy but museums and churches? And then I'm wondering, why take two ex-paramilitaries from Belfast all the way to Italy, and for something that takes three days of rehearsal, if the whole thing's so simple there's no risk?"

"You're the girl who likes to run with scissors," Kieran said, still with a smile. "Why the worry all of a sudden?"

"I'm not worried, Kiero," she said, leaning toward him. "I want it to be perfect maybe more than you do. But what I would have said if you'd have come back and we talked about it, like we agreed would happen, is, 'I was thinking it was something around here, and probably simple.' That's what I would have started with."

"I told you why we had to decide there."

"Had to," Crawl chimed in. "No way we could wait, Bren."

"Okay," Brenna said, nodding. "But I'll say it again. This man's taking you all the way to Italy. And you're thinking this is for something that's barely a crime. But I'm thinking ... Italy? And you need three days of rehearsing? He should have spelled out what's really going on, that's what I'm thinking. You deserve that. You deserve to know more than you know now. That's what your meeting should have been for."

"It'd all depend on what it is he's after," Crawl said. He took a quick drink of stout. "As far as risk goes, I mean."

"The Vatican museums would be out, for example," Kieran said. "The Vatican guards look stupid in their puffy uniforms and spears and bells or whatever, but they're backed up by the whole Italian army. Doesn't matter what he'd be after if he had something like that in mind."

Crawl agreed. "If it was the Vatican, he'd have to put more than fifty thousand on the table. Go in there for anything, it'd be worth a train load."

"But no big museum or famous art gallery or whatever is going to be no risk," Brenna said.

"Unless he's got it figured just right," Crawl said, raising his index finger. "That was the point I wanted to make. If you figure something out just right, your risk can go down to about nothing. You can do a lot with no risk, you get smart enough."

"And if you have enough money behind you," Kieran added.

"Well, he's got that," Crawl said. He slipped a small wedge of cheese into his mouth and pulled another drink from his nearly empty bottle.

"I'd never go into the Vatican with him, though," Kieran said. "Twenty million would be more like it, something like that was in the works."

Crawl grinned. "So you do have a price."

"What do you mean?"

"Twenty million, you said. At some point, we all have a price, don't we? Yours is twenty million for the Vatican. Or maybe something less than twenty million, what do you think?"

Kieran shrugged, tilting his head. Then he turned back to Brenna. "How about you, darlin'?" he asked. "Seriously. Twenty million might do it for me, even if it was the Vatican. What about you?"

Brenna leaned back in her chair, eyeing Crawl. Then she smiled and nodded. "Okay. Twenty million, I'd go into the Vatican. Is that what you want to hear?"

Crawl grinned and winked at Kieran. "Watch it, little brother," he said. "Lady's got expensive tastes."

Brenna laughed lightly and took another small piece of bread.

"I bet he has twenty million, though," Crawl said. "Could have twenty million connections, too. Some things depend more on connections than money."

"He bloody well knew about you two," Brenna said. "He had somebody asking questions."

"But we know some things about him, too," Crawl said.

"Like what?" Kieran asked. "Besides that he has a lot of money. And connections, or he wouldn't know all those things about us."

"What else?" Crawl asked, sitting up straight. "What else do we know about him?"

Kieran put down his sandwich. "Okay. I'd say he's German. He acts like a German. Click, click, everything in order; you know the way they are? He's that way. He isn't Irish, that's for sure."

"You think maybe he's Catholic, going to Italy to get something?" Brenna asked.

Crawl shrugged. "Could be. Maybe to copy something, like I said. But what nationality do you think he is? Where's he from? No, he's not Irish."

Kieran said, "And he's not Italian."

"Because?"

"No passion. Stone man. I'll stick with German."

Crawl pointed the neck of his bottle toward Kieran and said, "He's American."

Brenna tilted her head. "Why do you say that?"

"His accent, first of all. Like all the American movies. Maybe German blood, but he lives in the States. He's got that sound."

"That doesn't prove anything," Kieran said, shaking his head. His bottle was empty. He put the empty on the floor and reached for a fresh one. "Lots of people talk like him. It's all the American shows they watch."

"I know an American when I hear one," Crawl said. "More important than that, though. He was talking about you and Willy Doyle, and you lighting him up with petrol."

Brenna sat up like a shot. "Who's Willy Doyle?" she said. "And what the hell is this 'lighting him up with petrol'? Does that mean on fire? On purpose?"

"It was nothing," Kieran said. "It didn't even happen."

"Crawl knows about it, and the man from wherever-the-hell-he's-from knows about it, so it must be something. Why can't I know about it?"

"It's nothin'," Kieran said again. "So, no, you don't have to know about it." He looked sharply at Crawl. "You were making a point."

There was the hint of a fresh smile on Crawl's thin lips. He said, "I was saying, you noticed that the man said gasoline? He said something about the fire, but he used the word 'gasoline', not 'petrol'."

"He did," Kieran muttered. He nodded. "He said gasoline."

Brenna tried again. "Kiero, did you or did you not pour bloody petrol on a man named Willy and set him on bloody fire?"

"Put a sock in it, Bren," Kieran said softly, looking sullen. He took another bite of his sandwich and said, chewing, "We're trying to figure out important things here, and you're talking about nothin'. I already told you it's nothin', so don't keep talking about it." He paused briefly and added, "We can talk about it later. But it was nothin'."

"It's not nothin' if this stranger brings it up."

"Most important, though . . ." Crawl said, rapping his bottle twice, hard, on the table, "most important is, how did he know all that stuff about us? About you and me, Kieran? About my father and Maze Prison and your little sister, for God's sake. You don't talk about that, do you? Who knows about that stuff?"

"Hell, no, I don't talk about it," Kieran said. He took another drink, a long one.

"I don't, either," Crawl said. "Why would I ever talk about any of that to anybody?" He studied his bottle, looking at it as if it were a crystal ball. Then he said, "So. If he is from America, and somebody's told him about all that, then we pretty well know who must have told him, don't we?"

The two men were silent for several seconds, staring at one another. Brenna waited, holding her breath.

Kieran said softly, nodding to Crawl, "It must have been. Him or somebody else that he told, and they told Day."

Brenna asked, "Had to be who?"

Kieran continued, still staring at Crawl, "So what are you thinking?"

Brenna said it louder. "Had to be *who?*"

"Michael," Crawl told her. "It must have been Michael."

"Okay," she said, "thank you. Now who's Michael?"

"Probably braggin' about us, is all," Kieran said to Crawl. "Braggin' about his little brother back home in Northern Ireland."

"Somebody, please. Who is Michael?"

"Michael is Crawl's brother, Bren," Kieran said. "He's got an older brother."

Brenna beamed warmly and leaned to touch Crawl's arm. "Well, hell, Crawl, I didn't know you had a real brother. Oh, my goodness."

"Kieran's like a little brother to me," Crawl said, "but that's from our moving in with him and his mother and sister, Michael and me. But Michael's blood. He lived with Kieran, too, but he didn't stay long."

"Just a short time," Kieran said.

Crawl took another drink, emptying his bottle. Brenna reached down to get him another.

"He's older'n me by two-and-a-half years," Crawl said. "He married a tourist."

Kieran nodded. "Went to the U.S. with her. Blond-haired nurse, the lovely Sherri. Michael was a hard man, way deep in the Volunteer Force, but Sherri had a lot to offer, I guess. Got him out of there. He was only with us for a couple of months."

"Gone to California," Crawl said, "city called Oakland, by San Francisco." He raised his bottle as if for a toast. "Has a little boy of his own now, too. Roddy, named after our father. Michael drives a truck. Local delivery stuff. He wanted to drive national and see the country, but Sherri smacked him down on that one, I guess. He's just drivin' local, bein' a good boy."

Brenna asked, "Have you seen him since he went there?"

Kieran leaned forward. "Bren," he said, "we're not in a family tree discussion here, all right? The point we're talking about is, is Day American and did Michael tell him all that stuff about us? And why would he do that?"

"And what can he tell us about Day?" Crawl added. "That's the main thing. If it was him that told Day, which it almost has to be, what can he tell us about Day?" He suddenly looked at Kieran and asked, "Does your mother even know all of that? Not about Willy, does she? Or about what happened in Maze?"

"Hell, no," Kieran said. "And even if it was Michael, he was just braggin', is all."

"But this is good!" Brenna said. "You can just call him and ask him who he talked to. Unless he tells everybody he meets all about you two, he'll probably remember, don't you think? He might just say, 'Oh, yeah, that guy. His name isn't Day, though, it's ... whatever.'"

"I will," Crawl said. "It's the middle of the afternoon there now, though. He'll be busy deliverin' pink nightgowns to a dress shop or some damned thing, but I'll get to him later. He'll be straight with me."

Kieran nodded, thought about it, then took another bite of cheese. "Maybe Day is from right there," he said, "same part of California."

"But still," Brenna said, "why come all the way to Ireland to hire you for a B&E over in Italy? Why not just get somebody from America? Or Italy? Why come to Ireland?"

"But not to Ireland," Kieran said, "did he?" He paused, then sat up suddenly and added, "He didn't just come to Ireland, did he? He came to Northern Ireland! I think that could be important!"

Crawl was already grinning.

Kieran continued, now leaning forward and speaking quickly, "We're going into a country that's wall-to-wall Catholic, right? Catholic from the Pope on down. So Day comes to Northern Ireland to get two loyalist-connected ex-paramilitaries ... to do what? Maybe to do something that he knows will make a lot of Catholics get sweaty. Could that be it? Find some guys that won't mind going where he wants to go and taking whatever he wants to take and not get spun out by it."

Crawl was nodding now, as well as grinning, "Like you said, what have they got there but churches and museums?"

"A church," Kieran said, "or a museum, an art gallery, a monastery maybe ... or we go back to the Vatican again. What else is there?"

They had thought about it for just a few seconds when Brenna said, speaking very softly, "There's a person. There's a person, isn't there? There's the Pope."

They stared at her, letting that new entry sink in.

"Here's an original concept," she said. She inhaled deeply. "What if he rehearses both of you for what's just the set-up for something big, but not for where it's really going? What if he never pulls the curtain all the way back?"

Crawl said, "Are we talking now about ... what if he's after the Pope?"

"Bloody hell," Kieran muttered.

Brenna said, "Think about it. What would happen if two Northern Irish Protestant loyalists, both with histories in the Ulster Volunteer Force, one of them the son of a UVF commander who was convicted and did time and even got killed in Maze Prison, got caught blowing up the Sistine Chapel? Or the Pietà? Or yeah, maybe even the Pope. But it happened without them ever realizing what the endgame—which had actually been planned from day one—was really going to be? And then, after everything's over, nobody in the world could prove there ever was a Mister Whoever involved at all?"

4

It was 3:45 P.M. Immaculate Conception High School, located on the northern edge of Santa Fe, New Mexico, was being dismissed for the day.

Formed by the Blessed Sacrament Sisters in 1931 as a coeducational mission school on the poverty-riddled northern ridge of the then-obscure city, the academy underwent dramatic changes beginning in the post-World War II years. The changes were driven not only by the increased wealth of the area but by the movement of that wealth into the most scenic part, the northern ridge, where the foothills that eventually rose beyond the Pecos Wilderness and into the full-blown majesty of the Sangre de Cristo Mountains achieved their first tenuous steps.

The ridge's changing demographics led to an increased demand among the wealthier citizens of the area for excellence in education, which led to a sharp increase in the size and the number of financial gifts bestowed on the academy by grateful parents and other patrons. Significant upgrades in the academy became not only possible but mandatory.

By the late 1990s, the school was divided into two premier college-prep institutions: Sacred Heart High School for boys and Immaculate Conception High School for girls.

On this day, as on many days, one of its brighter students, a petite junior named Marie Groves, was feeling less than impressed.

Marie stood on the school porch near the student's court. She was thin and just five feet four. She kept her black hair short and brushed flat, making no attempt to appear taller than she was. With the exception of her eyes, which were so alive they dominated her pale, heart-shaped face, Marie appeared to be even younger than her sixteen years. Her large, dark eyes, however, held a settled air of intelligence and wisdom, as if they had already visited places the rest of Marie's body had yet to know.

On this March afternoon, she was tired of the long school year, tired of her teachers and tired of being the only sixteen-year-old at Immaculate Conception without a driver's license, let alone a car of her own. She was especially tired of the suffocating regimen of being driven back and forth from school to the fiercely restricted environment of her home in the Pecos Wilderness by her sixty-eight-year-old aunt and legal guardian, Mrs. Leah Ozar, who was even now rolling her whiter-than-white Lexus sedan into the parking lot.

Marie had little doubt that the reason Aunt Leah rushed to whisk her away from school each day, as soon after the bell rang as possible, was so that Marie wouldn't be tempted, in that short free moment between her classes and her long ride home, to take drugs, pipe-bomb the principal's office, or lose her virginity in the bushes with one of the boys from Sacred Heart who came to visit the all-girl school every afternoon.

Some days it was just harder to be pulled back home than others. Some days the girl's highly regimented aunt seemed so intrusive and domineering that evasion, however momentary, seemed to be the only way she could assert herself.

There were eighty yards of lawn between the parking lot and the porch where Marie waited in her mandatory plaid skirt and white blouse, with her black backpack hanging from her right shoulder and her fourteen-by-seventeen rag paper drawing pad tucked under her left arm.

Aunt Leah got out of the car and waved. Marie drifted backward, pretending not to notice. Nearly two hundred girls and forty boys peppered the school lawn and granite-block porch, so it was easy for her to delay her kidnapping, if even for just a few minutes, by seeming distracted.

Aunt Leah started across the grass, walking gingerly on her tender right knee, her head held high, her flowing dress as white as her car. An ornate, three-inch cross of gnarled gold wire swayed on her ample chest, as it always swayed on her ample chest—winter, spring, summer or fall—letting everyone see that she, perhaps even more than anyone else in the city of Santa Fe, held her faith in proper perspective.

Through the laughter and shouts and commotion, Marie heard her aunt call her name. Some of the other kids turned to look. Marie saw Theresa Wiles and Sean Taube laugh knowingly as she drifted toward a group of students gathered to the right of the smoked-glass doors of the school.

Marie's Uncle John, Leah's brother, occasionally seemed to show that he cared. But these moments fell far short of the love Marie had experienced from her parents. Whatever Uncle John or Aunt Leah did for her never quite seemed like real love, so she found herself carrying a seed of sadness. But at least her Uncle John filled the distance between them with some warmth. Aunt Leah filled the distance with more distance, it seemed. With a call to order. With insistences that the rest of the world be as restricted, and as restrictive, as she was herself.

Determined to delay the inevitable, and being simply hungry for new company, however short-lived, Marie wandered over to one of the boys from Sacred Heart, one she had seen before but not met, one who was taller than Marie by a foot, and blond. She smiled and said, "Hey."

"Hey."

"You're from Sacred Heart, I guess."

"Yeah. My name's Terry Kohl." He extended his hand.

Marie squeezed rather than shook it. "I'm Marie Groves."

On the lawn, Aunt Leah paused, as though sensing danger from sixty yards away.

Terry smiled. "I've seen you out here."

"I've seen you too. You're a friend of Diane Brooks."

"I know her, yeah. She goes out with a buddy of mine, over there." He gestured toward a group of students gathered just beyond the wall of the porch, four boys and four girls, all of them listening intently to a very thin girl with red hair who waved her hands in the air as she spoke. He said, "You know Dave MacInnes?"

Marie put up her hand to shade her eyes from the afternoon sun. "Yeah, I do. I know Diane kind of likes him."

"You dating anybody?" Terry asked.

"No, but I live a long way from here," Marie said, nodding her head toward the north. "Up in the wilderness, in the mountains. It's hard for me to go out with friends."

"Is that right?"

Aunt Leah called Marie's name again, now from just thirty yards away. This time she dragged it out so it wasn't so much a name anymore, but rather just a sound, like something from a tall bird. "Mrieeeee!"

39

Terry looked to see the source of the sound.

Marie didn't.

He said, "Is that your mom?"

"My aunt."

He watched the woman in white and waited, expecting more.

"She's okay," Marie said. "She's wound pretty tight, though."

"She comes and takes you out of here every day?"

"I live with her."

"With your aunt?"

"Her and my uncle. Her brother, not her husband."

He studied Aunt Leah again for nearly five seconds. "And they won't let you drive?"

"I don't have my license yet, but I will soon."

Looking back at Marie, he tilted his head. "Your folks around?"

"Died. When I was a kid."

"I'm sorry. How'd it happen?"

From twenty yards away: "Mrieeeee. I think we should be going now."

"Car accident. My uncle and I survived, they didn't. He was driving. I live with him now, him and her."

"How old were you?"

"Seven. I remember it. I have a scar from it over my knee. My uncle got one, too, on his face, so we both remember it, every day."

"Wow," Terry whispered. Quickly, eyeing the approaching aunt, he withdrew his phone from his pocket and asked, "Marie, right? Can I call you? What's your number?"

"I don't have a phone of my own, but I can give you my home number."

By the time Terry had typed the last digit, Leah was climbing the stairs to the porch. "Marie, it's really time to be going."

"I'm going to hug you," Marie whispered to Terry with a sudden sparkle in her eyes. "Follow what I say, okay?"

As Leah closed in on them, Marie said to Terry, "I'll see you tomorrow, honey." Then she reached for his neck with her free arm to pull him close.

Terry did what she asked him to do, and did it grinning. His arms went around her waist. He pulled her closer and squeezed, pressing his cheek into hers. He even managed to sneak a peek at the aunt's reaction.

But Aunt Leah didn't look shocked at all. She didn't even raise a eyebrow.

Marie pulled away. "I'll skip lunch again tomorrow," she said, smiling at Terry again. "I'll see you then."

"Yeah," Terry said quietly but sounding very much in earnest. "I'll see you then."

Marie, visibly pleased with Terry's response, turned, adjusted the weight of her backpack and walked past her aunt with a jaunty, "Better head out, Aunt Leah."

Leah said, "All right, dear," but she didn't move. She stared at the boy, who was still grinning but looking a little uncertain about whether he should be.

She appeared to be neither angry nor amused. She took a single step toward the boy and said in a voice that was firm and low and even, "I'm sure you're intelligent enough to limit this kind of thing to the show she puts on for her Aunt Leah."

Then she turned to walk rigidly with her only niece down the steps and back across the long green lawn.

For most of the ride back to their home on Bruce Lake, Marie listened to her CDs and stared out the window. She didn't use the earphones, since there was nothing in the music to launch her aunt into a discussion of the destructive power of negative lyrics. Just some easy Spanish guitar, and then, as they climbed to higher elevations, one of the many "Best" collections of Ella Fitzgerald.

They entered the Pecos Wilderness northeast of Santa Fe and moved into the hills of aspens and pines, where the Pecos River broke fresh from the rock twenty miles to their east and the sharp young heights strained to become the southern altitudes of the Sangre de Cristo Mountains.

"I say this lovingly," Aunt Leah said, suddenly breaking their silence with her most soothing voice, "but I am curious, Marie. Do you enjoy yourself tremendously with that kind of game playing? Or is it just so-so for you? Something to amuse yourself while I walk with considerable pain all the way across the lawn, calling out to no response like a doddering fool?"

Marie continued staring out the window for a full twenty seconds. "I may be in love with Terry, Aunt Leah," she said. "Is that what you call game playing?"

Silence.

A small, spring-fed lake named for a long-dead trapper's mother, Lake Roselie, slid by on their right.

Marie said, "I didn't think about your knee."

More silence.

"I know it hurts you sometimes, but I didn't think of it," she admitted softly, finally turning to look at her aunt. "I'm sorry."

"Thank you, dear." A long minute passed before Leah added, "And I would just ask, dear, please don't despair of your lifestyle. I know what goes through your mind, but you have no idea what you'll find springing up for you. Can you believe that? That wonderful things are going to spring up for you?"

Marie squirmed to sit upright. They were about to circle the southern tip of Rancho Del Mundo, one of the largest areas of private property in the wilderness area and the fifteen-mile mark from their home. She said, "I know," softly, hoping that her aunt would accept it as the end of their conversation and be quiet again, at least for a few minutes, at least long enough to let Marie stare out the window and not be distracted.

The clearing that spread wide and deep into the hillside came into view. Deep greens in tall grass moved in the breeze like the surface of a lake. Seventy yards from the road, a cold mountain stream tumbled lightly from north to south along a concave ring of trees, tracing a dazzling line through the clearing. The late afternoon sun glowed in the stream and in the grass and in the arms of the pines that walled off the interior like a curtain.

It was a place that Marie felt connected to in an extraordinary way. It gave her the feeling that it was where she herself was living, even now, although hidden from her own sight. It was as if who or what she really was had been magically knitted to this very special place, to those trees, to that grass, to that stream.

It was the strangest and most beautiful sensation.

She had one other "soul-place", as she called it, very much like this one. A place in the pines next to the lake just south of her home.

In fact, the sense of connection that she experienced in these magical places was so striking that she had once seriously wondered, when she was barely a teenager, whether places outside herself could actually have been created, or at least infused with something special, through her own will—as though she might have whispered her own magic into them. Maybe without even knowing it, but so that something of herself, something about who she really was and what she really wanted to be, was invisibly embedded there, maybe for all time.

She felt equally connected to her mother and father. Even though their bodies had died, she felt them with her, still. And, in these special places, the bond that still linked her with her parents felt stronger than at any other time, in any other place. It felt so strong and so real that as she gazed out of Leah's car she said to her mother excitedly, without sound, "Look how the stream by the trees sparkles today, Mom. It's like the field is wearing a necklace!"

It was those moments that kept her fed inside, even while she lived in a home without deep affection and without humor. It was the certain ground to her that no one could take away. It held her mother and father closer to her than her own breath.

The forest closed over the last view of Rancho Del Mundo. They were nine miles from home.

Clearing the top of a steep hill, the road began a sweeping curve to their right.

Marie said quietly, as if to the window, "I'd really like to see some of the people at school more."

Leah glanced at her.

"Am I going to get my driver's license soon?" Marie turned back to her aunt. "I don't need a car of my own, but I'm old enough to be using this one."

"Trust me, dear. You will have an extraordinarily full life."

"I'm not talking about a rich, full life, Aunt Leah. I'm just talking about driving the car. I'm asking you seriously, is there something the matter with my driving the car?"

Leah flicked another glance in her direction but remained silent.

"It's the only way I'll be able to make friends. That doesn't mean anything to you, but it does to me."

They traveled another half mile in silence.

"See?" Marie said, not bothering to hide her frustration. "You say things, but you don't really talk with me about them. I ask you questions, and you're just suddenly, 'Okay, I'm not talking anymore.' But you don't even say that. When you don't say anything at all for five minutes, then I'm supposed to know: 'Hey, my aunt's not talking to me anymore.'"

"Don't, Marie, please," Leah said, turning to her niece, looking both hurt and sympathetic.

"Well, what's the matter with questions like, Am I going to get a license like a normal sixteen-year-old? Or even, Could I get a car, like my only two halfway close friends have? It doesn't have to be a new one; I don't care. Or a question like, Am I ever going to get my own cell phone? Or, Is Uncle John ever going to sell this house and buy another one within five hundred miles of another human being, for Pete's sake? He's got enough money."

"Your uncle is a remarkably caring man," Leah said. "And I don't know about cars right now. I think this year, when school is out, we'll be taking a trip. Your uncle has talked about taking us to see South America."

"South America?"

"It would be premature to say anything definite, but he has discussed it, yes."

"South America?"

"We'll all talk about it. But wouldn't that be the chance of a lifetime?"

"We won't talk about it, though, will we?" Marie unhooked her seat belt and brought her knees up to her chest. "It'll all be decided and I'll just be told, 'That's it.'" Her arms circled her legs. Her hand absentmindedly pulled at the top of her sock. She leaned against the door and turned toward the window again.

Leah reached to touch her arm. "Just know that we love you, dear. Know that we believe with all of our hearts that you have a remarkable future ahead of you." She paused, looking at Marie critically, then added, "And you really must wear your seat belt."

5

For more than ten years after Kieran's father was shot and killed, his mother, Maureen, dulled the knives of her loss with alcohol. As she disintegrated more deeply into the disease, she left her children hostage to it, as well.

After a decade of dying slowly and to no one's surprise more than her own, things changed. On a warm Saturday night in Belfast's New Evangel Fellowship Church, Maureen Lynch found herself accepting Jesus as her Lord and Savior and Alcoholics Anonymous as her highest discipline.

She tried her best to share her faith in her own home. She read things from the Bible to Kieran and his older sister, Colleen, saying "Jesus promised you" this or that, or "God says to us in the book of . . ." this or that. She told them about Adam and Eve and Moses and Isaiah. She said over and over that Jesus died for them, to save them from their sins. She hoped it helped them, but she knew it helped her, as she lived simply and raised Kieran and Colleen as best she could in a home with no husband for her or father for the children.

Through all those years, though, Kieran had been a withdrawn and deeply angry boy, as he and Colleen—who, for reasons no one in the family ever understood, grew up somewhat mentally deficient—became not only brother and sister to one another, but in some ways father and mother and best friends, as well. Kieran was the protector, Colleen the listener, consoler and worrier.

But their youth made them a poor father and mother, and the bitterness of losing their father, as well as losing so much of their mother, given her need to work and her need to drink, which was replaced by her need for church activities, made them troubled best friends.

Kieran's brooding and sudden flights into rage, which had already exploded into violent clashes both in the streets and at school, seemed relentless. He refused to relate to his mother but chose,

45

instead, the company of Crawl, whom his mother had taken into their home in the naïve hope that male companionship might help to settle her son.

Colleen, physically attractive but nearly always sad, lived out her loneliness in the conviction that her failed attempts to enter the high-energy world of girls her age but not of her mental limitations proved that she was an inadequate human being.

She once confided to Kieran, on the evening of her fifteenth birthday, when it was raining for the third straight day, that she could never quite decide what she should feel sorry about next. Four months later, when she was barely sixteen, Colleen died in the deep cold of an early winter. She died alone.

Driven by the confusion of too much loss, Kieran's rage escalated. For more than three years, with Crawl as his mentor, he drove himself into the hard edges of the UVF, as well as into a series of other illegal adventures. But in those years, in the brooding times of looking backward rather than forward, Kieran also came to recognize something critical. Colleen, who had cried to him more than once because she could never do anything right, really did do something right, because she never stopped trying. Even when Kieran no longer wanted her help, she kept trying. Even when she embarrassed herself and embarrassed him, as she tried to keep up with the other kids her own age, she kept trying. Even when she ran away from home and everything that had gone wrong, she was still trying. She died that way: still trying.

He found he wanted to tell her so badly that she had done well to keep trying, and to tell her he loved her for it, that on the fourth anniversary of her death, with just a slight encouragement from alcohol, he did it. He shouted it out loud, through tears, standing on top of the concrete railing of Lagan Bridge at two o'clock in the morning.

It was a fruitless shout about things hoped for and doubted, but it opened a door. On that night, Kieran made a commitment to his dead sister. He determined that if Colleen had never stopped trying, with all that she had to overcome, he would, for the first time in his life, steel himself to do the same. For her, and for whatever else turned up in his life that might be as good as her, he would really try.

He pulled back from his involvement with the Force, which Colleen had begged him to leave a dozen times, always with no effect. He pulled back from his entanglement with Crawl. No more plots, no more breaking and entering, no more loaded guns with their safeties off kept close for clouded reasons.

He spoke again with his mother, trying to heal the distance between them. He even tried, for the first time in his life, to anticipate what she needed and to make it happen for her. Before long, his anticipation deepened into affection, his affection deepened into love, and his love deepened into commitment. He would not fail his mother in the same way he had failed his sister, who, he had finally come to realize, had always been his best friend. It had never been Crawl. It had been Colleen, all along.

And now, it was Brenna.

Kieran's arm wrapped underneath her shoulder, holding her close as they lay together in the dark. Brenna's head was on his chest. It was 2:25 A.M., but even the late hour and too many stouts couldn't overcome the energy of Italy and fifty thousand pounds and all the serious questions that were so clear to them now and all the answers that were not.

Was it a simple act of corporate espionage, a copying of records, a bugging of offices, a threatening of enemies? Was it really without risk or weapons or the chance of anyone being hurt or caught or killed? Or was it more? Was it more than they wanted? Was it so much more that they would have to drop the money on the table and walk away, regardless of Day's threats?

"That's where Michael is key," Kieran had said to Crawl. "If we know who Day is, where he lives, what he does, then we say to him, if he talks about seeing our heads in a box again, 'That's no good anymore, because we know where to get at you, too. And our friends know.'"

At least it was leverage.

But Crawl had taken it even further. "That's right. We tell him, 'If anybody comes after us, you're going to die, and your wife and kids too, and that's a dead-bolt guarantee.' And it would be. Michael would kill him in a heartbeat, something happens to me."

Kieran shifted his weight and eased a little more onto his side.

Why think about that? Nothing was going to happen. No weapons, no risk, nothing stolen.

Michael had only a week to find the man's identity, but he would have a good part of the money Day had already given to Kieran and

Crawl, enough of it to find out what they wanted to know. Michael, after all, was a man who knew what he was doing.

"Tell me about that fellow and the petrol," Brenna whispered, bringing Kieran back to the moment.

She opened her eyes and turned, looking at Kieran, barely visible in the dark. When he didn't answer right away, she glanced at the clock, then turned to him again. "Would you tell me?"

He murmured, "God, girl. It was nothing."

"Using petrol on a man isn't nothing."

"I was barely a teenager. Not even that old, I don't think. I didn't start a fire."

Thirty seconds passed.

Very lightly: "But why would you try?"

"If I really tried, Bren, I would've done it." He squeezed her shoulder. "Let it go."

She was quiet for another minute. Then she turned and propped herself up on her elbow. "But Crawl knows."

"Crawl lived with me for years. In less time than that, you'll know a lot more about me than Crawl. You already do." He found her shoulder and pressed her back down, this time with her head resting on his pillow, very near.

Another thirty seconds passed.

"Tell me something new about yourself," she said. "Something I don't know."

"Secrets?"

"No." She thought about it, then added, "Well, secrets if you want. I just meant, something I don't know."

"Do you have secrets?" Kieran asked quietly.

"Of course I do, I guess. Nothing huge. But you go away with yours, you know? I talk with you, but sometimes you're not even there." She placed her hand over his heart. "I don't mind that you have secrets. I just wish they didn't hang on to you so. I just don't like to see you sad."

She traced circles on his chest with her fingernails, slowly.

Nearly five minutes passed in the dark.

"I have my name in forty-seven different places," Kieran whispered. "All within three kilometers of Newtownberry."

Brenna stirred. "What?"

"Where nobody can take them off."

48

"I must have just slid back to sleep. I just now dreamed you said something about your name being written all over Newtownberry. Tell me I was dreaming."

He chuckled. "You wanted to know a secret about me. It's true. And nobody can take them off."

She laughed brightly and softly. Her fingernails began to trace the same slow circles on his chest. "Tell me."

"I like building fences. I told you that."

"Yeah." She propped herself up again on her elbow.

Kieran propped himself up too. His left hand circled her waist. "Well, I realized something, with the fences. All those jobs I've been in and out of for the past few years, everything I did disappeared like smoke. I never realized that before. Hell, I never worked before, how could I know that kind of thing?"

"What kind of thing?"

"I told you I worked in a warehouse?"

"Yeah."

"Everything I stocked disappeared in two weeks. Same with stocking and cutting in the lumberyard. Think about it. Everything I did went away. Bam, bam, people buy it, it's gone. Cutting grass for the city, they called me a landscape technician, I told you that. You ever hear of a landscape technician?"

"And you cut grass, and it grows again."

"So there was never a trace left to say I did anything. Anywhere."

"I have that at the beauty salon. I do their hair, I do their nails ..."

"And it all comes undone."

"God, that's depressing." She suddenly laughed. "That's right, though."

"I did that conditioning coaching for Devlon-South's soccer team? One day they all walk off the field and it's gone."

"But fences are different," Brenna said. "I like that."

"There's something physical out there now that says I was there, you know? The whole idea of fences is, they last. Like monuments. Fences stay like monuments stay. I put up a good fence—those people have all kinds of money—good wood, nice-looking fence, a trellis on some, fancy post tops ..."

Brenna ran her hand along his cheek. "God, love," she said, laughing again, "don't tell me you're writing your name on people's backyard fences?"

49

"No, no," he said, shaking his head in the dark. He started to laugh. "But those tops are all decorator tops. They're monuments themselves. So I write, with a big felt pen ..."

Brenna rolled away, then back again, laughing so hard she shook the bed.

"I do." He began laughing too, not so much about the fences, but at how hard Brenna was laughing. "All the way across the base of the post tops before I seal them in place, I write a big K-I-E-R-A-N."

"Oh, God, I love it," Brenna said.

"You like that?"

She laughed again, then leaned to kiss him on the cheek. "I love it," she said. "I love you." Then she sank back down to the pillow.

He settled down too.

Her arm rested across his waist.

"See," she said, "secrets are fun. Or, they can be. Oh, I liked that."

"Yeah," he said.

They were silent again. But this time, the silence lasted only a few seconds.

"We have to be careful which ones we share, though," Kieran said.

She turned her face toward his. "What do you mean?"

"Some secrets don't bring you together, like names on fence tops."

Again, "What do you mean?"

Kieran took the time to choose his words carefully. "I know secrets about Crawl, for example. And he knows things about me. You tell some secrets to get things out of yourself, thinking it'll help. But once they're out, that kind of secret, you find it didn't help at all. It just drove you apart."

"I don't understand."

"When I went to see Crawl after they blew up his leg, we had a few drinks. A lot of drinks. And we talked. And the first thing you know, there they were, these secrets, right out in the open where they shouldn't have been. Something about him nobody else should have known."

"Can you tell me?"

He ran his hand through his hair. He didn't answer.

"I can carry it with you," she whispered. "Would you trust me with it?"

He still didn't answer.

"Is it that bad?"

"No," he said, rising from the pillow. "That's just it. It's not bad at all, that's the whole thing with it. I mean, it turned out bad, but it wasn't like he did anything on purpose."

It was Brenna's turn to be silent.

He sank back down to the pillow. "It was just kid stuff. All hell breaking loose everywhere, but he was just a kid."

"Please. Let me carry at least one thing with you. Especially if it wasn't bad."

It was another thirty seconds before Kieran said, speaking quietly, "It was when he was eleven years old. His father took him on a robbery when he was eleven, and it was a big job. Serious crime. UVF stuff. No place for him at all."

"Why would he do that?"

"Michael was supposed to be there, on watch for them, but he'd broken his thumb, so Crawl's dad had him fill in. Told him to watch for the police or any nationalists while him and some others in the Force broke into the place.... He fell asleep, Bren. He was eleven years old. It was the middle of the night, he fell asleep."

"And they came when he was asleep?"

"They took his dad and the others. They almost got him, too, but he was small enough to hide."

"What happened to his father?"

"Somebody killed him. Stabbed him a month later, in Maze Prison."

"Oh, no."

"There were different stories, but the big one was, Crawl's dad got them all caught because he was stupid enough to put his kid out there like that, so there was a fight and one of them killed him."

"That's awful."

"So that's Crawl: the man who got his dad killed. And now I know it, because he told me about it that night. So now, there's a part of Crawl that hates me. I know what he doesn't want anybody else to know. I know what he doesn't even want to know himself."

Brenna touched his face, softly. "I'm so sorry, Kiero."

"There are just some things other people can't know about you, Bren. Not because they'll hate you for it, but you'll start to hate them for knowing it."

She whispered, "I understand. I really do."

"Some things, you just can't make them right by talking about them."

"I'd never hate you, Kiero," she said.

He took a deep breath and pulled her closer. "I wouldn't like that," he said, barely above a whisper.

She said, "I'll never hate you."

"I hope not," he said.

Her lips brushed his cheek. "I could never hate you, Kiero."

Kieran was breathing deeply. Steady breaths in the dark.

Slowly, very gently, so she wouldn't wake him up, Brenna traced her fingertips through his hair, close beside her on the pillow. She remembered the day she told him that his hair was so black his grandparents must have been crows. She remembered it because it was the day they first met.

She had just left work at the salon on Colson Street. She saw him walking toward her in a lightly falling snow in front of the Cantonese restaurant with a neon sampan in the window. He stopped and smiled and said, "Excuse me." So she stopped, too. But he didn't say anything else, as if it were her turn.

Smiling at him so he would know she was willing to play, she asked, "And why do you say that? What have you done that I'd want to excuse you for?" But he still didn't answer, so she said, "Or are you just thinking about doing something that you might want me to excuse you for later on?"

It was in the Oriental restaurant, where they spent an hour and a half getting to know each other, that she said to him, "Your hair is so black, your grandparents must have been crows." Looking far away and serious, he said, "I wish they were."

She wanted to ask him what he meant by that, but she hesitated. He might have said he wanted to be able to fly away from everything, and she didn't want to hear that. Maybe everything meant everybody, including her. She changed the subject, but she still went back and forth about it in her own mind, wanting to ask him if he wished he could fly away, but not wanting to push it. Back and forth, the whole time they talked about other things.

She didn't like see-sawing inside herself, and had, in fact, worked hard to overcome it: part of her was the little girl wanting to run with scissors in her hand, just as Kieran had said, the other part was afraid she would put her eye out. That second part had never quite been able to escape something that her mother told her when she was very young. She said, "Brenna, God's told the world to find a way to break your heart. And the world has to do what God tells it."

What the hell kind of thing was that to tell a little girl?

She turned to lie on her back, resting her palms one on top of the other over her midsection.

Fifty thousand pounds, for God's sake. If that wasn't worth running with scissors, what was?

The money didn't mean big spending on rings or new cars, either. Crawl didn't have a clue what she was all about. If she had a price, it was about finally getting a chance to secure roots so deep nobody would be able to throw her away, throw her out into the street or something, as if she were junk.

She realized that her heart was racing.

She twisted again, settling on her left side, facing Kieran. Her hand reached into the dark and settled on his shoulder. Kieran, bad boy turned her boy. But still wanting, she suspected, at least during those moody times of his, to be able to fly away from them all.

Kieran said it right out loud, and so abruptly that it startled her: "He was older than me."

"Who was?" she replied, blinking in the dark.

"Willie Doyle. The guy I set on fire."

He turned toward her.

She said, "Oh." And then, "Have you been awake the whole time?"

"On and off maybe." He found her hand by his side and grasped it. "He was thirty-five, at least," he said. "He hurt my sister."

"How'd he hurt her?"

"He just hurt her. I was ten, eleven, somewhere in there; she was older. He worked pumping petrol over on Lynchway, by the bridge. I knocked him down from behind with a pipe and sprayed him with his own pump. Then I chased him with a lit cigarette lighter."

"Oh, my God."

"I guess I did set fire to him, Bren. Isn't that somethin'?"

"Oh, God, Kiero."

"Me, not even a teenager."

"What happened to him?"

53

"He didn't die or anything. I threw the lighter at him and his arm caught fire, then his whole jacket. It scared me more than it scared him, I think. I could have just as easy lit myself up."

"But what happened to him? What happened to you?"

"He got his jacket off and people rolled him around on the ground. I was runnin'. I didn't see it. He got burns on his face and hands, his arms. I don't know. That's what I heard later. They chased me, some of the guys that hung around the station did, but I got back home."

"What did he do to you after that? What did the police do?"

"Michael had too many friends for any of that. No police. No visitors in the night. Michael was deep into the Volunteer Force, and his friends were hard people. He had a lot of them, and everybody knew it. He told Willy he'd light him up himself, he ever sent anybody to mess with me. Crawl told me about that. Crawl thinks Michael is God. Willy ended up leavin' the city, as far as I knew. That's what they told me."

He released her hand.

"But I did torch him," he said. "And it scared me more than him; I really believe that. Only it wasn't just that I could have been lit up, too. I just said that. But seeing what you're capable of, seeing what you're willin' to do, how everything can just turn around, just from one minute to the next ... My God, that can be a fearsome thing, Bren."

She eased closer.

"I wasn't scared about his being dead, though," he said, now whispering. "I hated him. I guess I still do. But I'm glad I didn't have that to carry around all these years on top of everything else. Not torching a man to death."

Brenna gave him another full minute, just making sure that he didn't have more he wanted to say, not wanting the closeness to end. Then she kissed him twice very lightly, once under his collarbone, once on his shoulder, and then, settling her head on his outstretched arm, she closed her eyes.

Several minutes later, in the deep dark, she whispered, "Thank you."

"Michael?" Crawl said it furtively, cupping his hand over the phone, wanting Michael to pick up on the fact that something was wrong.

"Crawl. What's goin' on?"

"I've got somethin' comin' down on me, Michael. I need your help."

There was a long pause. He pictured Michael moving with his phone to another part of his house, giving himself some privacy.

He heard a shuffling, then Michael again. "Tell me."

"I need you to help me find out about a man. He's talking about handing somebody my head in a box if certain things don't happen, and I think you're the only one who can tell me who he is. I have to know that before I see him again."

"What do you owe him? And why would I know him?"

"I don't owe him. He made me and Kieran an offer to do a job. There's a lot of money involved. But the thing is, he knows things about us, about the truck yard and H-block, the UVF, all kinds of personal things nobody knows except you and me. And I never mention inside stuff to anybody, you know that. The job at the trucking company, are you kidding?"

A long pause. "So you think I'd be talking about those kinds of thing to people? What the hell is this, Crawl?"

"I'm not saying on purpose."

"Are you drunk?"

"I'm just telling you—no, I'm not drunk—there's a powerful man who's threatened me with decapitation, for God's sake, and who's serious about it, and he knows secret things about us. About Kieran. It's stuff he can't know. No one knows this stuff except us. He got the information from one of us because no one alive, Michael, knows these things except you and me."

"And Kieran."

"Kieran's not talking about it, for God's sake. He's got locks on things as big as China. And you know I'm not out there telling anybody anything."

"So he got it from me?"

"Not on purpose, I said. But I have to know who this guy is. If you did slip some time and talk to somebody, about Maze or Kieran's sister or Willy Doyle or anything that so few people know about, I'm not mad. It's a one-time slip, I know that. But I'm counting on it being you, and on you remembering, because that way you might be able to tell me who he is. Maybe it wasn't to him directly, but if you can figure out who got the information, then maybe you can find out who it was passed on to. This is serious, Michael. Please. I need you to remember."

Crawl waited, but Michael was silent. "Michael?"

"About the night with the trucking company?"

"He knows."

Another long pause. "About Kieran and Willy, too?"

Crawl, speaking softly: "You know who it was, don't you, Michael?"

Again, a long wait.

Crawl said, "Tell me you know."

"No, I don't," Michael said, sounding like a man deep in thought. "But maybe I can stare at it awhile. See what happens."

"I haven't got much time. I'm willing to send you money if you need that to track somebody down."

"We'll see."

"Not only my head, but Kieran's, too."

"What's the job you said you're into?"

"I can't talk about that yet. Trust me. Find the guy and I'll tell you everything I know."

Michael sighed a long sigh. "I'll stare at it."

"That's all I'm askin'."

After Michael hung up, he stood staring at the phone for several minutes, not moving a muscle. He could hear the TV from the family room. His mind tuned in to it in bits and pieces. He heard announcers' voices bobbing up like beach balls in water, but he kept pushing them back down, letting his mind fly past possibilities like a scanner radio. Irishmen talking, sometimes in whispers. Where and when? Could he have been drunk, not thinking right, talking about even the dark things to people who had no business knowing?

A man on the TV was talking about a vacuum cleaner that uses hot water, and there was music that had bells in it.

But it couldn't have been him, not talking about those things. He liked his stout and he liked his liquor, but he was too well trained to spill things no one had a right to know.

Chevy pickups, he heard a guy say, had more headroom than any other pickup. The guy was trying to sound like a cowboy.

Irishmen laughing and drinking, talking in whispers. Where and when and who?

Synthesizer music on the TV bobbed and weaved over a laugh track that rose and fell, as a new show came on and a man shouted something about men with breasts.

The picture of what must have happened, and how and when, formed in Michael's mind so suddenly and so clearly that he held his breath: thirty or more Northern Irishmen packed in a bar with the lights low and the music loud. There were darts being thrown and cue sticks being waved. All of them drinking hard, some of them being loud. But not all of them.

And not all of them were men.

He thought it through, and, being satisfied, walked into the family room.

On TV a fat man in a bathing suit had a little kid in a bathing suit standing on his belly. The man was lying flat on his back in the sand with the kid looking down at him and jerking at his suit as if he were going to take a whiz; too young to know better. The laugh track spiked.

But the family room was empty.

He walked down the hall and looked into his son's bedroom, being careful not to make noise with the door.

Roddy was asleep, his head tight against his red race car headboard.

Crossing the hall, again being quiet with the door, he found his wife, Sherri, transferring clean clothes from a yellow laundry basket into the second drawer of her dresser. She glanced at him nonchalantly, then paused and straightened up. "Whoa," she said softly, looking alarmed. "What's happened?"

Michael shut the door behind him.

"We have to talk."

6

As Kieran mounted the dark wooden stairs of his mother's small house on Kennelroy Street, he found himself thinking: someday I'll knock on this door and she won't answer because she'll be dead.

He knocked four times.

He had thought the same thing the last time he visited to bring her a tin of her favorite mints and hear her talk about how Kieran would live in her house someday with Brenna, about how he would end up rich from inventing something incredible about building finer fences, about her latest choice of movies or quiz shows on television, and about what she thought about the last elections or England or the Middle East or boiled foods.

Someday, possibly very soon, her health being what it was, he would knock and she wouldn't answer. And, on that day, he wouldn't be anybody's boy any more.

He pulled on a small strip of green paint that was peeling from the door just above his head. It cracked and came off in his hand. He listened for footsteps and suddenly, there she was, with no sound from inside the house to give her away, pulling back the lace curtain and smiling out at him.

"I knew it was you," she said loudly with the door still shut. Then the chain came off and the lock twisted and she opened the door wide. "Four knocks. That's what you do, did you know that?"

She laughed and kissed him on the cheek as he bent down to hug her and say, "Hi, good lookin'. How you feeling today?"

She ignored the question, saying instead, "It's your signature in sound, I call it. Four knocks. Four knocks is Kieran, all of them even; bam, bam, bam, bam."

"Is that what it is?" He couldn't help grinning.

"That's your signature in sound," she repeated. Her eyes sparkled. "Four knocks. And I do love to hear it."

She coughed twice, hard, then regained her smile and ushered him past the dark stuffed furniture of the living room, where the flowers on the wallpaper were dull and the light was poor and the air was stale. She led him into the kitchen he had painted for her—a pale yellow that she said was like sunshine—nearly a year before.

It was their favorite place to sit and visit.

Maureen Lynch was only sixty-six years old, but her hard life had rounded both her back and her shoulders, and her once blazing red hair was now thin and gray. She moved slowly, with difficulty. She also had trouble swallowing anything more than liquids. The cough and swallowing problems were, Kieran had told her, conditions that needed a doctor's attention, but she wouldn't hear of it.

Someday, possibly very soon . . .

Her voice had stayed young, though. And her mind was still alert, a fact she attributed to having gotten into the habit of eating for sustenance, not amusement.

But even that fine discipline gave way to their biweekly ritual of the candy tin. It was one of the favorite exchanges of their visits together. Kieran would pull a small green tin of Dyno-Mints out of his pocket. It was her favorite sweet, and he would pretend that was a major discovery, one that caught him totally by surprise.

Then she would fuss and smile and say he shouldn't have, and she would hold the tin up to the light and read the advertising slogan that ran all the way around the outer edge. Then she would put her little hand up to her mouth and laugh out loud, as though she had never heard it before.

Today would be no exception.

Kieran said with eyebrows raised, "Well, what's this doing in my pocket?" and out came the newly discovered tin, which he set in the middle of the table. "Must be somethin' for that sweet lady," he said, "lives on Kennelroy Street."

His mother's eyes twinkled. "Oh, God love you," she said. "You're so good to me." Then, taking the tin in both hands, she held it up to eye level, tilted so that the light from the window fell on it, and she read as clearly as a town crier, "Like no other mint in the world. Only stronger."

Then she laughed, and Kieran did, too. The magic never seemed to fade.

But there was also tea to be made. The second stage of the familiar ritual. And so, taking the little tin box with her, she went to the cupboard.

"Whoop!" Kieran said loudly, catching her by surprise. He pulled out a second tin box. "What's this?"

"Oh, my goodness, the good times double!" His mother laughed and retreated to the table, moving slowly and smiling a puzzled smile. "What's this one for?"

"Ah! A third one!"

"Oh, my!" She laughed again and sat down, reaching to gather up her treasures. "What's this all about, Kieran?"

"And, God help us, girl, here's one more!"

"Oh, my, Kieran, thank you." The old woman giggled like a child and stood suddenly to shuffle around the table and give her son a hug. "Are we celebrating something?"

"Well," he said, helping her back into her seat and walking across the room to get their cups and saucers from the cupboard, "I'm getting a vacation in Italy with a few guys I work with. A reward for how many fences we've done and things like that."

"Oh, that's wonderful! I'm so proud. An award!"

Kieran poured her tea. "I'll be gone a week or two, so I thought I'd get you a supply this time."

"When do you leave?"

"Day after tomorrow. I won't get a chance to come back before I leave, though. I've got a few more arrangements to make. There's some things I have to finish lining up. You know how that is."

"Is Brenna going with you?"

"No. Just two guys from where I work." Kieran had settled into the chair opposite her, hot tea in hand. He reached to open one of the tins of candy. "One does fences, the other works on houses. Building new rooms, additions, things like that."

"A lot of people must be getting fences," his mother said. "Two of you going all the way to Italy for building fences. My goodness."

"A lot of people are getting them, that's right. You don't want a fence, do you?" he asked with a smile.

She shook her head. "Just my mints will do." She grinned. "Like no other mints in the world, only stronger."

And so it was underway one more time: nearly ninety minutes well spent among the rituals of mints and tea and news and small talk, and Kieran checking out the house for things damaged or broken or just not working right.

At one point, he noticed she swallowed her tea with a turn of her head. She did it not just once but three times.

"Are you having worse pain in your throat?" he asked.

"No, dear. Why do you ask?"

"Because it hurts you to swallow. You winced."

"No, it doesn't."

"Why did you turn your head when you swallowed? You did it every time."

"I don't know. It doesn't hurt, though. Watch." She took a sip and swallowed without turning her head. "See?"

"Honest to God, girl," he said softly.

"It doesn't hurt me, Son. I'll be all right."

Kieran glanced around the room. "It isn't just a doctor you need. It's a better place to live. It's too damp in here. It leaks so bad it's got you coughin' and God knows what else. Wincing when you swallow."

She thanked him for caring, then deflected his concern by asking him a series of questions about Brenna. How were they doing? Was she still being good to him? Was she still a beautician's aide? Had they talked about a date for getting married yet?

"I want to see that day," she said, looking serious and glad and worried, all at the same time.

"I know."

"I only want it if it's right for you, though."

"I told you about the trip. But I'm getting a bonus, too. I'll have it in just a week or two."

She glowed through tired eyes. "Oh, Kieran, I'm so bloody proud of you."

"Some of it is going into a new place for you to live in," he said. "I don't want you to argue about it. We'll get a doctor that you can see regular, too, one we can trust."

"Aw, darlin', you don't want to be doin' that."

"It's not a problem now. It's really a big bonus. I swear, that's the truth."

She nodded, then lowered her eyes, gazing sadly into her tea cup. "Well," she whispered. She didn't say anything more, she didn't raise her eyes for a long time.

So Kieran told her about Italy, speaking slowly, laying his hand on hers. Told her safe things. He would see Genoa and Milan on the vacation tour, churches and art museums. He knew the weather and scenery were things she would enjoy a lot, so he wished he could take her, but he couldn't this time. Maybe someday.

She agreed that a trip someday would be nice and asked him to take pictures while he was there. He said he would try, although he wasn't very good at remembering to take pictures.

They talked about the game shows she watched and why she didn't like goat's milk cheese. She asked him why he thought even young children these days had to have tattoos everywhere and holes punched all over their bodies. Then he walked through the house to finish inspecting the leaking windows and notice the bubbled paint on the ceiling of her bedroom and say a quick word about what it was telling him about her roof, but not pushing it.

And then, when his obligatory inspection was finished, it was time for the last and most important ritual. He promised he would be back to see her soon, and she promised she would be there. Then he bent over to kiss her on the forehead, and he stayed bent over.

It was time to let her give him her blessing, that favorite blessing of hers right out of the Bible.

Her right hand rested for a moment on his cheek, as it had so often over the last several years; so much missed affection, so hard to make up. Her left hand moved to the top of his head and dragged softly through his thick hair. Then she rested her right hand on his head too, and closed her eyes, and began to pray in a soft and solemn whisper: "The Lord bless you and keep you."

He wondered if her prayer ever seemed to her like a blessing she wanted for herself.

"May the Lord make his face shine on you and be gracious to you. May the Lord turn his face toward you and give you peace."

Her prayer settled on him like an absolution, and he wondered if she was not really saying, "I've asked the Lord to forgive me for causing you hurt, Kieran, and I'm asking you to forgive me too."

Her hands withdrew, and then Kieran did something he had never done before. He placed his right hand on his mother's gray hair. He held her shoulder with his left hand. He waited in silence for several seconds as she stared at him wide-eyed, then blinked and closed her eyes and lowered her head.

A tear slipped slowly onto her cheek.

"The Lord bless you too, Mum," Kieran murmured. "The Lord make his face shine on you ... and give you peace."

As he walked down the steps of the porch and turned to wave his quick goodbye, Kieran realized that, of all the rituals in their visits, it would be the blessing he would miss the most if he knocked on her door when he got back from Italy—finally with enough money to help her—and she didn't answer because she was dead.

Terry Kohl's phone rang three times before he answered with a simple, "Yeah."

He always answered that way, Marie realized, as if he were answering a question instead of a phone.

She smiled, as she had begun to smile whenever she heard his voice, either on the phone or in person, although their in-person contact was still limited to brief meetings at school.

But that would change soon, and they both knew it. It was one of the reasons she continued smiling as she slowly lowered herself to lie flat on her back on her bed. She brought her feet up, resting them on the dark green bedspread with her toes just over the edge, and glanced to make sure that her bedroom door was shut.

On the walls around her, charcoal drawings brought her earth, sea and sky together, in more than three dozen unique ways.

"What am I interrupting?" she asked.

"Hey. Nothing." There was a smile in Terry's voice, too.

"What are you doing?"

"Wait a second," Terry said. There was a pause, then, "Okay. Actually, you saved me."

"Saved you?"

"I just started watching a really bad movie. What are you doing?"

"I just thought I'd say hi. Which really bad movie, of the many?"

"*The Last Glass Fence.* Ever hear of it? About fifteen years old, no big stars."

"No. But that doesn't mean much."

"I guess. Your uncle and aunt wouldn't like it, but this time they'd be standing in line."

"What's it like?"

"What's it like, or what's it about?"

"Either way. I just wanted to visit with you for a minute."

A pause. "I'm glad."

63

"You get me out of the house," she said.

"I'd like to."

"You do," she said, speaking softly. "Inside. You get me out of the house."

"Sometimes I wonder about you," he said. "Are you out of the house now?"

"Yep. Tell me what the movie's like."

He paused to think. "Okay. Let's see. Movie review. *The Last Glass Fence* is a tongue-won't-work, edge-of-your-seat, wet-your-pants-scary, wanna-be of a movie, shot in that suburb where all the people who really can't act very good go to live and make bad movies."

Marie laughed, but kept her voice low. No sense letting Uncle John and Aunt Leah hear her. She said, "How about economy of script?"

Terry laughed with her. "Definitely economy of script. Economy of script in a ma-and-pa, wooden-swing-on-the-back-porch kind of fallen-neighborhood whodunit."

Marie, reaching for her pillow with a laugh louder than she intended, said, "Fallen-neighborhood whodunit?" And then, pulling the corner of the pillow to cover her mouth, she broke into a nutty-feeling laughter.

Definitely, Terry Kohl got her out of her house.

Aunt Leah stood high and straight beside the doctor's dark-leather easy chair. Her right arm was held tightly across her waist. Her left hand was grasping her right wrist like a bodybuilder on a magazine cover. Her voice was as tight as her posture. "The boy is on the phone again," she said. "He's talking to her right now."

The doctor was seated near the ceiling-high window of his library, facing the deep blue water of Bruce Lake. The late afternoon sun was winking from a thousand ripples across the surface of the water. Birds were flitting over the natural glitter, looking for food. Three ice cubes melted in a half-empty glass of water on the mahogany table to the doctor's right. It was his thinking place, his planning place, his praying place, and, at this time, his reading place.

Without turning to look at her, he raised his eyes from the latest of the more than a dozen books he had read on the art of war. Agincourt, Waterloo, Gettysburg, the Somme, Stalingrad, Midway—he was a devout student of all the great battles.

He lowered his reading glasses, holding the frame between his thumb and forefinger as carefully as he would a scalpel. He said, "By 'the boy', you mean Terry Kohl?"

Leah's eyelids closed halfway under the severe weight of her disapproval. It was hard, trying to drag a man as stubborn as her brother through the necessary disciplines. It was hard, and it was wrong that she had to. "He's the only boy who calls her," she said. "At least, that we know of."

His expression was stern, as if he were finding a reason to be critical of the light dancing on the water of the lake.

"He'll be here one of these days," Leah said, swelling her chest with a deep breath. "He'll be here very soon. Here. At this house. I know it. You know it, too."

"What I know," he said, "is that the world as we know it will very soon be changed forever."

"He has a car, John. He will show up at our door tomorrow, or the next day, or next week. Let me deal with it and I will. But don't continue to do nothing."

"Listen very carefully, Leah," the doctor said, turning to look at her. "We've discussed this more than enough. I will handle any visitors. For your part, settle it in your mind that Marie is trustworthy."

Leah returned his hard stare without blinking.

"Settle it in your mind," he repeated, this time leaving no doubt that he was giving an order, not making a suggestion. "Marie is worthy," he said. "And she is trustworthy. She has to be trustworthy!"

The two-story building, yellow-bricked and orange-shuttered, stood at the corner of Hayes Street and Escondido Parkway in east Oakland, like a place not wanting to be noticed. Even the sign was diminutive: five-inch black letters on a redwood-stained pine slat above a door with wire mesh over its glass. It read: Brennan's North-Irish American Club.

The proprietor, Patrick Brennan, opened the door four inches on Michael Connell's second knock, which was hard and persistent. Patrick, short, balding on top and already widowed twice, although he was just fifty years old, was a glad-hander hell-raiser, who so much needed a constant flow of company that he could think of no better way to go through life than serving the social instincts of the San

Francisco Bay Area's small but zealously close-linked Northern Irish population.

It was a good life, and he was convinced that his social club did only good in this world. So he had no reason to be apprehensive when he saw two of his regular customers, Michael Connell, who was married to Patrick's niece Sherri, and Michael's even larger friend Haley-Joe O'Marron, standing at his door two hours before opening, looking like the bulls they were, only smiling.

"Well, what have we got here?" he exclaimed, closing the door in their faces just long enough to release the security chain, then opening it wide. "Two of the city's brightest, not able to wait for legal hours." He laughed and stepped aside as the two men, Michael in a dark gray sport coat, Haley-Joe in a light tan jacket, stepped into the bar-and-gaming side of the club.

Both men lost their smiles as they entered.

The neon beer and stout signs glowing behind the bar were the only lights, making the dart boards, pool tables and all three of the men glow with soft reds and blues.

"I know you're not this hard up for drinks, boys," Patrick said, shutting the door behind them and following them to the nearest table.

"Can we sit?" Michael asked in a husky voice, pulling back a chair.

"It's a meeting you want?" Patrick said. His smile faded into a quizzical look.

"A favor," Michael said.

Patrick glanced at Haley-Joe, who was also sitting down, only on the other side of the table, not next to Michael. He paused and said, "Well, I'm up to favors. You know me." Then, sounding uncertain, he added, "Should I break out anything for you?"

Michael shook his head. "We need a favor, Patrick," he said. "Sit yourself down here, please."

Patrick did, between the two men, which was the only choice they left him. "You're lookin' serious today, Michael," he said, shifting nervously in his seat.

"Patrick," Michael said. He placed his thick arms on the table and lightly knotted his fists. "Sherri told me something last night that was hard for me to hear."

Patrick shifted in his seat again. "A wonderful girl, Michael," he said, nodding appreciatively. "You're a blessed man, and I'm not tellin' you anything you don't already know. A wonderful wife. And a wonderful niece to me. And a wonderful son she's given you, too. Let's not forget little Roddy."

"She said that she made a mistake, Patrick, and told you some of what I call my family secrets. Here at the bar, she thinks it was. You being her only uncle and all, and her trusting kin like she does."

Patrick blinked and stared, folding his hands on the table.

Michael eased his chin a single inch closer. "She tells me she was feeling a little light-headed, and you and her were talking. She said how you told her about your first young wife in Ireland, the one you ran out on. Before the other two you had for awhile over here. She said you started in on your poor father and mother, and on the killings in the streets, and on, oh, what a lonely man you are, and poor Patrick, and Lord-knows-what-all. And, God love her, Sherri was feeling all close and sympathetic with you. And so, she told me, she's hearin' all these secrets, and next minute she found herself telling you certain things about me back in Ireland. Some of what were very private things I'd told her. But you see ..."

Patrick noticed Michael's fist slowly clench. He felt his heart speed up. He made a point not to swallow, not to move.

"I told her those things in strictest confidence, Patrick. Stone-dead confidence. Like a husband and wife love-offering or some such thing, just something very personal between her and me. You know what I mean?"

Patrick tried to smile, then settled for a shrug. "I'm afraid I don't, Michael, no. A love-offering?"

"That's a dumb way for me to put it, isn't it?"

"No. No, it's not." Patrick swallowed hard without thinking.

"No, it was. You can say it was a dumb way to put it, because it was a dumb thing to do, though I didn't see that when I told her those secret things, which were not even all about me, but about my dead father back in the Force, and in prison, God rest him. And about my brother, Crawl. Even about a fellow we lived with named Kieran and a certain Willy Doyle, if you remember those names."

Patrick twitched his head left-to-right and back again, twice.

"Well, you do see, though, it was to show her I'd trust her with anything. That's the only reason I told her things like that. You see what I mean? So that was real private."

Patrick leaned suddenly forward, his eyes wide. "You know, I don't remember any of this," he said. "I really think this must be a mistake, Michael."

Michael stared harder at the smaller man for a moment. "But it was to show her that I trusted her, Patrick. Are you listening to me?" His voice rose and grew hard. "I love the girl, and so I trusted her, and I wanted her to know that. But while I still love her, I have to admit, I'm not happy at all that she told you what she did. I wouldn't give a damn if you were her long-lost father. And you know what else? I'm especially unhappy that you told whoever it was you repeated those things to. Right down to the smallest detail, Patrick. Why did you do that?"

Patrick's head shook harder. His index finger became a flag again, flapping in an unfelt wind. He sat bolt upright. "Oh, no," he protested, now speaking loudly. "I didn't tell anyone, Michael. Honest to God, man." He started to rise from his chair and then settled down again. "Maybe she made a mistake, isn't that possible? Because, I swear, it wasn't me she talked with. I don't know a thing about you, other than what you've told me yourself over a fair river of good stout, right here in my own home."

He tried a hearty laugh but came up with something less.

"Don't call my wife a liar," Michael said flatly.

From Patrick's right, the first words Haley-Joe spoke: "That was a mistake, Patrick. You shouldn't have called the man's wife a liar."

Patrick's eyes suddenly flashed with anger. "Look here!" he shouted.

Michael reached out suddenly, without changing his expression. He wrapped his fist around Patrick's raised wrist, holding it tight.

Patrick tried to pull away but couldn't.

Michael glowered at him in the blue-red light.

"Shouldn't have called the man's wife a liar," Haley-Joe repeated softly in the background.

"I'll ask you this one time, Patrick," Michael said, squeezing the man's wrist. "I would like to know who you told. I know you remember because there was too much detail to be just something you said as offhand remarks. And I know you well enough to know that you aren't a man who tells private details about your friends' lives to people you don't know, and know well. It was stories you told. It was conversations about things you heard in confidence. So don't lie to me, here, Patrick. We're good friends, we can stay good friends. But I need you to show me you're still my good friend, and good kin to my wife, by telling me who it was you told about me and my family."

He released the wrist slowly.

Patrick sat back in his chair.

"Who, Patrick?" Michael said softly. "Name. Address. Phone number. E-mail. Everything you've got. And you'd better have more than a vague kind of description for me."

The anger in Patrick's eyes had melted back to fear, and now the fear was naked. For a full half minute, he didn't speak. Then he practically whispered. "I'm trying to think, Michael, but so help me God, I swear I can't remember even hearing anything, let alone telling anybody anything that might sound like family secrets. I swear it before God. Was I drinking too much to remember? I don't know. But you're a valued friend. Why wouldn't I be telling you if I remembered?"

"Because they told you not to tell me," Michael said. "Because they paid you not to tell me." He rose slowly to his feet. So did Haley-Joe. "Because you're more afraid of them than you are loyal to your family or your friends. Because you're more afraid of them than you are afraid of me. So far."

He pulled open his sport coat and reached back, waist high.

Patrick muttered, "Oh, God, man."

He heard Michael say, "But we can bloody change that." He noticed Haley-Joe closing in to stand nearer to his side. When he turned his gaze back to Michael, he saw a black snub-nosed revolver in his right hand.

He shouted, "Oh, hell no!" and jumped to his feet only to be caught in midair by Haley-Joe's massive hands on his shoulders, pressing him back down. "What the hell do you think you're doing?" he shouted at Michael.

Michael methodically emptied the six chambers, placing the cartridges on the table. "Tell me," he said.

Patrick tried bolting a second time, but Haley-Joe drove his open right hand into the back of the man's neck, his fingertips digging into soft muscle on both sides. Patrick cried out with pain and grabbed at the strong fingers with both hands, but Haley-Joe hammered his shoulder with his left hand and drove him back into his chair.

"You know this game, don't you?" Michael asked quietly. He placed a single cartridge into the revolver and spun the chamber. "We'll play it until you remember who has the information," he said, eyeing the cartridge chamber from behind.

Even in the soft light, he could see the heel of the lone cartridge. It had spun to the second chamber, left side. Too close to firing position.

"You'll get six chances maximum," he said, buying a few more seconds. "And then ..." He spun the chamber again. "Then you'll be dead, Patrick. And I'll go to your funeral and I'll say to your niece, 'Now who could've done a thing like that to Patrick Brennan?'"

With the flick of his eye, he glanced one more time at the back of the revolver's chamber. This time, the heel of the cartridge was safely settled on the right side, four pulls of the trigger away from firing.

"Michael," Patrick gasped. "For the love of God, man. There was nothin' to it!"

Michael's lips curled. "I want the name. And more." Leaning forward, he dug his fingertips into Patrick's yawning cheeks, jammed the barrel of the revolver deep into the terrified man's mouth, and squeezed the trigger.

7

The countryside of Italy's Piemonte region struck Crawl as the prettiest country he had ever seen. Ireland was green and rocky and lush with hills, but this was everything: green, rolling hills, neat rows of grapevines as far as he could see, forest areas, long, flat plains, and rushing rivers fed by the snowcaps of the Maritime and Cottian Alps that stood like neighboring planets not many miles straight ahead.

Until then, all he had seen about Italy was in the movies and travel brochures and a few magazines, and they all stuck to pictures of grapevines and girls on beaches and things in Rome, like the Coliseum and the Vatican and that big town square with the fountain and all the pigeons.

But this was different. This, a man could come back to someday. Take his time. Get to know somebody. Mountains in front, beaches behind, grapes in the middle.

Antonio, the thin, thirty-something Italian who had picked Crawl up in Genoa a little more than half an hour ago in his little white Fiat, looked bored. And he obviously didn't like to talk. Even when Crawl had asked him if Kieran got picked up okay, Antonio just nodded and said, "Got him."

"How long before we get there?" Crawl had asked.

"Hour. Little more."

That was it.

Another small town came up quickly on their right.

The towns surprised Crawl, too, but not because each offered something new every time, like the countryside. Just the opposite. He was surprised at how they all had a church right in the middle, in the courtyard, and how their three- and four-story stucco buildings all looked so much the same. The same yellow walls. All the roofs the same orange tile. Even all the shutters, the same dark green. He must have seen six hundred window shutters since he went into his

"I found a girl and I love her" routine and left his tour in Genoa, and it seemed like every one of them was the same dark green.

He found himself wondering where the Italians' reputation for being so creative came from. He decided they must have had a few great artists like Michelangelo and a few great architects that built the big cathedrals, but the rest of the country must have been designed by the same three or four families, or family-owned companies. Or maybe it was all owned by the government. However it happened, whoever owned it came up with one specialty. They did square yellow buildings with orange roofs and green shutters. And nobody cared.

At least the Irish use different colors, he thought. Go down a street in Belfast, you see green buildings next to pink ones next to orange ones next to white.

"I saw palm trees in Genoa," he said. "Where are all the palm trees along here?"

"Somewhere," Antonio said. He opened his right hand in the silent question: What the hell do I know about palm trees?

Crawl quietly repeated, "Somewhere," and went back to observing the countryside and resting his hand on the new phone in his pocket. He had two phones now. The "best of everything" new one that he and Kieran had each bought with part of Day's money, and his older basic one, for just in case Day pulled a "Leave your phones with me until after the rehearsal and the job are done" move on them.

It didn't hurt to play it safe.

Or to have the best equipped phone he could get, especially for here in Italy.

The country around him was starting to flatten out. A plains area now, with the mountains still in the distance but looking bigger than before. He saw people on horses way off to his right and he noticed how, with his window open in the heat of the day, the air smelled sweet.

Antonio swerved to avoid a wooden box on the road, and he muttered something like a curse in Italian. Crawl smiled and wondered if he should try to remember it. Say it later if he gets mad.

At least he knew that he and Kieran were ready. They had opened separate Banca d'Italia accounts they could access in either Milan or Genoa. If the rehearsal told them the job was good to go, they would have Day transfer the bulk of their additional forty-five thousand to their accounts. That, and they would each take a couple thousand in cash.

Most importantly, Michael had given them enough information on Day to pin the guy to a wall if they had to. Now, if Day said, "Okay, the job is, we're going to blow up the Pope," Crawl would spell it out for him. Just say, "We're out of here. And by the way, our friends know who you are, where you live and how many tiles there are on your kitchen floor, so don't even think about raising bumps on our heads, let alone dropping them in a box."

"Name is Dr. John Cleary," Michael had said. "Big in biotechnology, and I mean *big* in biotechnology. Has his own company, and he has a lot of heavy connections, which is part of the way he got rich. Another way was his wife's money, but she's dead now."

"How and when?"

"Ten, fifteen years. I don't know exactly. There's a lot I don't know yet."

"John Cleary?"

"C-l-e-a-r-y. He was in internal medicine originally, but just for a year or two, way back. Then he dove into biotech, big time. Now he has more money than God."

"That's good to know," Crawl had said, grinning. "So what about his company?"

"He's founder and chairman of Jerron—J-e-r-r-o-n—then a second name, N-a-s-h. Jerron-Nash. You can look it up. It's all R&D now, and focused on DNA stuff. It's in New Mexico, which is a pretty wild state not too far from California. And in fact, the guy lives in what they call the Pecos Wilderness. In the mountains. He has his sister living with him, name is Leah, and a niece named Marie, sixteen years old."

"This is good stuff, Michael. You get the Free Drinks Award, boyo."

"One more thing. You can look this up, too, but he was nominated for the damned Nobel Prize six years ago. Didn't get it, but he was up for it."

"For doing what?"

"Doing things only ten people can understand. His big-deal paper was called—are you ready for this?—it was called 'New Horizons in the Search for Spindle Protein Protection in Mammals'."

When Michael said it, he laughed. "I thought it was a really good read, but you must have read it too, didn't you?" He laughed again.

Crawl laughed. "It sounds like muscle building for sewing machines," he said. "Doesn't it?"

"So that's a start," Michael said. "Let me know if you need more. And let me know what you're into as soon as you can."

"Probably not on a cell, but I'll let you know. For now, I've got Cleary. Jerron-Nash. New Mexico. Pecos Wilderness. DNA. And something called spindle proteins."

That was all Michael had told him, but it gave him all the muscle he would need in case he and Kieran had to back out and stay in one piece.

Antonio cursed again as the Fiat swerved hard when a red van coming from the opposite direction wandered into their lane for a split-second. It was a woman driving. Long black hair with nobody in the seat next to her. She looked angrily at Antonio as she sped by.

"How much farther?" Crawl asked.

The Italian shrugged. "Not much."

"How much in minutes?"

"Not much."

Crawl tried again.

"Where'd you learn English?"

"I don't like use it."

"You talk good English."

"Think so?"

"Better than I talk Italian."

Antonio nodded, satisfied.

"So use it to tell me, how'd he come to contact you? Day, I mean."

Antonio shrugged again. "He just came," he said.

"He just walked up to you in the street?"

"Something like that."

Crawl wiped sweat from his forehead and cheeks. The Fiat wasn't air-conditioned and the day was getting hotter. "So how long's it been?" he asked.

"What's been?"

"How long's it been since you met him?"

Another shrug. Which, Crawl realized, Antonio seemed to do as naturally as breathing. Most Italians talked with their hands, this one talked with his shoulders.

"Look," Crawl said. "Let's just talk like we're friends, how's that? We'll make it a nice little trip together in your no-air-conditioning car. Tell me, what do you do for him, other than picking up Irishmen and delivering us wherever we're going?"

Antonio looked young, in his early thirties, tops, but he was already balding in the middle of his head. He pulled a dark blue handkerchief out of his left-side pocket and rubbed his bald spot and forehead and said, "I get things. I do things."

"Did you get things to set up this job? What'd you do?"

Another shrug. "Just things."

They came up behind a slower-moving truck. Antonio swung around it, studying it as he passed it by.

"You like that truck?" Crawl asked.

Another shrug. "It's a truck."

"Okay," Crawl said. "I'll talk. You listen. Then you can just nod your head and shrug when I get to a good part."

No response.

Crawl guessed he obviously wasn't at a good part yet.

"I'm making a lot of money for this whatever-the-hell it is we're doing," he said. "I imagine you are, too. Our friend seems to be real generous, so now I want to be generous, too."

He reached into his pocket and pulled out a small wad of folded bills. Then he peeled a few off and held them up close to Antonio's cheek and flagged them for a second before pulling them back.

"This is seven hundred pounds," he said. "That's got to be a long way past five hundred euros here in Mother Italy. You tell me."

The Fiat slowed noticeably, but Antonio said nothing.

"It's yours, if you find me—just between you and me, now, not the boss—if you find me a semiautomatic handgun. Seven to ten in the clip, .30 caliber or better. I don't give a damn what kind, Italian or whatever, just so it works smooth and I've got the rounds to go with it. An extra seven hundred euros."

He wasn't thinking about how dangerous the job might be. He wasn't thinking about the American doctor's intrigues. He was thinking about how he would soon be trying to get away from a crime scene in the middle of Italy with a couple thousand pounds in his pocket. And he was thinking—for the first time because it was just hitting him—about the man driving the Fiat. He had known an Italian would be part of the job, but he hadn't been smart enough to think about the man, not until now, seeing him sweating with his right hand clenching the top of the Fiat's steering wheel and his thin neck pushed forward as he watched the road, and every five seconds shrugging at something.

He realized that Antonio might have already been told about him and Kieran getting a good chunk of the money as cash up-front. Why hadn't he thought about that? Antonio could easily have family in the area; brothers and cousins and friends. This skinny Italian, who spoke English and who knew how to break the law, how to get things done, could already be planning on hitting him and Kieran after the job was over, or have part of the family do it; hitting the two Irishmen in what was already getting to be the middle of nowhere, in Italy.

He held the money out again and said to Antonio, "It's a deal then, right?" at the same time that he said to himself, "There's no way in hell this guy's going to get me a gun!"

Antonio didn't answer but he was clearly thinking about it. He finally said to Crawl, "But you won't need a weapon."

"I know. No risk, no one gets hurt, I'm sure. So the weapon won't even come out. Which means Day never even knows about it, I guarantee you." He held the money up next to Antonio's right hand. "It's just my way of feeling safe. I'm not going to have to use it, you know that."

"So why get it?"

"If this whole thing is as safe as Day says, and we both know it is, what's the difference? So. Seven hundred euros, simple as that."

More silence, the Italian wiping his head again with his handkerchief.

Crawl kept at him, the money held high, well in sight, knowing that if the guy were really going to turn on them, he wouldn't do it for five times as much. "Is it a no risk job or not? What are you saying? You saying there's a big risk here, after all?"

Antonio said, "He's a serious man, Mr. Day."

"I'll give the weapon back to you after the job is done, too, how's that? You get whatever he's paying you, plus what's left of the seven hundred, plus the weapon. So are you smart or not? How can you go wrong?"

"I don't think so."

"Why not?"

76

One more shrug. "I made my deal with Mr. Day. I don't want to do this."

"No risk, it never comes out," Crawl repeated.

Antonio studied Crawl with dark and settled eyes in his rearview mirror. "Now I'll tell you what," he said. "Now let's not talk like we're friends anymore. How's that?"

Crawl set his jaw, lowered the money and sat back, staring straight ahead.

Mountains in front, beaches behind, and now he didn't know what, driving him to who knows where.

It was four o'clock. The sun was nearly touching the tallest point of the Alps to the northwest. A road sign said that they were sixteen kilometers from the city of Turin, straight ahead.

Crawl's heart sped up.

"Is that what we're heading into?" he asked Antonio. "Into Turin?"

"Not into," Antonio said quietly. "Just near."

His heart beat even faster. He didn't know exactly what the job was going to be yet, but he sure knew something important now about the doctor, and he knew something that was lying in Turin.

"Holy hell!" he whispered.

For another fifteen minutes they drove without hurry and without speaking over gentle hills leading closer and closer to a solid backdrop of mountains in the distance. Antonio suddenly slowed and turned right onto a well-worn path that led them down and to their right, around the base of a tall but gently rising hill. They followed the path, holding to the base of the hill, until a two-story house emerged on their left.

It was yellow stucco with orange tiles on the roof and green shutters on each of the six visible windows. At another time, Crawl might have laughed, it was so predictable. But not now.

The house had a chimney but no garage, and an archway built over the front entrance. It looked to Crawl as if it had at least ten rooms. There were two other cars parked near the entrance, a black Mercedes sedan that looked like new and another little sedan, a green Opel that looked even older than the car Antonio was driving.

"Who drove the two cars?" he asked Antonio.

They pulled to a stop. Antonio turned off the engine. "The Mercedes is for Mr. Day," he said. "The green one will be mine. You'll take this one after the job, over to Milan."

77

"I said who drove them here? Is there anybody here besides Day and Kieran?"

"We got them here so you'll have one of your own after the job. It'll have directions, where to leave it in Milan, in there." He pointed to the small glove compartment. "It'll be easy for you."

He opened the driver's door and began to squeeze out. He said, "The whole job will be easy."

"The house is quiet," Crawl said. "Nobody's comin' out or anything?"

Antonio closed his door and bent down to speak through his still-open window. "It's not a visit to grand-mama's house," he said with the beginnings of a grin. "No one's going to rush out and hug you."

Crawl said, "Go to hell," as Antonio, grinning wider, started toward the house.

The two doors opened at the same time; Crawl swinging open the Fiat and stepping out, and Kieran opening the front door of the house and starting out to meet him. He wore a white T-shirt, blue jeans and a tight and serious expression.

The doctor was right behind him, wearing a beige linen suit and a white shirt that shimmered like silk and the same straight expression he had worn throughout their first meeting. This time, he had no tie.

He stopped as Antonio approached him, then put his hand on the Italian's shoulder and began to speak to him in a low voice. But he kept his eyes on Crawl, looking interested but showing no smile to welcome him.

Crawl emerged from the car, scrutinizing the doctor in return.

There was still no greeting signaled from anyone, and what Crawl noticed most clearly about Kieran as he drew closer was that he didn't look all that thrilled about whatever he had already seen inside.

"Did you get in touch with Michael?" Kieran asked, now near enough to speak in a hushed voice.

"A while ago."

Kieran whispered, "Do we know who Day is?"

Crawl glanced past him. The man he now knew to be a doctor in biotech was patting Antonio on the back and turning, finally, to Kieran and Crawl.

"We're all right," Crawl said. "We even know where he lives."

"I guess we're all right," Kieran said. "But see what you think, inside."

"What about it?"

"You'll see."

It was all he had time to say. The doctor was already near enough in his perfect tan suit and perfect white shirt to extend his right hand to Crawl and to say in a voice that sounded perfectly genuine, "Welcome, Mr. Connell, to an adventure which, I promise you, you will never regret, and never forget!"

Crawl noticed that Dr. John Cleary from the Pecos Wilderness in the U.S. of A. was the only one among them who looked very sure about that.

8

Kieran was relieved that Mr. Day, or whatever his real name was, wasted no time, but led them directly into the house. Relieved, too, that there was no time wasted to point out wash rooms or offer some food or drink or sit down for small talk about Crawl's trip or stay standing for a tour of the kitchen or bedrooms or grounds.

With Antonio walking close behind them like a guard, the two Irishmen were led through a dimly lit front entrance hall rich with dark wood, potted palms and assorted works of art. The art included a pair of twenty-four-inch brass vases on four-foot-high marble pedestals. To their right, a statue of a helmeted centurion stood like a guardian knight next to two large interior doors.

The doctor paused in front of the two doors, as if to gather himself. The others stopped behind him, waiting for the first words to be spoken inside the house.

Kieran watched Crawl. Crawl watched the doctor. Antonio stood behind them like a second statue.

The doctor murmured in a reverential whisper as he grasped the door's shining brass handle and said, "Behold the man."

Kieran swallowed.

Crawl raised his eyebrows.

The doctor pulled the doors open and added, "He does not keep silent!"

The only lights in the long room were a flood of small spotlights positioned to illuminate three heavily encased tan panels—each more than fourteen feet long and three feet wide—that had been mounted sideways, six feet from the floor, with one on each side wall and one on the rear.

Under each one, also wedged tightly to the wall, was a thick, six-foot-long altar-like platform.

Immediately to the right of each of the altar platforms, mounted vertically rather than horizontally, was a far simpler but equally large black and white panel.

Unlike the tan panels, which were encased in heavy polished metal casings and covered with thick transparent lids, the three vertically mounted panels were simply identical copies of the same negative-image photograph. It showed the faint, white-on-black features of a naked male corpse. He was lying face up. His feet were several inches apart. His eyes were closed in death. His hair was long and disheveled. His hands were folded together over his groin. His folded thumbs were hidden from sight.

All of him looked blotched and speckled and ghostly.

Kieran's eyes darted back and forth from the panels to Crawl, who was holding his breath.

The doctor remained silent, watching their reactions.

Antonio moved to where he could see their reactions too.

"Do you recognize it?" Kieran asked Crawl in a strained whisper.

Crawl muttered, "I think so."

"You recognize it?" asked the doctor.

Crawl said, "It's that shroud."

"The Shroud of Turin, yes, the most studied artifact in all of human history. The burial cloth of Jesus of Nazareth."

Crawl said, just loudly enough for Kieran to hear, "We're takin' it?"

Kieran shook his head no.

Crawl's eyes swept the room.

The doctor announced, "Each full image is fourteen feet, three inches long." He walked in solemn steps to face the first tan panel on the right wall. "Each is three feet, one inch wide."

His eyes were half-closed. His voice rose slightly as he began to move deeper into the room.

"Jesus was five feet, eleven inches tall," he said. "He weighed between one hundred seventy-five and one hundred eighty pounds. His body was anatomically perfect. This figure, his figure on the shroud, is the only human figure in medical history known to be perfectly proportioned throughout the entire body. The only one."

The doctor's words leaked out slowly. "Only in the negative photographic images, only on the white-on-black, do we see his figure clearly. We see that he was crucified through his wrists, not his hands. We see that he had a large contusion on his right cheek. He had another contusion under his right eye. His nose was fractured. His left nostril was swollen and deformed. His cheekbones were swollen. Trails of blood traced down from each nostril, and it was a man's blood, type AB." He stared at the nearest image for several seconds, then added, "The highest concentration of type AB blood in the world is found in the Middle East. It is the most prevalent blood type in Israel."

Kieran stared at Crawl, wondering when he would interrupt and ask the man flat out what the job was. He knew that he would at some point. Crawl wouldn't be put off too long by the man's narration, or by the reminders of the dead lying or hanging all around them.

The doctor kept speaking; his voice never speeding up, never slowing down.

"He had deep three-inch wounds over his entire body, back and front. The principle wounds are round at the ends and straight in the middle, like barbells. They are perfectly matched to the metal flagellums that archeologists have discovered on the Roman whips of his day; metal balls that exploded the skin. That's how archeologists describe those metal balls. They were purposefully designed to explode the skin and splinter the underlying bones.

"One hundred and twenty flagellum lesions are clearly identified over the length of his body. The wounds were delivered by two men; one taller than the other, so the direction of his blows were more severely angled. 'He was whipped, so that we might be healed.'"

Kieran liked it less every time the man went through it, which the doctor had, for Kieran, at least twice over in the last two hours.

He had even told Kieran that he and Crawl were there in order to help him get to the real thing, which was in the cathedral in Turin. What he hadn't said was why.

"His head was punctured by thin, pointed objects. Twenty visible punctures can be seen across the forehead and temporal areas. The forehead was punctured over the frontal branch of the temporal artery, so he had blood streaming into his eyes."

Kieran looked at Crawl and saw that his eyes had narrowed again. He's thinking hard again, he thought. Watching, putting things together, probably planning something, because Crawl Connell was always planning something.

The doctor's sad eyes glistened. "He couldn't have seen well," he continued, dropping his voice until it was barely audible. "Not with the blood in his eyes. He wasn't able to wipe it away because his arms were pinned to the crossbeam of the cross. Both his shoulders were wounded, too; his right more severely than his left."

He fell silent.

No one moved.

The doctor's voice was still just above a whisper as he again started inching forward. "The crossbeam weighed between one hundred and one hundred twenty pounds. It was oak. There are microscopic tracings of oak fiber from the cross still on the shroud. Oak was the most abundant tree in Israel at the time of Jesus.

"The carbon dating that was attempted in 1988 could not have been accurate. It's been since demonstrated that the fibers of the shroud are coated with a bioplastic compound. Bacteria caused it. In 2005 the shroud's fibers were tested by chemists from the Los Alamos National Laboratory who took all the previous findings into consideration. They found that the 1988 tests were conducted on a patch of cloth that had been applied to the shroud in medieval times. They dated the actual age of the overall shroud at between 1,300 and 3,000 years."

Stretching his arms across the wooden altar toward the second of the tan replicas, he slowly tapped at a rusty blotch on the linen's bottom edge.

"No one knows how the image could have been made on the linen cloth. Even today, we have no idea of how it could have been made. Every painting and staining technique known to exist has been considered and disproved. A nuclear reaction of some kind is, from a purely scientific perspective, the most probable causal event. Whatever it was, it's known that it must have happened very quickly. The linen was only on the body for a very short time. The stains would have been markedly different if the shroud had stayed on the man's body for an extended period of time."

Kieran realized that he was listening more intently this time than he had the first few times the doctor had played it out to him, before Crawl arrived.

"Among the many traces of other things still on the shroud," the doctor continued, "twenty-eight flowers have been positively identified, through still-intact physical tracings, as having been laid on the shroud with the body. Several of them grow only in one small area near Jerusalem. All twenty-eight bloom only in the spring, only in the Passover season. 'Before the feast of Passover, Jesus knew that his hour had come.'"

When Crawl finally spoke, he didn't do it quietly. Kieran thought it might have been the bit about the flowers that did it, but Crawl asked abruptly, "What are you going to do with it once we get you in to it?"

Again, the doctor didn't seem to notice, "Fifty-eight pollens still exist in trace amounts on the shroud. Pollen can survive for thousands of years. Nearly half of the original pollens don't even grow in Europe, which means the shroud could not be a later European artifact."

Crawl said it louder. "What are you going to do with it once we get you in to it?"

"But every pollen found on the shroud grows in Israel. All fifty-eight."

Crawl moved into the doctor's line of vision and positioned his face just inches from the doctor's. He said, speaking calmly but looking agitated, "Don't tell us anything else about flowers and pollen, okay? Because we don't really want to know about flowers and pollen. What we came all this way to find out is, what are you planning on doing to it once we get you in there with it? 'Cause that's what we're here to do, is that right?"

The doctor stared at him, seemingly trying to focus.

Antonio eased closer.

Kieran moved in front of the Italian.

"It's really time for you to just tell us what the job is," Crawl said. "Because to tell you the truth—and I'm sure I'm speaking for my friend, Kieran, too—we're not sure that we like some of the possibilities that come to mind. So it's time to cut to the chase. What we want to know is: What are you going to do with the real thing once we get in there with it? And if we don't hear that little part of it mentioned soon, I gotta tell you, we're out of here."

The doctor's eyes widened. "You can't go," he said. "Why would you want to?"

"We can and we will," Crawl said. He looked proud to have actually gotten the man's attention. "And we'll do it in about one minute from now. So put it on the table for us. And don't even talk about seeing our heads in a box, or whatever it was you said that was supposed to be scary for us, because we have friends all over the world too. Even in the U.S. Even near Jerron-Nash and your house in the Pecos Wilderness."

Kieran came to attention. He glanced at Antonio, then looked quickly at the man from a place called the Pecos Wilderness who had just gone as stiff as one of Kieran's fences.

Crawl added, "They can even get near your sister and your niece, doctor, if you don't play totally straight with us."

Kieran's heart pounded. He hadn't known that. The guy was a doctor, with a sister and a niece, and a man who didn't like it at all that Crawl knew who he was and where he lived.

He looked again at Antonio. The Italian looked like a cat caught in traffic—on edge and uneasy, but looking more surprised and uncertain than mad or dangerous.

The doctor had straightened to his full height. He said, sounding calm, "You made an agreement with me. That agreement stands. I told you that. Why are you talking about leaving?"

"Why are you looking afraid that we'll do it?" Kieran said. "You can always get somebody else."

He was ready for a "Because you already know too much", but he didn't get it.

"Time is important to me," the doctor said. His eyes were dark and alert. "I told you that when we met in Belfast. Time is important to me. Why are you even speaking about this?"

Crawl said, "Because I'm asking you, what are we going to with the shroud once we get you in, and you keep on not telling us. And now's the time. We know we're going after the shroud. What the hell else would you have all this up here for? But nothing stolen, you said. Nothing stolen. So what are you going to do with it once we get you in to it?"

The doctor paused, thinking hard behind hard, wide eyes. He said, "I just want to touch it. That's all I'll do. I swear it. What comes to a mind like yours? What did you think I would do, after I told you nothing would be stolen?"

Kieran had moved backward, positioned now to watch Antonio nonstop; close by him, ready to move.

"Well," Crawl said, flashing more impatience of his own, "let's move on to something like the game you played in Belfast. That's how you put it, right? 'Let's play a children's game'? Only now I'll be the one that counts to three. And if you haven't told us what you're going to do with the shroud once we get to it by the time I say three—if you haven't told us more than, 'Oh, I only want to touch it'—then we're taking your little rent-a-car and the money you've already given us and you'll never see us again."

He paused for a full five seconds. Then he said, "One. And remember, our friends know where you live. We don't call them at the right time, they go after your sister and your niece."

The doctor wet his lips but didn't answer.

Kieran swallowed and watched the doctor's eyes. He saw no surrender.

"Two."

Silence. With Kieran thinking, "Holy God, what's going on?"

"Three!"

Crawl turned to Kieran and nodded. "We're out of here," he said sharply. "Let's go find Milan."

The doctor blurted out in a low whisper that was as tight as a rope, "I need the blood. I just need a sample. A trace, on a piece of tape."

Crawl stopped and turned. He tilted his head.

"You know about me and my family," the doctor said, speaking quickly, "so you know about Marie."

"That's right," Crawl said, lying.

"What you may not know yet is, my niece has terminal cancer." The doctor turned slowly to lay both hands on the altar platform to his left. He stared at the marks left by the face on the shroud. "She doesn't know it," he said softly. "She just knows she's felt very sick. But it's too late to save her through any medical means."

"How long's she got?" Crawl asked.

"Maybe thirty days. Maybe a few months. It's very hard to tell."

Kieran said, "And you think the blood will do something to save her?"

The doctor turned to Kieran. His eyes appealed for understanding. "If I can take even a trace of it and touch her with it, I know she'll be healed. I know it! It really is the blood of Jesus! It must be!"

Crawl wondered what it was that just went off the tracks. Something was wrong with the last three minutes, but he wasn't sure what.

"You're a scientist, right?" he asked. "Why do you believe that?"

"I'm a man of faith who happens to be skilled in a medical science. I believe it because I know that miracles happen. I know that. As a scientist."

Crawl said, "So you're looking for a miracle, is all?"

The doctor stood at his full height, looking at Crawl. "You say 'is all'. But God in heaven, man, that would be everything!"

"So you're not planning on taking the whole shroud?" Kieran said.

"God help us! Not at all! I'll press a little tape to it and draw off a trace of the blood so infinitesimal no one will even know anything's missing!"

"We're going to have to break into it, though," Crawl said. "That's what all these cases are for, right? These are here so we can practice getting into them. Are these cases duplicates of the real thing?"

"Perfect replicas," the doctor said, looking slowly around the room. "Once I have a trace of the blood, that's all I'll need. Or I should say, that's all my niece will need. It's the blood of Jesus, I'm certain of it. One touch, that's all I need time for. I don't expect you to understand, and I certainly don't ask that you agree with me, but I believe that with absolute conviction. And I'm willing to pay you a hundred thousand pounds to help me get it."

They were silent for a moment.

"Virtually no risk," the doctor said, shifting his eyes to Kieran. "No weapons will be necessary. No one will be hurt. Nothing, at least nothing anyone will ever know about, will leave that chapel."

"And then you'd never see us again," Crawl said. "And we'd never see you again. That's a part of it, too, isn't it? Little local boys from all the way over in Ireland; and you vanish, and we just scratch our heads and go home. Which is a long way from the Pecos Wilderness."

"You asked me what the job is, and I told you. I just need a trace of the blood. I don't understand what you're talking about now."

"Okay," Crawl said. He pursed his lips, nodded, and said it again. "Okay. All you need is a trace of the blood."

He caught Kieran staring at him. He nodded again, this time at Kieran. He said a firm "Okay" one more time, clapped his hands together once, loudly, and turned to look again at the cases around the room. "So let's move on," he said.

With that, he walked to the nearest of the horizontal replicas and reached up to rap on its transparent cover. "If it's protected as much as they want it protected, this stuff isn't easy to get through, is it?"

Kieran spoke up. "The cover," he said, "was designed by an Italian aerospace company. He told me about it. That's an inch of polycarbonate, with some kind of gas pumped into the real thing to preserve the cloth. It will have an aluminum cover over it too, when we get there. A duplicate of the cover is in the other room. The cover's easy, but the polycarbonate is so strong that fire and gunshots and even most bombs won't hurt it. But he's got two lasers from North Korea that will."

"From South Korea," the doctor said quietly.

Kieran said, "The lasers are special forces design." His hands began to gesture, drawing small squares in the air. "They're no bigger, each one, than maybe four fists put together, but they cut through this stuff like butter. I worked one a half hour ago. He wouldn't show me what we were going to do once we cut our way in, but he showed me the lasers are rigged to run along the top and side edges of the case. They cut at an angle so we can take the whole cover off in about ..." He looked at the doctor. "How quick again, to have the cover off?"

"Two minutes, fifteen seconds. With both units cutting."

"How about the aluminum cover-thing?" Crawl asked.

"Less than half a minute," the doctor said. "It's secured with latches. They just hold the cover on, they don't protect it from anything serious."

"So less than three minutes total to take it all off and get it all out of the way," Kieran said.

Crawl was biting his lower lip, the right side. He said, "Why do you need four of us?"

Again, Kieran answered. "There's a window of just a few minutes, is all, before the alarms click in again. Two or three of us might not be quick enough."

"But four will?"

"Four will nail it," Kieran said. "It's worked out good, Crawl. The lasers are so new the Korean military isn't even using them yet. At least not that they admit. Cost him a fortune."

"Good for him," Crawl said, as if unimpressed.

He turned to the doctor. "So answer this. Why take off the whole cover, if all you want is to touch the shroud and take a sample of the blood?" His right arm swept across the nearest replica. "You wouldn't do the whole thing for that. You'd cut a little square, is all

88

you'd need. You're wasting two or three minutes, at least, and maybe more. That's a lot of time with alarms about to go off."

The doctor shook his head. "You can't cut a hole with a laser over the shroud itself," he said curtly. "It would burn a hole in it."

Kieran said, "We cut the whole cover off at the sides, he told me, so the laser just scorches the case along the edges. Smoke but no fire. Then we lift the whole cover off and we're in. Cut it any other way and the shroud gets burned too."

"So nothing hurts the shroud?" Crawl asked. "That's a big deal to you?"

"Nothing and no one," the doctor said. "Absolutely not. That would be unthinkable."

Crawl thought about it for a few more seconds, then turned to Antonio. "So what do you think about this, Italy? You think the man doesn't want to hurt the shroud?" He didn't give Antonio time to answer before he said, "I know. You'll shrug. What do you know, right?"

He looked at Kieran. "All the man does is shrug. You notice that?"

Kieran shrugged himself.

Crawl threw up his hands. "You see that? You do it, too. Must be the air around here. Everybody shrugs."

He nodded several more times and said, "Well, little brother, do you buy this, what he's telling us here? You've been with him for a while now."

"He did say that to me," Kieran answered. "About the one thing we have to be sure of is not to touch the shroud with the lasers."

Crawl turned to the doctor, paused for another few seconds, then nodded again and said, "We'll need two things. One, show us the plans you have for getting us in and out. No more talk about how secret things have to be, not to us. Because we may have ways to make them even better. Second, we search all three cars and whatever gear you're carrying just before we leave for the job."

"Why would you do that?"

"We'll want to make sure: no extra backpacks with a few loads of explosives, no secret South Korean special forces flamethrowers, no big surprises. How's that for honesty between friends?"

The doctor's lightning scar quivered as he forced a grim smile. "Do you seriously think that I, of all the people in the world, would want to destroy the burial shroud of Jesus?"

He let them think about it, then he added, "I'll let you have everything you've asked for, but I'll add one condition myself. I am the only one who touches the shroud. You don't touch it. You don't even breathe on it. You don't poke it with your finger or with anything you're carrying. You don't touch it in any way, shape or form. When the cover is off, you both stand back. Your work is done."

"Well," Crawl said, nodding agreement, "unworthy as we may be to breathe on your shroud, we do deserve to eat when we're hungry, so why don't you ask Antonio here to break us out something to eat and drink, 'cause I'm standing here starving. Then let's look at a schematic of the cathedral, which you must have, being a smart man with almost a Nobel Prize. And then tell us whatever Plan A is to get us in and out with no risk and no one getting hurt."

Kieran nodded his agreement. He even managed a half smile. He was finally ready to believe it: they were going to do a job for fifty thousand pounds each, with no weapons and nothing stolen and no one hurt and hardly any risk at all.

Crawl turned to him. "Of course," he said, sounding deadly serious, "if that really is the burial shroud of Christ, we just might burst into flames."

Kieran's smile faded, then spread again as Crawl winked at him and laughed out loud.

They shared a quick meal of couscous and stir-fried vegetables that neither Crawl nor Kieran enjoyed, then spent the next seven hours, until nearly 1:00 A.M., studying the schematic of Turin's Saint John the Baptist Cathedral and reviewing the plans and materials at their disposal.

The materials included multiple duplicates of the polycarbonate and aluminum casing that protected the shroud, the two handheld South Korean military lasers that would open the casings to the doctor, and the cigarette-pack-sized digital video camera that Antonio had planted in the cathedral to record the night schedule and the checkpoints of the security guards.

The plans were so well thought out and so expensive that Crawl found himself thinking that he could never care enough about anybody to go through all the doctor was willing to go through for his niece. He thought of all the work and the time and the planning and the mountains of money, plus all the could-end-your-life risks, and he thought: no way. No way he'd ever care enough to do that much, not for anybody in the world.

He even wondered, just for a few seconds, if that was something he should feel bad about.

At 1:15 A.M., satisfied that the operation was not only possible, well planned and well equipped, but that it did, in fact, seem relatively risk free, they ended their day with an agreement that on their next day together, the equipment would be much more than items on display. The next day, and much of the day after that, would be dedicated to rehearsals.

The doctor ended their session by giving each of them three sets of manila folders to review and discuss together as necessary. They were labeled: Entry Rehearsal, Shroud Rehearsal, Exit Rehearsal.

As they headed toward their bedrooms at the end of a long first-story hallway, Crawl jabbed Kieran's arm and said, "Let's talk. Outside."

The night air was filled with muted clicks and chatters of more insects than they would hear in a whole summer in Belfast. A waning moon was suspended over the Alps, which was good, Crawl thought. In a few more nights there would be nothing but a sliver of moon to illuminate Turin.

He and Kieran were quiet as they backtracked along the way they had come. The house slipped slowly behind the hill. They walked a hundred yards more when Kieran stopped abruptly and asked in a hushed, rapid-fire sequence, "So what do you think, Crawl? This blows my mind. What did Michael tell you? Doesn't this blow your mind?"

Crawl stared at him, sucked in his lower lip, bit it for a moment and said, "The kid's dyin' with cancer, my ass. That's what I think."

"What?"

"I think it spun his head around when I told him we know his name, his company, what he does there; we know about his niece and his sister, where he lives, all of that. I think his brain was tumbling down the stairs so fast that for a few minutes one idea was bumping into another. He got it back, but for a minute there he lost his ground. And it showed. I think he was scrambling and that's what came up. Maybe on the spot, 'cause he's not used to scrambling, or maybe it was in his pocket so it would be ready to use whenever he needed it, but the kid's not dying of cancer. Uh-uh . . ."

"Hell, Crawl . . ."

"But he is smart. Probably a genius. And he's thought it out right. And it looks like it'll actually work. I think it'll work and I'm all in. But—and this is what he said—the girl doesn't even know about her cancer yet. Right? That's exactly what he said. You heard him say that, right?"

Kieran thought about it, then nodded, just slightly.

"So she's dead in thirty days if he can't get the miracle blood to heal her," Crawl said, "but she doesn't even know she's got damned cancer yet?"

"I feel bad for her," Kieran said quietly. "Is that what you mean? She's only sixteen."

"Listen to this again," Crawl said. "And this time put your brain in gear. He says he loves her so much that he's spent a year or two, or whatever, finding the right people, and researching the shroud, getting measurements and building exact replicas of everything, which must have cost a fortune, and getting this house, and building polished metal cases, and designing indestructible polycarbonate covers, and bringing in special-ops lasers from Korea, for God's sake . . . because, he says to us, 'Oh, I have to save my niece, I love her so much!' But he never got her into a doctor about the cancer? He never got her any treatment? Never even asked her if she wanted any? She never got any meds that she might ask about, like, 'What's going on with me, Uncle John?' Never an IV? Never any chemo or anything else? And all the time, with all his money, he could have taken her to anybody, any place in the world, any time he wanted?"

"Hell," Kieran whispered. He was staring. His mouth was hanging slightly open.

"And his sister doesn't tell her, either?" Crawl said. "Like . . . what? She doesn't know, either? And the girl's just a few weeks away from dying, and she can't figure it out for herself? Have you ever seen anybody who's just a month away from dying with cancer who doesn't know they damn well better see a doctor?"

He brought out his phone.

"Michael?" Kieran asked.

"That's why we got the thing, right? Yeah, Michael."

"The kid could be mental," Kieran said. "Maybe he's mental too. But the sister would have to be too, wouldn't she?"

"The point is," Crawl said, pausing before entering Michael's number, "if getting the kid cured of cancer isn't the real reason behind this operation, it means he's doing it for some other reason. End of story. If it's not her, it's something else. And that something else is really, really, really important to him."

He looked down and entered Michael's number. He muttered, "She's not even a part of this. No way."

Michael answered on the fifth ring.

Crawl cupped his hand over the phone. "It's me, Michael!" He wandered another five yards away from the now-distant house. "Everything's going good, but we need to find out a couple of things again, soon. Two, three days, max."

"Everything's okay, though?" Michael asked.

"Yeah, we're with the guy, and it's okay. We think. But we need to know something right away or it might be going totally sideways."

"What's the job?"

"No names, no details, all right? Not over a phone."

"Okay. So what do you need?"

"You said the man we talked about has a niece ..."

"Yeah. Lives with him."

"I need the kid's medical history."

"The girl?"

"The niece, yeah. Last few years, last six months, even. We need to know if she's spent any time in a hospital, or missed any school, and when, and for how long, because he says she's so sick with cancer she's dying, and we don't believe him. And it's important we find out for sure."

"He says it's cancer?"

"Cancer. She's dead in a month from now is what he says. Like they've started the countdown on her."

"Their hospital would probably be in Albuquerque. It's a lot bigger than Santa Fe's, which would be closer. Don't know if it's better, though. They wouldn't have many choices except those two, unless he flew her somewhere for special treatments. But even if he did that, they'd have had her in the one in Albuquerque or Santa Fe first."

"And she'd miss a block of school."

"Oh hell, for sure."

"Find out, okay?"

"Databases are easy."

"Let me know if it costs you."

"Can't be much, if anything."

"Fly in if you have to. It's that important."

"You need it by when?"

"Sometime in the next three days. But don't call me. Keep your phone close and I'll call you."

"Any time."

"If you can, find out something else for us too. You can get it from there, straight as a rope, and it's just as important."

"What's that?"

"How long does DNA last in dried blood?"

Kieran's eyes were suddenly wide and staring and pounding with questions.

Crawl glanced at him and grinned.

Michael asked, "This is serious stuff, isn't it?"

"Serious but not scary," Crawl said. "I'm not talking anyone's blood in particular. But I'm asking you to do a dive into it, as quick as you can. Dry conditions, warm temperatures, just laying in something and drying out. In fact, blood, and maybe tiny bits of bone, too. Tiny stuff. How long does the DNA stay good, or whatever they call it? So they can try and do something with it before it rots away?"

Michael didn't answer for several seconds. Then he said, "Where are you calling from? In Italy, I know, but where in Italy?"

"Not now, Michael."

Kieran whispered, "What the hell?" and began to pace: five feet away, five feet back; five feet away, five feet back.

"Okay," Michael said. "I'll get you details as quick as I can."

"And I'll call you, right?" Crawl said. "Not the other way around."

Michael paused. "Later," he said and was gone.

Before Crawl could put his phone back into his pocket, Kieran was all over him. "Tell me what the hell you're thinking, wall-to-wall, top-to-bottom," he said. "Now's the time, damn it."

But Crawl didn't answer immediately. He went back to biting slowly on his bottom lip and turned to stare again at the darkened house with the pictures of the shroud and with the doctor who was lying to them.

When he finally spoke, he spoke cautiously, like someone who knows where he wants to go but has to feel his way in the dark to get there. "The man is willing to risk everything he has just to get at that blood," he said. He paused, thinking. Then, "The same man has put twenty years into a worldwide company that's focused on one thing. The ins and outs of DNA. What can be done with DNA." He paused again. "The same man is a genius, probably. State of the art company, state of the art facility, state of the art research, and just two feet away not that long ago from getting the damn Nobel Prize."

When he finally turned to look again at Kieran, his eyes were narrowed and dark and sharp. "I don't think he wants the blood so he can heal his niece," he said. "I think he wants the DNA that's in the blood. I think he wants the DNA that's in the blood because he thinks he can clone Jesus, and he knows more about it than we do. And he knows, for sure, that if he can clone Jesus once, he can clone him ten thousand times!"

The picture was on Marie's dresser, framed in silver: an eight-by-ten color print of her mother and father standing in front of a wall of orange rock in Sedona, Arizona; her mother holding one-year-old Marie scrunched close to her cheek, and her mother and father both smiling warm, broad smiles, their eyes radiating affection.

Her mother, whose name was Katie, looked the way Marie thought she would look someday, maybe in a second sixteen years. At least she hoped so. Older but not old. A little heavier. Her black hair longer. Beautiful though, at least in Marie's opinion, largely because of the way her mother's eyes smiled as much as her lips.

She remembered her mother's smile. Her touch. The warmth of her body. Her hands being warm even when it was cold outside. And she remembered the sweet rhythm of her voice, which, Marie felt certain, must have been embedded into her while she was still in her mother's womb, and which would always resonate with her in ways she could neither know nor understand.

Her father, Hugh Groves, was also good-looking, somebody she would have been proud to walk into school with. He was muscular and taller than her mother by a good six inches, with short brown hair that wasn't parted, and thick dark eyebrows.

About her father, Marie remembered, in order of importance: first, he played games with her in the backyard and laughed a lot and made her laugh; second, he had scratchy whiskers she liked to rub; third, the muscles on his arms made her feel safe whenever he hugged her; and fourth, he smelled different from anyone else. Not bad, but very different.

She didn't realize until she was seven or eight that her father's unique aroma was actually the smell of cigarettes.

While her current room was filled with charcoal drawings that she had sketched and still treasured, the photo was her prized possession. Not only because it showed Marie and her parents together, but also because of the way they were smiling. She was convinced that even though they were smiling at a camera lens, they were consciously, really and truly, with forethought, meaning those smiles for her, today. They knew the picture would be kept. They knew she would be the one keeping it. And they were smiling for her now, exactly where she was in this moment. She drew so much strength from the power of this conviction, and from the love in their smiles, that there was simply no other possibility.

She lay on her bed, gazing at her strongest hold on life for nearly ten minutes. Then, strengthened, she got up, put on her black sweat shirt, grabbed her layout pad and a thin box of charcoals and slipped out of the room. She was quiet going down the stairs, and she left by the front door, not the back. The back would have taken her too close to her uncle and aunt. She circled the house on the south side and walked into the woods.

Pines towered around her like guardian soldiers. Their fallen needles, long and brown, muted her steps like a rug. Bars of sunlight shined in air that smelled as sweet as herbal tea. To Marie's right, the lake, emerald-blue in the afternoon sun and barely wrinkled along its edges, sent baby waves inching up the soft, grassy shore in a slow and peaceful rhythm.

In this place she loved most of all the places along the lake, she sat with her back against her favorite grandfather pine, drew her knees up to her chest and opened her drawing pad to a picture she had already begun.

Like nearly everything she drew, it was a coming together of varied elements, animate and inanimate, earth, water and sky, the old and the new, everything in the soft lines of black and white communion.

She withdrew her charcoal, studying her rendered hill of tall trees blending to become the sinew and veins of an old man's muscular neck. His lean, smiling face was Marie's picture of a grandfather's face, bearded and serene, the person inside eminently accessible, always. Accessible. That had to be seen in the eyes. That was what she would try to capture more clearly today, in her soul-place by the lake.

Tomorrow, and the next day and the next, until the drawing was complete, the grandfather's gray hair would flair into needles and leaves, as if he were the greatest of all the trees that had ever been; and all that he was would be folded into the clouds with a single bird in the air above, as there was so often a single bird in Marie's charcoal world.

And it would endure. She would have it captured on paper, and so it would all endure: the earth and the trees, the grandfather and the sky, the clouds, the bird, all the beautiful things, all knitted together one more time.

She liked that, bringing everything together, and keeping it that way, so she smiled.

Beyond the water, two Pecos Wilderness mountains parted to form a perfect valley. It was as if they had taken their places intentionally so that she and others like her could come into the wonder of this place and enjoy a perfect view of South Truchas Peak—the more than thirteen thousand feet of granite skyline, where bighorn sheep outnumbered people and the elk roamed as free as the birds swooping and swirling in the "V" of the valley, close to the water.

High overhead, framed by the valley with the great mountain as a backdrop, a single large bird soared, its wingspan seven feet, at least. She had seen this one before, perhaps a dozen times, and her heart soared at the sight of it. It hovered for the longest time, then it dipped and slowly turned, so smoothly, and then it rose again and hovered again, and all without any apparent effort.

Marie let her eyes close.

She would miss the magic of this place near the lake when she flew away, as she knew that she would, certainly in another couple of years. She would miss this special place very much.

She would have to bring Terry here, too, she thought, when he came to visit her.

When she opened her eyes, nearly fifteen minutes had passed. The old man of the mountain and the tree was smiling at her. She smiled back. Raising her eyes to look at the sky between the mountains, she was surprised to see a second long-winged bird, the same size, the same kind, gliding very close to the first. It was something she had not seen before: two of them together.

She watched them for a long time, admired their hanging in mid-air, gliding earthward, turning, rising and then hanging again like pieces of a mobile. So beautiful. But where had the second one come from? Where had it been all the other times she had been to this special soul-place by the lake?

"Not as planned," she whispered with a soft smile. "But two is really nice."

9

After three days of rehearsals, three days of studying maps and detailed schematics of Turin's Saint John the Baptist Cathedral and its Chapel of the Shroud, three days of studying the routes in and out, three days of practiced lasers and practiced timings and practiced individual roles, and three days of getting on each other's nerves and finding measured ways past those minor flash points, they were ready. They each knew what to do, they each knew how to do it and they each knew, with agreed-upon reasons why, what not to do along the way.

Crawl and Kieran had what little gear they needed gathered and in the Fiat by 1:50 A.M., and they left for Turin, traveling in between the doctor's Mercedes and Antonio's green Opel, at exactly 2:00 A.M. on Thursday morning.

They hadn't yet talked again with Michael, but they weren't about to pass on the doctor's additional payment of forty-five thousand pounds each no matter what the outcome of Marie's health or any details about DNA housed in blood. The job, they had confirmed yet again, was well planned, well equipped, well practiced, and, while there was some risk, certainly, what little risk they could anticipate did not, in their minds, outweigh the treasure now parked in the bank and waiting for both of them.

In a small cloth bag, they were taking with them two pairs of blue surgical gloves, each with a dab of gel inside the end of every finger, and two pairs of black cloth shoe covers; everything fingerprint-proof and easily disposable. Their two travel bags were on the floor of the Fiat's back seat, ready for their return to Milan. A separate backpack rested on the back seat of the passenger side, ready to go to work in the presence of the shroud. Everything else that any of them would need was either in the backpacks Antonio had in his Opel or in the case the doctor would take in to extract his needed traces of blood from the shroud.

Crawl and Kieran had already driven their route to the cathedral in daylight, both to get used to driving on what, to them, was the wrong side of the road, and to practice their exit from Turin toward Milan.

Given their planned speed limit to Saint John the Baptist Cathedral, they would be face-to-face with the figure on the shroud in fifty minutes, at exactly 2:50 A.M.

Crawl was driving. Kieran was beside him, bobbing his right knee up and down mechanically; something Crawl had never noticed him do before.

The three vehicles didn't bunch together too tightly. They just kept in sight of one another at a little over the speed limit; not fast enough to get stopped, not slow enough to attract unwanted attention.

After the job was finished, they would all be on their own. Crawl and Kieran would drive to Milan, Antonio would go to God-knew-where with the two lasers, which were going to be his payment for his part in the job and which, Crawl and Kieran had decided, would give the Italian more for the night's work than both of them combined.

The doctor, they believed, although without being told for sure, would be going back to New Mexico to see his niece, who may or may not really be dying.

For their part, Crawl and Kieran had already confirmed that forty-three of each of their forty-five thousand pounds had been transferred into their bank accounts on schedule, as promised.

"Remember," Crawl said as they drew nearer to the city, "one of us watches the doc the whole way through. That's all we can do."

Kieran's knee slowed, but only slightly, and only for a second. "Antonio, too," Kieran said. "Don't let him leave early, whatever you do."

"He won't leave early."

"He goes out early, fifteen brothers and cousins drop on us."

"He won't leave early," Crawl repeated.

"We need a weapon."

"We'll have one."

"What do you mean?"

"We'll have one. Trust me."

"I love it when I don't know what the hell's going on. You going to tell me?"

"Don't worry about it," Crawl said. "Your knee'll fly off. Look at that thing. When did you start that?"

Kieran noticed his knee. He stopped shaking it.

"I'll stay on the doctor," Kieran said. "Make sure all he's doing is pushing some tape against the thing."

Crawl nodded.

Traffic was light. What little there was seemed to be leaving Turin rather than heading in

Crawl looked again at Kieran's right knee. It was jittering up and down again, even faster than before.

Turning the empty corner from the Plaza Castello, they drove past the Turin Cinema Museum onto the Via Roma on the west side of the cathedral at 2:48 A.M., the doctor still in the lead, his Mercedes moving slowly.

The square bell tower of the unadorned sandstone cathedral, with its red-tiled roof, rose sixty-five feet off the ground in front of them. It was near the southwest corner of the building, forty yards from the iron-reinforced front doors. Tall, narrow stained glass windows lined the sides of the darkened cathedral. There were no windows on the front wall. At the top of the tower were a pair of open belfry windows.

Kieran checked his watch. In seventeen minutes, at exactly 3:15 A.M., the armed security guard inside the cathedral would shut off the sanctuary's motion-sensor alarm system to make his second security round of the night. They would have to be inside and in position to take him out before 3:10.

His knee was steady but his heart was pounding. He pulled again on his tight-fitting gloves and held his backpack to his chest as Crawl rolled the car next to the tower. Kieran's free hand was tight on the handle of the door. He checked the roads, front and rear, quickly, and said, "Clear."

Crawl checked the roads as well, then slowed the car to a full stop.

"Go for it," he said, and Kieran was out of the car, running to the base of the tower.

Crawl pulled away, still following the doctor, Antonio now at his rear bumper.

Directly across from the northwest corner of the cathedral, he knew the vehicles would turn left onto the Via Basilica and park facing away from the cathedral. Parking was never a problem on the Via Basilica in the middle of the night.

At the base of the bell tower, already breathing hard, Kieran clipped a thin black rope to the base of an eight-fingered arrowhead. His glanced up every three seconds. He wished that his heart would stop pounding so hard, but it didn't. Biting his lip, he forced himself not to rush too fast, to be calm, to remember that everything was going to work out fine.

No weapons. No one hurt. Nothing stolen but traces the police wouldn't even notice. And, if each kept his head and did his job, maybe some risk, but not much.

He fit the arrowhead into the fat barrel of what looked like a long flare gun and checked again for oncoming traffic or late-night pedestrians. Seeing no one, he stood up and fired the arrowhead at the open belfry window at the top of the tower.

The window was large, six feet high and four feet wide, and he had practiced well. The eight-inch-long hardened-steel fingers of the arrowhead released on impact, latching onto the shelf at the window's base on Kieran's first try. The rope hung like a spider's silk from the window to the ground.

Kieran heard a horn blow in the plaza and crouched down, ready to lie flat, holding his breath. But five seconds trudged by, seeming like twenty, and no car appeared. He heard himself mutter, "Please, just two more minutes."

He stuffed the firing device back into his backpack and extracted two fitted handclasps, which he locked onto the rope. He thought of Brenna, and he wondered what she was doing while he was in Italy using clasps to pull himself up a rope to an open belfry window, his breath exploding in short, sharp bursts. Was she thinking about him? He hoped that she was. He would tell her what he was thinking about as he reached the top of the tower, if and when he got home again.

Inside the tower, he caught his breath and took out a black rope ladder with four-inch studs that would hold the ladder out from the tower wall. He hooked the ladder to the belfry's ledge and tumbled it out for the others, who were already moving from the shadows of the north wall of the cathedral to the base of the tower.

He heard himself whispering out loud again, saying from what seemed like far away, "Give us one more minute."

Suddenly lights swerved around the corner from the plaza in front of the cathedral.

The doctor was at the base of the tower, already reaching for the ladder. He dropped flat to the ground in the shadow of the wall. Crawl and Antonio did the same against the north wall of the cathedral, near the chained and bolted northern sanctuary door.

The car swung onto the Via Roma and drove past them without slowing down.

More importantly, it was a light blue Opel sedan, not the Turin police.

The doctor went up the ladder, struggling with his footholds. Crawl went second and made it up quickly. Antonio was right behind him, moving just as quickly.

Kieran pulled the ladder up, as the Italian tumbled to the floor with a grin and gasped, "That went good."

Crawl pulled a sheer black cloth from the pocket of Kieran's backpack. The doctor helped him hang it over the opening of the window with adhesive putty. Kieran stuffed the arrowheads and ladder against the wall of the belfry, out of their way. They would leave them; they couldn't be traced. Antonio had the two lasers out and was already hunched over the bolted trapdoor that would give them access to the staircase of the tower.

With the window shield in place, the doctor flipped on a small flashlight.

Antonio had one of the lasers in hand. Kieran took the second and knelt beside him.

He would tell Brenna about this part too. Her eyes would dance like a little girl's.

It took them nearly four minutes to cut through the door. It took another thirty seconds to descend with flashlights to the heavy ground-level door that separated the tower from what had long ago been converted from a small clergy-vesting closet into the cathedral's souvenir storage room, tucked into the northern corner of the cathedral vestibule.

The door to the souvenir room took another four minutes to open, but suddenly, there they were: together with miniature flashlights and black backpacks and dangerous plans in the crammed company of countless small boxes of holy cards and brochures and miniature plastic replicas of the shroud with paper photos pasted on their front. Mounds of four-color leaflets about the holy and mysterious artifact and the ancient cathedral that housed it lined the shelves on either side.

"Clockwork," Crawl said, checking his watch, obviously pleased.

The doctor checked his watch too. "We have eight minutes," he whispered. He got down on his knees in front of the door that would lead them into the front vestibule of the cathedral, and lit a small fluorescent cartridge he placed on the floor next to the door, illuminating the room with a yellow glow. "Be ready to go immediately, just in case."

Kieran surprised himself by thinking about picking up a souvenir pamphlet. He decided against it.

"Absolute silence." The doctor slipped a stethoscope from the side pocket of his backpack. He inserted its earbuds and pressed its hard black circle against the door leading into the vestibule and the main body of the cathedral. Then he waited.

Antonio, who was squatting next to a large opened box of rolled linen miniatures of the shroud, pulled a black ski mask from his backpack.

Crawl and Kieran picked up the lasers and went into a silent crouch, Crawl to the left of the door, behind the doctor, Kieran to the right.

Kieran listened to himself breathe. He told himself, don't think about Brenna, don't think about anything except what you do next. No mistakes, no risk.

They waited, glowing yellow from the light. The pamphlets, postcards and little linen shrouds glowed yellow behind them. No one moved.

Seven minutes went by. Seven and a half.

The doctor stiffened and hunched forward, listening to a distant thud: the door that led from the cathedral rectory to the sacristy behind the main altar at the other end of the church being closed and echoing through the empty cathedral. Then he heard the popping of switches in the sacristy, fourteen of them, as the security guard turned on the cathedral's lights before making his rounds.

"Motion sensors off," he whispered. "Mark the time."

They did. Their countdown had begun. In exactly twenty more minutes, if the guard did not turn the motion sensor system back on from its secure location in the rectory, the system would engage automatically and a cautionary alarm would sound in the clergy's quarters.

"Lasers," the doctor said, quietly but sharply. He slid away from the door, making room. Kieran and Crawl closed in. As they cut through the two sliding bolts on the souvenir room door leading into the corner of the vestibule, the doctor prepared a hypodermic needle.

The guard, they knew, would still be in the sacristy, which was directly behind the main altar and separate from the main body of the cathedral. But he would be in there for less than a minute more. At that point, his round would take him in a counterclockwise sweep of the cathedral, starting at the ivory pillars and gold-framed glass doors of the Chapel of the Shroud.

He would check the security of the chapel first, then move to assure the well-being of the saints and the angels and the Jesus figures portrayed in the six stained glass windows of the cathedral's north wall. He would glance through the nearly blackened wooden pews and red-curtained confessionals near the back of the nave. Then he would enter the front vestibule to check on the chains and bolts of the front doors.

From there, on every night but this one, he would go back toward the main altar area, moving this time past the south confessionals. He would return to the sacristy and turn off the lights in the main body of the cathedral itself, leaving just two as security lights. Then he would reenter the secured rectory, where he would turn off the sacristy lights and reengage the motion sensors and alarm system. The entire round was mapped to take him just under thirteen minutes. It would take him two of those minutes to double check the Chapel of the Shroud and work his way to the front vestibule.

The door leading into the vestibule was open in two minutes, twenty seconds. The doctor and Antonio slipped on ski masks and moved out. They crossed the gray stone floor on padded feet and stood behind the nearest of the four twelve-foot-high doors to the sanctuary. Each door was magnificently carved and as thick as a man's arm.

Soft steps in the church, but still far away.

They didn't look. They didn't have to. The guard would come to them.

A humming sound. The guard was a tenor.

Inside the souvenir room, Kieran rubbed his forehead with the back of his hand. He was sweating.

The doctor and Antonio braced themselves, the doctor standing, Antonio crouching low.

Crawl and Kieran stiffened too, unblinking and silent, ready to spring if there were any sound of trouble.

The guard, a blue-uniformed middle-aged man with a thin mustache and a pudgy build, checked the north confessionals, swept a worn glance through the church's last half-dozen pews and walked casually into the vestibule, just as he had done a thousand times before on a thousand other nights when there had been no one hiding in a ski mask to grab him and to thrust a hypodermic needle into his neck, freezing his throat and sinking him to the floor, unconscious.

After the guard was subdued, the doctor said, "Move quickly now." He sounded out of breath.

Kieran rushed past him and handed one of the lasers to Antonio. Together they ran down the side aisle toward the chapel.

The doctor jogged after them.

But Crawl stopped. In a single quick sweep, he removed the guard's Beretta 9mm 92D from its holster and stuffed it under his belt in the small of his back. Then he pulled his hunter's vest down to cover it and ran after the others as silently as he could, as fast as he could, given his limp.

The Chapel of the Shroud was tucked into a small alcove between the main altar and the north wall of the building. It was adorned like an architect's vision of the gates of heaven: red velvet and gold plating and white marble, with great winding pillars marking the entrance and six-foot gold-plated candleholders lining the side walls. The aluminum cover of the shroud's encasement was mounted sideways against the back wall of the chapel, as if the man whose blood had made the stains was lying down directly over the white marble Altar of the Shroud.

At the chapel's locked doors, Kieran forced himself not to look at the gold and velvet and aluminum and marble. Just focus, he told himself. He held the laser waist high and cut through the first of two brass bolts that held the chapel doors locked.

Antonio cut the other at the same time, a smaller bolt located at floor level, built into the lower gold-leafed panel of the doorframe.

Crawl came up to stand next to the doctor, first surveying the altar in the chapel, then turning to examine the chains on the nearby side door of the church, through which they'd make their exit.

The doctor stood like a man transfixed, staring at the long molded casing of the shroud on the chapel's wall, with its raised, shining figures telling so clearly the terrible, wonderful story of the passion and death of Jesus, and, on the far right, the wrapping of his body in the shroud itself.

The doors swung open like great glass curtains.

Kieran rushed for the altar, Crawl and Antonio right behind him.

Antonio said, "Twelve minutes, forty seconds left."

The doctor blinked, hesitating for the briefest moment, then rushed forward with the others.

Stripping the altar of its candles and cloth, all four of them climbed on it to stand face-to-face with the shroud's aluminum casing.

The others heard the doctor breathlessly whisper, "Concentrate!"

Kieran turned, then realized the doctor was saying it to himself, not to them. He looked at his watch.

Crawl and Antonio locked the roller-guided lasers in place at the top of the two sides of the encasement, then turned them on.

Antonio announced, "Twelve minutes, ten."

Crawl and Antonio moved the lasers straight down, top-to-bottom. The beams cut through the aluminum covering and the four hinges that held the covering in place easily and quickly, just as the doctor had promised.

Together, the four men lifted the covering and slid it to their right across the top of the altar. Kieran and Crawl jumped down to prop it up against the wall.

The doctor didn't move. Still on the altar, he stared at the shroud. He was captured by it, wide-eyed and ashen in the presence of the cloth and the history and the mystery and the blood.

Kieran snapped him out of it. "Eleven and thirty."

The doctor whispered it again: "Concentrate." Then he willed himself to nod to Crawl and Antonio.

Kieran shook himself loose from his own desire simply to stare at the shroud and its possibilities and helped Crawl to lock his laser to the top-right corner of the polycarbonate cover. Antonio locked his to the bottom-left corner.

The lasers' red eyes clicked on again, this time with their beams angled to allow the removal of the polycarbonate once it was cut, but not angled so severely that their beams would touch the shroud itself.

Crawl moved left, Antonio moved right.

Kieran knew the job would be this way when it actually happened: the simplest tasks would seem as though they were taking forever; his breath would be harder to keep slow and steady; his heart would be pounding too hard and racing too fast; every background noise, no matter how slight or insignificant, would sound like the police storming the chapel. He tried to think about the fifty thousand pounds to steady himself, then told himself, no, think about removing the polycarbonate once it's cut. Everyone does his job. No mistakes, no risk.

The doctor opened his backpack. He handed Kieran two power-suction handles, which Kieran positioned firmly on the shroud's fourteen-foot polycarbonate cover. Then two more, and two more, and a final two.

By the time Crawl and Antonio finished cutting the shroud's protective cover across the top and bottom and moved to cut down the two sides, eight handles spanned the face of the cover.

Kieran checked his watch, his heart pounding. He whispered, "Six and forty-five."

"There's time," the doctor said sternly.

"Foot to go," Crawl said softly.

The doctor whispered, "Don't rush."

Antonio finished cutting down the right side and backed off. He lowered the laser carefully to the altar and positioned himself next to the doctor and Kieran, who had each grabbed two of the suctioned handles.

Crawl said, "Done," and dropped his laser to the altar to grab the two remaining suction handles.

"Together now," the doctor said. They braced themselves and pulled.

The heavy cover lifted out more easily than they had expected. They lowered it to the altar, then let it lean forward as they lowered it to the floor.

"My God," Kieran whispered, staring at the shroud, breathing hard, "there it is."

Crawl stared. Antonio stared. The doctor whispered, "What's our time?" without taking his gaze from the shroud.

"Four and fifteen," Antonio said.

The doctor said, "Quickly," and mounting the altar once again, opened the canvas case which hung from his side. His face was nearly as white as the marble of the altar.

Antonio grabbed the two lasers, one in each hand, and walked quickly out of the chapel.

Kieran started after him, but Crawl told him, "No. Change of plans." He started after Antonio, pulling the guard's Beretta from his belt and saying loudly to Kieran, over his shoulder, "You watch the doc."

Kieran hesitated, stunned to see Crawl with a weapon, then turned just as the doctor removed a four-inch roller tape from its casing. Pressing it against one of the eight major patches of blood on the shroud, he rolled it quickly back and forth one time, pressing hard. Then he did the same, with the same roller, to another patch of dried blood, after which he quickly put the roller back into its case and withdrew a second roller, identical to the first, from a case of its own.

Kieran scrambled up to the altar to stand beside him, staring with the surprise of what was happening rising to a low boil inside. "What's that?" he whispered loudly.

The doctor rolled the second roller quickly over the side-by-side third and fourth major patches, returned the roller to its case, and withdrew a third.

"What are those?" Kieran asked, this time even louder.

The doctor completed rolling patches five and six without answering. He replaced the roller without answering. He drew out a fourth roller without answering.

Kieran didn't know what to do except to leave the doctor alone and to get out of there with his money. But he knew that the game had been changed, that things were in play that they had not talked about, that Crawl had been right. He said, "You got enough now?" as the doctor zipped the bag at his side shut and started down.

First Crawl with a gun, and then four damn rollers, Kieran thought. He realized that he was not only trembling but sweating, and that he felt out of breath.

When Crawl reached Antonio, the Italian was beginning to laser-cut through the steel chain that reinforced the two alloy bolts on the northern doors of the cathedral, just twenty yards from the chapel. The chain was giving way without serious protest.

Crawl approached Antonio slowly, the Beretta at his side.

From the chapel, they heard Kieran say in a voice louder than necessary, "Two and forty-five."

The chain banged once as it separated, then settled to hang like a dead snake. Antonio slammed open the door's two bolts. He bent down to stuff both lasers into his large backpack. Holding the backpack in his left hand, he mumbled a quick, "Good luck," to Crawl and reached for the handle of the door.

Crawl had the Beretta in the Italian's face before the door opened five inches, with the muzzle of it just an inch from the startled man's right eye. "Two minutes left," he said quietly. "Then we'll all go out together."

Antonio spat out a single expletive in Italian and pulled back; his eyes flared with shock and anger.

Crawl said, "You don't go now. In a minute you'll walk with me all the way to our car."

"What the hell are you doing?" Antonio broke into a sweat.

"I get in and drive away, then you get into your car and drive away, too. One, two. Like that. No surprises."

The Italian's dark eyes flashed, then narrowed. He looked at his backpack, then at Crawl. "You think you can take these, too?"

Crawl shook his head. "I don't want the lasers. You get them. I just want you beside me when I get to my car. That's all. If you try and run, I won't kill you, but I will take out your legs."

"But we're out of time!" Antonio whispered, practically squeaking.

Kieran and the doctor sprinted from the chapel.

Crawl spun to look at Kieran, who understood the question in his friend's eyes and said loudly, "Just tapes. That's all. We're done with it."

The doctor froze when he saw the weapon in Crawl's hand. "What are you doing with that?" he asked, straining to remain calm.

Crawl flashed a smile. "A minute and change left," he said. He grabbed Antonio's left shoulder. "Let's go, friend, but not running."

The doctor was trying to push past Kieran to reach for Crawl's Beretta. "Put it away!" he hissed. But Kieran held him back with both hands and shook his head with such a fierce expression that the doctor quieted.

Crawl opened the door a foot, saw that the road was clear of traffic, and with Antonio at his side, started for the cars as quickly as his limp would allow.

There were no brothers of Antonio waiting in hiding. There were no police. There were no middle-of-the-night pedestrians. There was no traffic.

By the time the motion sensors clicked back on and the cautionary alarm sounded in the rectory of Saint John the Baptist Cathedral, the three cars had started up and were pulling away, unnoticed by anyone at 3:33 in the morning.

10

Kieran was behind the wheel as they turned onto the Torino–Trieste Highway and headed toward Milan, and he was practically shouting, "He took four rolls! Four rolls of tape, four of them, five inches wide, each one, like paint rollers! All over the damn thing, back and forth!"

Crawl clapped his hands and laughed. He said, "He used paint rollers?"

"Not paint rollers, but like paint rollers. Small ones, but all over it, back and forth!"

Crawl laughed again, clapped his hands five times more, fast and hard, and shouted, "That's not for his niece! He didn't want all that just to touch his niece with a speck of blood! He's making sure he's got enough, but it can't be for her!"

"He must've got two square feet of it," Kieran said. He was checking his mirrors more than looking at the road ahead. "He could wrap her head with it, all he got!"

"That's what he said he wanted, right, was blood," Crawl said. "Said what he meant, meant what he said." He laughed again.

"He told us one touch."

"And we got fifty bloody thousand pounds," Crawl said. "And the police will get there and find nothing missing. That's the best part. Damaged stuff they can replace, but nothing missing. If he'd have burned it or spray-painted his message to the world on it or something, they'd be after us in armies."

He laughed again and reached into the travel bag to get his phone. "We gotta call Michael," he said. "Right now."

Again, Michael answered on the fifth ring.

Crawl put him on speaker. "Michael!" he shouted, "We're good! What about the girl? Is there any reason to think she's dying from cancer?"

"She's probably healthier than any of us," Michael said.

"I knew it!" Crawl shouted. He slapped Kieran on the arm and grinned wide.

"She's only missed one day of school in two years," Michael said. "And she spent a couple hours at the hospital in Santa Fe last year with a broken finger, but that's it. Her uncle was in there, too, a couple of years back, for a hernia op, and again for a routine physical last year."

"So both of them are okay?"

"From what I could find."

"Do they have a cancer wing or something at that hospital?"

"A Cancer Center, yeah."

"What about the DNA?" Crawl asked. "Did you get how long it can last in blood, or in tiny bits of bone?"

"In blood, it's not long. Depends on temperature and all, but in water it breaks down in maybe months. Not like fifty years or anything. But bone keeps DNA like a vault. And the wildest thing about bone is, with the tech they got goin' today, they can get a whole sample, full strands of it, all connected, from just one nanogram of bone. And do you have any idea how bloody small one nanogram is?"

"Ten people probably know that. Just tell me."

"There's like five thousand of them in a single grain of sugar. That's five and three zeroes of nanograms in one grain of sugar! There's a billion of them in one gram, and they can find and pull out your full DNA from one nanogram of bone dust! Honest to God. That's wild, isn't it?"

Crawl stared at the phone. Then he looked at Kieran and smiled, and his smile spread. He was thinking about the doctor from the Pecos Wilderness, and how hypnotized he was about the beating the man on the shroud took from the Romans, "exploding his skin" with metal balls and pounding down on his ribs and thigh bones and collarbones and arm bones and hip bones. He was thinking about bone splinters pounded into vaults too small to be seen with a naked eye.

He inhaled and said to Michael, "Yeah, that's wild. But after two thousand years, could any of it still be good to go? Good so they could still work with it and do things with it?"

"After two thousand years?"

"Do you know? Or, can you find out?"

There was a long pause before Michael said, "Okay. Here's what I got on that. DNA in bone breaks down—"

"What does 'breaks down' mean?"

"Comes apart. Not connected anymore, one part to another. It says it breaks down by fifty percent every five hundred and twenty-one years. You notice that? Not five hundred and twenty years, or five hundred and twenty-two, but five hundred and twenty-one years. What the hell's that about, they got it down to that one more year? But that's what it is."

"Two thousand years, Michael."

"I'm figuring your two thousand years now, they got that formula. So, that long ... you should have ... something between, like, seven to nine percent or so, still good to go. Still connected. They've found DNA in bone that's a half million years old, talk about a vault, but nothing still good to work with."

Kieran had slowed the car and turned to stare at Crawl.

Michael said, "That what you wanted?"

Crawl was staring too, straight ahead, not moving, not answering, barely breathing, whispering, "Oh, my God ..." again and again.

Michael said, "I won't press you about it right now, and I understand what phones are good for, but you gotta get me the detail on what you're into as soon as you can, whenever it's okay." He paused. When they didn't respond, he said, "Do you hear what I'm saying, and are you going to do it?"

"We may hand-deliver it," Crawl said, still staring straight ahead.

"That'd be good, too. Why don't you do that?"

"We gotta look at some things first, Michael," Crawl said. "We'll let you know about travel plans, but we have some serious thinking we need to do now."

When Crawl's next silence had lasted almost fifteen seconds, Michael simply said a subdued, "Have fun with it, boys. I really want bad to hear, though. But stay safe," and he was gone.

Crawl lowered his phone and looked at Kieran and grinned. Then he laughed and pumped his fist in the air and delivered a wildly hard slap to Kieran's thigh and shouted, "We got him! Maybe seven percent! We got him! We got him! I don't know whether to stop for a drink or run around the car a few times or wet my pants or get out and hug you till you pass out, but we got him!"

Kieran laughed and slapped the steering wheel hard, five times, and Crawl laughed with him. Then they settled in, both smiling as if they would never stop, and drove on in silence, still watching for police and listening for sirens, but no longer expecting them. Just feeling good and dreaming and thinking about what the information Michael had passed along meant; about Dr. John Cleary from the Pecos Wilderness in the United States, and about his plans, and about his money, and about what the next day might bring to them, or the next month, or the whole amazing rest of their lives.

Then, no more than fifteen kilometers farther down the road, Crawl began to think about what their next couple of months might turn out to be like, for him and for all of them, if they were really smart.

"Kieran," he said, finally, shifting in his seat.

"Yeah?"

"Think about everything we know."

"You don't really mean 'everything' we know, do you?"

"No, but this much for now. We know who Day really is. We know he's richer than a crooked king. We know he believes the blood on those tapes is Jesus' blood. We know he thinks he has a real chance of doing what he wants to do with those tapes. And we know something about how much they must be worth to him."

"How much is that?"

"Six million, do you think? Should we settle for six million?"

At first, Kieran just eased his foot up a bit and looked at Crawl. Then he guided the Fiat to the side of the road and slowed to a stop in front of a large and expensive-looking residence that sat thirty yards back from the road. A stone lion crouched on a pedestal on both sides of its glass and wrought-iron front door.

"Spit it out," he said.

Crawl said, "Think how he acted walking around that house back there, like even the pictures on his walls were holy, right? And now he's got the real thing. The blood, man. And we know where he lives, or Michael does anyway, and we could soon. So, how quick do you think he'd be to pay six million or so to a few good-lookin' Irishmen who happened to get into his lab to borrow those tapes for just a short little while?"

"Wow. You don't quit, do you?"

"I'm talking about barely a crime, Kieran. A fifteen-minute operation. Hardly any risk at all. Nothing stolen, just borrowed. No weapons used. Nobody hurt. What kind of crime is it if we threatened to mess up a few pieces of tape? Which he broke the law to get in the first place, remember that. Which means, who's he going to complain to if we hold his tapes for ransom? The police? After tonight?"

Kieran was silent.

"If getting them was worth a hundred thousand to him on top of all he paid for those lasers and God knows what else, now that he's got the real blood on those tapes, with the real bone dust in the blood, they're worth, like I said, I'm guessing at least six million. Two million for you, two million for me, two million for Michael, all cash money."

Kieran inhaled deeply.

"What would you do with another two million pounds?" Crawl said. "Or two million dollars, make it? Seriously. Somethin' you never thought about in your life before. Two thousand, thousand real-life U.S. of A. dollars? For you and Brenna. You and your mother."

Kieran still didn't answer. He just looked out the windshield. No other response. Yet.

Crawl said, "Two million dollars, dropped into your lap. Honest to God. What would you do with it? Really."

"I think," Kieran said, finally beginning to relax, and even smiling again, "I think I'd get the prettiest ten or twelve acres of meadows and streams and trees in Ireland. And I'd build a fence of fine wood in it, somewhere close to the stream. And I'd write my name under the top of each post there. And then I'd take my mother there, and I'd tell her that all of that fine meadow, and all that fine fence, and the stream and the trees, it was all hers to keep now; to have for her very own. And then I'd say, 'Oh, and that beautiful new house in the middle? That belongs to you, too.'"

Crawl gave the picture time to grow quick roots, saying nothing.

Kieran smiled again and turned the car back onto the highway. When he got up to speed, he said, "What would you do?"

Crawl didn't hesitate. "Fast cars, beautiful women, and see the world." Then he added, "Not all the world, though. Most of the world is a dump."

"Do you think he can actually do it?" Kieran asked. "Clone Jesus?"

"He thinks he can, and that's the only thing that counts. He's feeling pretty damned sure, what he knows and what he's got, or he wouldn't have risked the cathedral. That's what's driving this whole thing so far, and that's what will make getting money for the tapes a cakewalk, too. He feels sure he can, and he knows a hell of a lot more about what he can and can't do than we know, right? So who are we to argue?"

"He wanted it bad," Kieran said. "He looked like he was ready to pass out just looking at it, back in the church."

"So we spend whatever it takes for Michael to get as much more information on him as we need. Where he goes, when he leaves, when he's back, who else comes and goes, and when, and how often, and for how long ... and how everything's protected, for sure. Everything we can get about him and about his sister and niece. I think he's certain to keep the tapes in his home, too—in his own lab, or safe, or something. I can't see him leaving them in his company buildings and driving away, can you? Not a chance of that."

Kieran said, "Michael can line up a place for us somewhere near those mountains of his."

"We can head for the States ourselves in a day or so," Crawl said. "Drop out of the tours. They won't give a damn. They're paid for all the way through, anyway. I'll tell 'em my fiancée got in a car accident; you tell them your mom got sick. Or, whatever you want. They couldn't care less. And then, when we get to the U.S. with our new friend, Dr. Almost-a-Nobel-Prize, it's as simple as we just go in and put a gun in his face. We find the tapes and say, 'Okay, we're gonna burn the tapes right now if you don't transfer X amount to this account.' Or, 'Get this much cash back here by whatever.' Just keep it simple. People over think these things, sometimes they screw everything up. If we want it transferred, we hold the tapes close to a fire to make sure he does it, and when we check it all out we call and hide it in other accounts before we leave his place. We do that, and we leave the tapes there for him, all safe and sound, and that's the end of it. Who's he gonna go to? What's he gonna do?"

"Go ahead and clone Jesus, probably."

"So he's mad at first, but then still feeling good, and we are, too."

"You think two million each, though? Really?"

"We get the information, we get the place, we get the tapes, we get the money. That's how it'll go."

"We just break in and find them?"

"It's in the middle of nowhere. It's not like he's got neighbors dropping in. We'll take our time. We'll find them."

"What if he's figured out we're coming? We told him we know where he lives."

"He'll never think about us again. He's got his own baby Jesus on the way, that's all he'll be thinking about."

"That's a lot to think about."

"We're part of history now, you think about it," Crawl said. "Someday they'll have cloning clinics all over the world. Sally Citizen will be able to order up her granddaddy's clone, like at a restaurant. Or movie stars. I bet they'll be selling movie-star DNA all over the place. Once it starts it'll catch on big time. A lonely lady will walk into her local cloning clinic someday and say, 'I'd like to have a Laura Vavoom baby.' Or whoever, pick your star. They'll say, 'Well, wouldn't you know it? Laura Vavoom's estate just put her DNA on sale this week! For one week only. Hey, we'll give you forty percent off!'" He nodded, punctuating his certainty. "It's going to happen, man. There'll be a whole new world of money in it, and it's going to happen, whether we get rich first or not. But for now, we get the tapes. That's the plan."

They drove in silence again, the only break being when Crawl laughed suddenly and said, "We'll tell him we'll shoot the tapes if he doesn't pay up."

Kieran laughed with him. "If he goes to the police, he's fried. He'll have to admit he stole the DNA."

"Have to. Get himself arrested. International case. Ruin his reputation."

"Put him in jail where the Italian government and the Vatican will see to it that he stays put forever."

"No, this guy won't go to the police. And count on it, it'll be easier than what we just did."

Kieran thought about it, and he kept thinking about it as they drove on in silence.

They were just thirty kilometers from Milan, driving alongside the foothills that were quickly growing into the Alps not far to the north, with the sky beginning to warm behind them in the east, slowly getting ready for sunrise.

Kieran said suddenly, quietly, "I hope he can't do it, though."

"He thinks he can do it," Crawl said, "so he'll pay."

Five minutes later, Kieran said it again, still quietly, "I hope he can't do it."

The sign told them that Milan was fifteen kilometers ahead when Kieran suddenly announced, "He's not going to wait for us, Crawl!"

He slowed the car and said again, "He won't wait for us."

"What do you mean?"

"He's not going to wait for us to get our act together—for Michael to scout his place and get all his details, and for us to get over there and get all set up, with all the watching and scouting and planning and everything we'd have to do. He's going to put on his gloves and get the pregnancy going before we even get there! What could be more for sure? He'll get the DNA ready as soon as he gets back, which will only take him a day or so, for all we know, and we're not going to have any chance in the world to get those tapes before it happens."

Crawl was just staring at him. He blinked a few times, staring and thinking.

"He came over here for four or five days is all," Kieran said, "and now it's a total fast track. He's not going to wait for a couple of bad-boy Irish nobodies to come and figure out where the hell the damned tapes are! 'Time is important to me.' Remember he said that? Why did he say that? He said it because he's on a schedule. By the time we can run up and put a gun in his face, he'll say to us, 'Hey, good luck, cowboys. I've already got the baby growing and doing just fine!' "

"Shut up," Crawl said sharply. "Give me time to think."

Kieran did. Then he said quietly, "Thinking won't change this, but have at it." He sped up without saying anything more.

They had just a few kilometers to go. Milan and the hotels and the tours were straight ahead. But Crawl was suddenly grinning again.

"Maybe," he said, "maybe it just got even better."

"Better how?"

Crawl said, "There's no doubt it's Marie, right?"

"Ninety-nine and nine-tenths of a percent chance."

"It's Marie," Crawl said. "He even got the name right, did you notice? I was just thinkin' about that. I wonder if he even worked that out on purpose, to get her name right, thinking about it even sixteen years ago. 'Marie' is just another way to say 'Mary'. What could be more perfect?"

He stared at Kieran, waiting for the light to go on.

It did. Quickly.

Kieran slowed the Fiat again. He said, "Don't go where I think you might be going, Crawl. Whatever happened to no risk?" Then he said it again, this time even louder. "Don't go there!"

Crawl said, in his best "I'm calm, so you be calm, too" voice, "Just answer this one question before you go nuts on me, okay? If he'd pay six million to get back a few rolls of tape, how much quicker will he come through with six million to get back Mother Mary and her boy-child, Jesus Christ, who she'd already be carrying, alive and growing?"

Kieran took the first right turn, eased to the edge of the road, slowed to a stop, turned off the engine and said, "You're talking heavy, serious, go-away-for-the-rest-of-your-life stuff now, you know that."

Crawl's tongue ran slowly across his lower lip. "Yeah," he said, "'serious' would be a good word for it."

"And how would we even find out for absolute sure if she's really the one? How can we be positively sure?"

"Go through it again. Nobel Prize—"

"I know all that. He's smart, he works with DNA, he's got some blood he thinks is Jesus. How do we know it's her?"

"He's a microbiologist, he lied to us about the cancer, he paid a fortune to get a sample of the right DNA, he takes the risk of dying in prison, he does nothing at all without thinking through every detail, his house is in a wilderness, and in that house he's got a sixteen-year-old virgin named Mary. And he's probably crazy. That's how we know."

Kieran's voice rose another notch. "How do you know she's a virgin?"

"I don't give a damn if she's a virgin, how's that? He's got a sixteen-year-old named Mary, and she's as healthy as you are. And he's got a lab. And he's going to do what he knows how to do, right there in the wilderness, in his own house. He's going to clone the damned DNA, Kieran! And you know it! And he's not going to do it with press coverage! He's going to use her to do it when nobody's looking, and if we take her for a while, we have it covered both ways. If he hasn't got the DNA in her yet, he still needs her back. If he does have it in her, all the better. At that point, he'll do anything he has to do to get her back. And she's better than the tape in other ways, too. We know where she is! We don't have to hunt for some secret safe in his house, damn it! We know when she leaves the house. We know where she travels, how and when she gets to school and back again. We know she's out in an area where we can get her, and get her easy, and no one's going to see us. And it's for six million U.S. dollars now, Kieran! Wake the hell up!"

Kieran exploded. "He could be planning on doing the whole thing in a glass jar, for all you know! You're talking about kidnapping, Crawl! Kidnapping a live person! In the U.S.! Kidnapping! On guesswork!"

"I know that's why he took the sample," Crawl said, "and I know it's for her. And you do, too."

"They might have a death penalty over there for all you know, kidnapping a sixteen-year-old in America."

"For six million dollars, I'll take that chance. Because it's a good chance. It's a perfect chance. And I know it's a lock because I know he'll pay that. Easy. So what if it's six million. He'll never miss it!"

"But it's serious, hunt-us-down stuff!"

"It's fifteen minutes to take her. Half a day, maybe, to keep her away from the house and get the money. Fifteen minutes to take her back. It's no weapons. It's no one hurt. It's not that much risk, as isolated as they are, and him being a criminal himself now. And it's six thousand, thousand dollars! Certain! He'll pay it!"

Kieran stared at him, stone-faced.

"But you know, you don't have to be in on it," Crawl said with a shrug, calming down again. "We don't need you. Michael and me will do fine. Why do we need you? But I swear, I'm going to make Michael so rich he'll be smiling for the next fifty years."

Kieran rubbed his face with both hands. He inhaled as deeply as he could and exhaled slowly. He stared at the morning skyline of a city he had never seen before. He said, "I didn't say I was out."

"Brenna would be smiling at you for it, too," Crawl said. "Wouldn't she? And your mom in the new house you talk about getting for her? With the new fence around it? But, like I say, we really don't need you. You can walk and it's okay, you know that. It really is."

"It's just ..." Kieran rubbed his face again, hard. "It's just, we're so far past 'barely a crime' here, we can't even see it in the rearview mirror. And you shouldn't just flip it off with, 'I know all this for sure.' That's all I'm saying."

They were silent. A full minute passed.

Kieran said, "I didn't say I wouldn't be with you. It's just gotta be thought out."

More silence.

He said, "I just want to make sure we're as certain as we can get, that's all. Before we do something like kidnapping somebody. You agree with that, right?"

Crawl scratched his cheek. He nodded. A moment later, he practically whispered, "Nobody gets hurt. We treat the girl like a jewel. We take Brenna, if you want. She can take care of the girl. She'd be good for us that way. We'll take Brenna."

Kieran inhaled and exhaled slowly. He said, "Creating Jesus, for God's sake."

Crawl said it again, "You can bring Brenna along."

"People decide they want to be God, bad things happen."

"Brenna can take care of the girl. And take care of you, right?"

"Try to play God, it's like setting off a bomb. It's like a blast area. A shock wave goes out."

"Cleary talked about running out of time. I wonder if he's crazy enough to try for Christmas."

"They call the blast area the 'kill zone'. Everybody in it gets fried, doesn't matter who they are."

"Do you think his 'time is important to me' is about actually trying for Christmas Day?"

Kieran blinked. He looked at Crawl and said, "What?"

"I said, wouldn't that be perfect for Dr. Crazy? Mary's boy-child, Jesus Christ, born on Christmas Day?"

11

The doctor was seated near the window of his library, facing Bruce Lake. This time there was very little light. Just a glimmer from the moon, nothing more. This time it was four o'clock in the morning.

He had not yet slept, and he would not sleep. His sister, Leah, would not sleep either. Not on this night.

He was sitting upright. His eyes were open. His arms were as straight as stakes. They reached to his knees, where his hands rested in motionless fists. His breathing was long and deep and regular.

He knew that he had done everything that could possibly be done to see Marie safely through the triumph of the day. He knew that the ovum had been properly removed and prepared. He knew that the DNA he had retrieved from the microscopic bone shards extracted from the shroud had been successfully introduced into the ovum's nucleus without destroying the priceless spindle proteins that enable the cells of a new organism to divide and thrive. He knew that this single achievement had overcome the last great obstacle to the cloning of a fully developed human being. And he knew that he had successfully implanted the embryonic clone into the womb of his niece, Marie.

He felt spent.

He stared in silence at the soft glow of the lake and the silhouetted beauty of the trees in the subdued light of the partial moon. He inhaled deeply. He thought of Marie. She would be giving birth to more than the child already growing within her; she would be the mother of a whole new age of purposeful human cloning. He thought also about his own role, and he let himself smile, although just slightly, as he wondered which of his two accomplishments would be recognized as his greatest achievement and his most enduring legacy: his cloning breakthrough or his conjuring of the second coming of the most perfect human being who ever lived.

Marie heard the alarm but couldn't locate it. It sounded as though it were coming from behind the curtain in the auditorium, where so many people had gathered, pressed closely together, to see something Marie hadn't been told about. When she tried to squeeze past them and to climb the stairs of the stage, her legs wouldn't move. She wondered why, but she didn't feel afraid. A fat man next to her laughed and said something in a language that sounded Native American. She thought he was telling her how to shut off the alarm, and that led her to realize, even there, in that place where she could still see the blue curtain of the Immaculate Conception High School auditorium, that she must be dreaming, and that it was her bedside clock that she was hearing.

She worked to wake herself up and succeeded. But she didn't quite wake up all the way. She turned to look at the clock that was still making noise and saw that it was blurred. Her bedside table was blurred too, and the windows across the room.

She pushed herself up on one elbow and reached to shut off the alarm. Then she pulled down her covers.

A twinge of fear came over her. Was she still dreaming, or did her legs really not want to move as they should when she tried to swing them out of the bed?

She realized that she was sweating and heard herself moan, and she tried even harder to focus. She was aware that her heart was beating faster than normal. She forced herself to a sitting position and stared again at the clock. It said 6:00 A.M. The right time for it to go off. The right time for her to wake up.

She was in her own bed and knew she should be moving now, but her legs seemed to belong to somebody else. She struggled to slide her legs over the side of the bed, and did so, but very slowly. When she was sure her feet were on the floor she leaned forward and forced herself to stand. There was feeling there, but what was wrong with her legs? Were they just asleep? How could both her legs be asleep at the same time?

As she stood up, becoming more and more concerned, she felt dizzy, then nauseous.

Inhaling quickly with deep breaths, she pressed one foot in front of the other, making sure she could feel the throw rug and hard wood floor until she entered the door of the bathroom attached to her bedroom. Once inside the bathroom, she sank to her knees and vomited

124

in the toilet. Once. Twice. A third time, the last time with nothing but air and noise and saliva.

Shaking and wet with sweat, suddenly very afraid she wouldn't be able to get up again, she grabbed the side of the toilet bowl and called out to her aunt. It was a weak call. She began to cry, but forced herself to stop. Then she called even louder and more desperately, this time to her aunt and her uncle, too.

No one came.

She cried out as loudly as she could, this time in as close as she could get to a scream, "Help me!"

The scream made the room move, and she buckled over suddenly to retch again into the toilet.

Voices sounded behind her. She felt herself being held by her upper arms and steadied. Her aunt was on her knees beside her, offering quiet assurances that she was okay, that her uncle was coming right in, that he would know what to do, that she was going to be fine and shouldn't be afraid.

But she was afraid. Something was really wrong.

She felt a hand press to her forehead, heard her uncle say, "My goodness, she's got a fever starting," then, "Are you going to be sick again, Marie? Or do you want us to help you get to your bed?"

She breathed deeply and thought about it, finally shaking her head no, still determined not to let herself cry. Then she tried to stand.

Her uncle and aunt helped her, but she felt incredibly shaky.

She said one word: a whispered, "Sorry."

Even that sounded distant to her.

"Don't be silly," she heard her aunt say. "You have a flu or something, that's all it is."

Her uncle was talking, too. "You'll be all right," he said again and again.

They were leaving the bathroom. She no longer felt as if she were going to vomit, at least not right away, but nothing else was really in focus, and she felt so weak.

They helped her past her dresser, where she saw her mother and father watching her from their photo framed in silver.

Her aunt said to her uncle, "Can you give her anything that will help?"

"I'm sure I can," her uncle said. "Get my case from the office, please. And get a half glass of milk."

Leah left the room.

Her uncle helped her until she was sitting on the edge of the bed, then he swung her legs up and eased her back onto her pillow. He sat down next to her, tall and serene. "Tell me exactly what you're feeling," he said quietly. "Do you feel any pain at all?" He probed her abdomen gently with the practiced fingertips of a physician.

Marie shook her head. "I don't hurt at all," she said weakly. "I just felt so dizzy and sick. And my legs felt almost numb. But I think they feel a little better now."

"It came on strongly, didn't it?" her uncle said. "And I'm afraid it's probably not done with you yet." He looked carefully at her eyes and felt her throat in several places.

He was, Marie thought, like a different man when he was acting as a doctor. He was certainly gentler and more attentive.

She closed her eyes and tried to relax. At least the room wasn't moving any more. And she didn't feel as nauseous as she did before, just a little queasy and incredibly weak.

She felt the doctor move at her side, then heard him whisper so close to her ear that his very nearness, as well as his words, startled her. "I love you, Marie," he said, "more than anything in this world."

She opened her eyes. Her lips parted, but before she could speak her uncle rose to a sitting position, and all she could do was meet his gaze.

His eyes looked so soft they actually seemed moist.

What was it that was making her feel afraid?

"You'll be all right," her uncle said once more, now in his normal voice. "But you may be in for a few uncomfortable days."

"How can you be sure it's just the flu?" she asked weakly.

"Oh, I'm sure, dear," he said.

Her aunt Leah entered with a black attaché case in her left hand and a half-filled glass of milk in her right.

The doctor said, still looking at Marie, "If I wasn't sure, I wouldn't have said so."

He opened his case and withdrew an ear-reading thermometer. "I'm afraid you may be home from school for a few days," he said, taking her temperature. "This could be the latest Asian strain." Withdrawing the thermometer, he said, "Not quite as high as I thought, but still, a hundred and one has meaning."

"That's not that bad," Marie said quietly.

The doctor put the thermometer in his medical bag and withdrew a small bottle of milky fluid.

"What's that?" Marie asked.

"It's a name you wouldn't recognize," the doctor said. "But it will settle your stomach, for one thing." He emptied the bottle into the glass of milk. "Yes, you'll be home for a few days, and sleeping, I'm sure." Then he and his sister propped Marie up so she could drink.

The milk tasted like peaches.

"In fact, don't be surprised if you sleep a lot," her uncle said, speaking quietly again.

"It won't make me throw up?" Marie asked. "I feel like I might."

Her aunt reached for the glass. Marie handed it to her.

"I would think you're done throwing up," the doctor said, now whispering and staring hard into her eyes.

"I feel terrible."

"Just rest, dear," her aunt said, bringing Marie's sheet up to her waist. "You don't worry now, about this, or school, or anything."

Her uncle helped her back down onto her pillow.

"You'll be fine, sweetheart," he said.

Her answer was weak. "I'm sure I will."

Her aunt pulled the sheet up to her chin.

"I'm sure you will too," the doctor said. His voice was confident, but seemed farther away.

Marie's eyes were half-closed.

The doctor smiled.

Aunt Leah smiled.

Marie closed her eyes.

Her aunt was saying something else.

But was that her aunt?

Someone's voice. Only, this time, from very far away.

12

Not many years ago, Michael Connell had been hard as a tree, and lean. Now he was growing into a much different man. Just thirty-two-years-old and still generally solid, he had rounded out in recent years, top to bottom, but especially in the face, which was also growing more ruddy. He had rounded out so much, in fact, that looking in the mirror continued to take him by surprise. His belly was so pronounced that when his wife, Sherri, begged him not to spend the three weeks away from home on his mysterious business trip eating and drinking, he patted his paunch and remarked with a laugh, "Bein' pregnant puts a glow in my eye, but it's damned uncomfortable, isn't it?"

Sherri smiled at him now from the photograph he had pinned to the visor of his red Chevy pickup. Her long arms were spread wide in the picture. The Pacific Ocean churned behind her.

Michael missed her whenever he left home for more than a few days.

He raised his bottle of imported stout and drank to his blond-haired wife.

He missed his son, Roddy, too, the proudest mark he would ever leave on the world, even if he lived to be a hundred. Now four years old, Michael's dark-haired boy was laughing at him from the second photograph pinned to the visor, the lad dressed in a Disneyland T-shirt with his head leaning forward in mock surprise and his eyes as wide as searchlights.

Another long drink. This one to the finest son God ever gave a man who sure didn't deserve it.

He glanced at his watch. One in the afternoon.

He had left Arizona and was making his way past Gallup, New Mexico. More desert lay ahead—dry red land as far as the eye could see interrupted occasionally by little towns with Native American names. But I-40 was a good road to travel, and the Chevy was running fine. He would arrive in the Pecos Wilderness between five and six o'clock to join Crawl, Kieran and Brenna at the A-frame he had rented near Monastery River in the Sangre de Christo Mountains.

The others, he knew, would be getting there before him.

He reached up to pat the photos of his wife and son with his fist. With any luck, he thought, he would do them so fine in the next few days they would never have to worry about anything. "Not ever," he whispered, thinking especially of Roddy "Not in your whole sweet life."

The music on the radio was fading. He hit the scan button, listened through five stations, all of them with commercials, then turned off the radio and began to sing in a clear tenor voice "The Sash My Father Wore".

He had already spent the better part of the last three weeks in the Albuquerque and Santa Fe areas, he and his GPS, the first time he had ever been to that part of the country. He had paid some good money and made some good contacts and forwarded the others a full dossier on the doctor and his niece and sister, including details he had dug up on the mechanics and timelines of cloning, which he had found fascinating.

He had also gotten detailed maps of Santa Fe and the whole northern wilderness area, and he had taken photographs of the doctor's house and its surrounding roadways back where the mountains began in earnest, north of the city. He had even talked with real estate agents in the area. There were just a few private properties. Private land was scarce in the wilderness area, therefore expensive. The few permanent homes that existed, including the doctor's, which had been built just a dozen years before, were powered with generators. Satellite was used for phones and the Internet.

Michael had photographed the doctor's entrance roads a hundred yards at a time, even visited and photographed a second house, which was down and around the bend at the southern end of Bruce Lake. It was the only other building from which anyone could see the doctor's house, and then only as a sighting of lights at night. Situated at the base of the high hills at the south end of the lake, the other home was owned by a retired couple who were traveling in Europe, according to the men Michael had found putting the couple's pontoon boat in the water for the approaching summer months. They wouldn't be back, the workmen said, for another three weeks.

Everything was working out better than fine.

He had detailed the doctor's work schedule. Three days a week in Albuquerque, the rest at home in the wilderness. He had a lab in his house, the real estate agent had mentioned. On the three days the doctor spent at his company, he left his house north of Santa Fe at 5:30 A.M.; he left Jerron-Nash to return home at 5:00 P.M. and arrived at about 6:15 or 6:30. When the traffic or the weather was bad, his drive was extended by anything from twenty to forty-five minutes.

The doctor's sister, Leah, had a lot less distance to cover, but she took her time. She dropped straight down to Santa Fe to pick up the girl from school at 3:45, but she often ran brief errands on the way back, sometimes not arriving at home until after 5:45. And on Mondays it was even later. On Mondays, she and the girl stopped at a shopping center on Farrell Avenue to spend an hour or so buying groceries. It was, Michael observed, their only shopping day, and it put off their Monday arrival until 7:00 P.M. on the first Monday he followed them, nearly 7:15 on the next two.

Who could tell, something like that might make a difference.

He had rented the A-frame for the whole month for him and the others, and he had forwarded them detailed driving directions.

Finally, he had purchased a six-year-old Chevy Malibu from a Pentecostal minister's wife in Albuquerque. He paid her cash, then gave her an extra hundred dollars to hold the car for his brother, who, he told her, would be showing up from Ireland for a visit on May 10.

She had protested the extra hundred dollars, but he insisted. It was an Irish way of doing things, he assured her, but his brother would call her the day before arriving so she wouldn't be worrying about when he would show up, and she could use the extra money for her and her husband's ministry at their little church.

How could she refuse?

He had also insisted to Crawl, in the conversation they had when the first details of the plan were put together, that Kieran's idea of bringing his girlfriend was a bad idea, that Michael would only accept her on two conditions: one, that Crawl was sure Brenna would actually help and not be there just as company to Kieran; and two, that her being part of the plan wouldn't cut his full share of the three-way split they had originally discussed—no splitting four ways because of Kieran's girl. If Kieran wanted a soft body, let him buy one in Santa Fe.

"It wasn't Kieran's idea," Crawl had reassured him. "It was mine. Brenna's got a sharp mind, which is always a help. And the aunt will stop for Brenna: sun going down, young girl with car trouble. She won't stop as easy for one of us, and with this job we take no chances. That's rule one."

The job that took no chances, as Crawl described it, would go like this: "You're with Brenna," he said to Michael. "You set up the grab on Monday, when the girl and her aunt are always late getting back home. Not night, but close enough, in a remote enough spot where the aunt won't be able to pass up a scared young lady with car troubles, and where cell coverage runs out because of how the road cuts below the thick tree line of the mountains right there."

Michael agreed. It would be a good setup.

"When Brenna gets her stopped," Crawl continued, "you wave a weapon at them, tell them no one gets hurt and all that, but the girl leaves with you. It's not only simple, it's safe as a cradle. We don't try and root her out of the house. Too many chances for hiding places, hidden satellite phones, guns lying around, other stuff we might not know about. The things you have to make sure of are, she doesn't have a weapon and her car's out of commission somehow so she has to hobble back to the house, which is close by, and which she'll do as fast as she can on a bad leg. But Kieran and I will already have been at the house, making sure the doctor understands the rules of the game. He'll keep the old lady from calling the police or anybody else. We get caught, he gets caught for the cathedral in Italy. Simple as that."

Crawl said the doctor wouldn't risk being caught for the DNA heist for several good reasons. "One, he won't last in jail. Two, he won't be around to see his prize baby born; won't get to take care of his niece and won't get to play grandpa to his own private Jesus. Three, he's disgraced on top of everything else. Even if he doesn't go to jail or he outlives his sentence, his reputation is gone, and you think he doesn't care about that? Four, the girl is hounded to hell and back by TV people, and they don't stop comin' down on her once nine months rolls around. It gets even worse then. And five, he can't be sure we won't kill the girl if the job gets screwed up. We know we won't, but hell, for all he knows, we might have friends who would go after the girl and the kid just to even the score if he puts us all in jail."

Michael wondered at the time if so much money was making his head go soft, but it really did seem bulletproof. And he hadn't seen anything to change his mind since.

"No," Crawl said, "he may be crazy, but he's not crazy enough to let the old lady call the law. That's why we have to let him know it's us, and let him know exactly what's going on, because that's the only way there's no police; the way he knows he has no choice but to pay us and get on with his Jesus deal in secret."

In the end, they all felt good about it. Even Brenna, who, according to Crawl, would be able to take care of the girl better than himself or Michael or Kieran by a long shot.

Only the money changed. They were now going to hold out for seven and a half million U.S. dollars, and the three of them were going to split it evenly: two and a half million to Crawl, two and a half million to Michael, and two and a half million to Kieran. Almost two million pounds each, with Brenna dependent on Kieran for whatever he wanted to share with her.

The one hitch so far had happened on the week before, when Michael's wife, Sherri, tripped with a laundry basket and tore the cartilage in her right knee. She went into surgery the next day, so Michael had to do the two-day drive back to California and be there with her and his son for a few days, at least.

While the interruption didn't make any real difference to any of them, since their schedule could bend from one Monday to the next, it had bothered Michael. Like having a worm all of a sudden living in your brain and wiggling when you didn't want it to. The worm kept reminding him: things can always go wrong. You can get all the information you need and make all the plans you want, but things can always go wrong.

Not a good thing to keep popping into mind when you're on your way to kidnap a teenage girl and hold her for seven and a half million dollars ransom, and you and Crawl and Kieran have histories in a group some people called terrorists.

He drained his bottle of stout, lowered it to the floor, being careful not to break it on the others that were already there, looked again at the prized photos on his visor and began to sing another song.

This time, without really thinking about it, he sang a sad one about a girl whose father wanted her to quit seeing the young man she loved, and so she did. But just for a few days. Then the guy got killed just as she was leaving home to find him again. All she had left of him was the old scarf she had borrowed from him in the rain the day she told him about her father, which, as Michael stopped to think about it, hardly seemed worth mentioning, even in a song.

The deep-woods cottage that Crawl, Kieran and Brenna pulled up to at 3:40 on Sunday afternoon was nearly two hundred yards from Monastery River, and, according to Michael's directions, exactly forty miles from the home of the doctor.

"Forty miles," Kieran said, as they stepped out of the car. "Maybe we should go and take a look at it tonight."

"We'll see it tomorrow, early, just a pass-by to get a feel for the drive," Crawl said. "When we go back serious, later, we'll see it inside and out. Tonight, we'll just make sure we got our act together."

Kieran agreed, as he had with every decision since that moment when he had told Crawl he was definitely in. He had been agreeing with Crawl for years before that, he realized suddenly, and he felt not only surprised but unhappy about it. He recalled when they were young and he followed Crawl as he broke into houses they knew would be empty because the obituaries in the papers said the family had a funeral going on someplace far from home. He remembered trying to be another Crawl Connell, a bad-ass paramilitary in the Ulster Volunteer Force.

All the time, Crawl was just trying to be another Michael, and Michael was just trying to be his father. Was everybody just trying to be somebody else?

He circled to the back of the car and picked the drinks out of the open trunk. Then he placed his black athletic bag on top of the cooler and walked to the cabin. It was a pine-log two-level A-frame built for genuinely rustic living. A well in a small riverside clearing supplied the water. Butane supplied heat to the stove. A not-quite-erect outhouse stood thirty yards into the woods on the backside of the cabin, opposite the river.

Inside, there were none of the carved bear statuettes or mounted antlers or framed paintings of leaping fish that invariably showed up in the typical hideaways where laughing men gathered to drink and play cards and trade half-true stories before and after they hunted down some of the area's wildlife. There were simply a worn couch with a tan waterproof slipcover, two equally worn matching chairs (also with slipcovers) and two round throw rugs of browns and blues and the sandy color of the area's soil. A circular metal fireplace sat almost in the center of the room, but there was no wood in sight. Three oil lamps were on the floor in the corner nearest the front door. The half-sized butane stove stood beside a small well-water sink against the back wall. An old oak table was covered with polyurethane and surrounded by six wooden folding chairs. Plastic plates, cups and glasses hid in the cupboard above the sink. Two dull carving knives and four serving spoons were in the small drawer beside it, along with a can and bottle opener.

On the loft level, five aluminum-tubing cots were lined up in a single row, with no wall or curtains to separate them.

"This is perfect," Crawl said with a grin, throwing his blue athletic bag on the floor next to the fireplace and moving around to study the room. "Out of the way. Perfect distance from Dr. Crazy. End of the bloody road, if you call that trail a road. No reason for anybody in the world to drive back here. And look around," he said, sweeping his hand from left to right, "in the corners, especially—no spider webs."

"That's always good," Kieran said, putting his bag down on the table. "What do you think, Bren?" Turning, and with a smile, he said to Crawl, "She hates spiders worse than you do."

Brenna put her black bag on one of the folding chairs and ran her palm over her hair, which was pulled back tight into a thick ponytail held by a bright green hair band. "I hate anything that crawls on my body with more than two legs," she said. She absentmindedly brushed the dark gray sweater that draped loosely over her worn jeans, checking it for crawling things, then put her hands on her hips and looked around more closely. "Reminds me a little of home," she said. "Not lush, is it?"

Kieran sat down, stretched out his legs and opened a bottle of stout. "The air's sure better," he said to Brenna.

Crawl motioned to Brenna to grab him a bottle of stout, since she was near the cooler.

He and Brenna joined Kieran at the table. "Spiders sneak around, though, like cats," Crawl said. He took a long drink and let out an equally long, "Ahhh."

Kieran said, "Cats don't tie you up and suck your blood, though, like spiders."

134

Crawl laughed, and Brenna did, too. She checked her sweater again.

"Why are we sitting in here?" Crawl said. He got up, grabbed his folding chair and headed for the long grass in the clearing that stood between the cottage and riverside woods.

Kieran and Brenna shrugged to one another and followed, Kieran carrying two chairs so that he could put his feet up.

He thought again, as he came back in to grab his bottle of stout, about always doing what Crawl said. Even simple things, like going outside to talk. Simple things like saying you want tea when they offer you stout or you want stout when they offer you tea. The game was always on with him; he would move you a little so he could move you a lot.

They sat silently for several minutes, just relaxing, taking it in. They couldn't see the river, but they could hear it. What they saw was the forest, and above the pines and aspens and junipers, the tops of the Rockies to the west, high and white-capped and purple in the distance under fat, white clouds.

"You think this cabin is like your apartment, huh?" Crawl asked Brenna.

"I like this neighborhood better," she said.

"Know what you should do?"

"Hmmm."

Kieran thought, there it is again. Crawl's going to tell her what she should do. He closed his eyes and leaned his head back and thought, instead, about how much he did like it here, listening to the birds calling and the insects clicking, and to how Brenna said, "Hmmm," in that soft, special way.

"You should get a picture of home," Crawl said, "if that's what you call that apartment you got. Take it with the camera you'll buy after tomorrow. Download the picture into your new computer, which you'll also buy. Then, when you get out on your new yacht ..."

She laughed and looked at Kieran, who still had his eyes closed. "Me and Kieran," she said.

Crawl barely paused. "Then you bring the shot up on your phone and look at it right there, in the middle of the Mediterranean. 'Cause that's where you'll be if you're smart, just off the coast of Italy. So you can look at the shot there, with a tall drink in your hand, and

135

you can remember how in-the-toilet your life used to be. Before tomorrow happened."

Brenna laughed again.

"No more Belfast for me," Crawl said with a hard stare at the mountains. After a long moment, he looked at Brenna again. "I meant the part about Italy. You've got to see Italy, Bren."

"You liked Italy better than Ireland?"

"It didn't have factories," Crawl said. "Not where we were. It was pretty, and it didn't have people blowing each other up every two months." He thought about it for a few seconds, then added, "I like it here, too, though. This is great country."

Kieran opened his eyes to rejoin them. "This is really nice," he said. "I like it better here, in this spot, than Italy." He stared at the Rockies and studied the sky. "Even the clouds don't feel like moving," he said. "Like they just want to stay where they are and enjoy things. Don't make anything else happen."

"I might even buy the property between here and the river and build a house right down on the water," Crawl said. "Just for vacations in the right season of the year." He leaned forward, suddenly laughing, and jabbed Kieran's arm. "But that would make it too easy, wouldn't it, little brother? All teenage Jesus would have to do to find me is drive an hour from home, and, poof! . . . I'd be up in flames."

Michael arrived laughing and shouting nearly two hours after the others. He brought more food and drink, and two fluorescent lanterns. He also placed two heavy green backpacks against the wall by the door.

There were bear hugs and more laughs, with a hard kiss on the cheek for Crawl, a hard handshake and hug for Kieran, and a gentler but firm handshake, and then a laughing hug and another hard kiss on the cheek, for the beautiful Brenna.

For the next hour and ten minutes they sat grinning and talking around the table as they ate sandwiches and drank good, thick stout and told stories of Ireland the way it used to be and about California the way it was now. Then they shared a short but enjoyable showing of Michael's prized few photographs of his wife, Sherri, and his only son, little Roddy, Crawl's nephew.

At six o'clock, the smiling stopped.

Then there were maps, and more photographs, dozens of them, but not of Michael's family. This time, of the doctor's house, rising in the deep woods by a lake, of the highways in the area and the dirt road leading from the highway to the house. There was the doctor himself: a dozen long-lens shots like the one he had sent to Crawl's e-mail, these taken both as the doctor arrived at and left from his office on two successive Fridays. The aunt was there, too, prim and proper, with a big gold cross hanging around her neck, shot as she exited her car at Marie's school and shot driving past Michael with Marie in the passenger's seat of her Lexus. And there was sixteen-year-old Marie Groves, as well, twenty-four shots in all, taken either with her Aunt Leah or with students outside of her school. Black hair, short. Alert expression. Soft-looking around her eyes, harder-looking in the set of her thin lips. Only smiling in one photo—one in twenty-four—taken as she ran down the steps at school with two other girls.

"You've already got copies of a few of these," Michael said. He put the maps in one pile and the photos in three separate piles. "But we'll look through them again to make sure there aren't any questions or concerns."

"Take us through them," Crawl said.

Brenna noticed that Kieran's right knee was bobbing steadily and that he was still staring at the photographs of the girl, not the maps. She reached to rest her hand on his.

"This," Michael said, pointing to a circle drawn on the map in red, "is where we are now. By this river and little lake." His finger traced a line to the highway, then around several long curves on the highway and up a smaller line representing a dirt road with another lake. There was another circle, also in red. "Forty miles," he said, "the man's house."

He pulled out several close-up photos of the house and the parking area in front of it, then two of the lake behind the house. "Bruce Lake," he said. "They live on the west shore. Another house is down in this direction, but that won't come into play."

"How do we make sure?" Crawl said.

"People are gone. They had some workers setting it up for summer, boat in the lake kind of stuff, but they're all done. People won't be back for a week at least, guaranteed."

His hand swept over the map. "All this," he said, "is mountains and woods. A few campers, rangers, whatever. A few hikers, maybe, watching out for brown bears, which is the kind you want to stay away from. Black, you say 'boo' and they go away. Brown bears eat you for lunch."

"Black, boo. Browns, lunch," Crawl said, smirking. He winked at Kieran, who looked at him but didn't change his concerned expression.

"The doc and this old couple own the only private property for about ten miles. There's a ranch south of here, but it's way out of the picture. And no cabins like this one, not on Bruce Lake, which is about three-quarters of a mile across at its widest and pretty long. End to end, about a mile and a quarter, something like that."

His finger traced sideways across the map, moving slowly on a line from the doctor's house to State Highway 10. "Now this little thread here is very important to our future well-being," he said. "This is Ridge Road. And this, this point right here, is where we get the girl." He let them ponder the spot his finger pointed to for a long moment, withdrew his finger, then continued. "Cells are dicey, territory like this, so I have radios for us too, just in case."

"He can still make a transfer of the money, though, right?" Brenna said.

"He doesn't have to get out. He has a satellite dish as big as a lake," Michael said. "Phones, web, whatever."

"How'd you get detail on him and the place?" Crawl asked.

"Realtor. Wanted me to know I'd be safe when I bought my next house from him."

Crawl nodded.

Michael noticed that Kieran was looking at the photographs again. Looking at the girl, Marie. Looking sad.

"So anyway," he said, "the radios are good for keeping us in touch with one another if we need them. Then Ridge Road runs past this point, a mile or so from where we get the girl, and right here this private road goes three, four hundred yards back to the man's house. Right here. By the lake."

He studied Kieran again, just for a few seconds, then said, quietly, "You're right, Kieran. The girl looks like your sister, Colleen."

Brenna pressed forward.

Crawl whispered, "Yeah. She does."

Kieran said quietly, as if in a trance, "Not really. Her face is different. This one is thinner. And she looks twelve years old. Her hair isn't as long."

"Right," Michael said. "All in all, she's a pretty average kid, I guess. Independent. I guess she would be, from the looks of the aunt, anyway. Kids at her school confirm she's kept on a pretty tight rope at home, so probably has to make do on her own, you know? But there's nothing you have to worry about as far as holding her for a few days." He smiled. "No black belts or anything."

"You talked with kids at her school?" Crawl asked, showing surprise.

"I said I was the owner of a photo gallery down in Albuquerque, there to talk to the school about getting some of their graduation picture business. It was easy. Kids like to talk about other kids, like it's all good gossip. And they all know about Aunt Leah." He pulled out two photos of the aunt. "They've got names for her: Hell-a-Leah, saying it like Halleluiah. And Fire Ant. Stuff like that. She drops the girl off in the morning, picks her up after school. You know the routine."

Crawl said. "Yeah, we do. So let's look at the road again, where we borrow her for awhile. You got photos of that, right?"

Michael nodded and spread them out.

At the spot where they would take the girl, the road looked like a dry riverbed running between walls of pines that rose up like cliffs on both sides. Michael pointed out just one break in the trees along the stretch where they would grab the girl, and that, he said, was just a marshy area with standing water.

"Tomorrow night," Michael said, "after the shopping and all, the girl and her aunt will get to our spot about seven o'clock, give or take twenty minutes, just to be safe." He was tracing his finger over the point of the abduction. He said, "That would put us in place by 6:40 at the latest."

Crawl looked at Brenna, then at Kieran, then at his brother, Michael. "So, have we been over that part enough in the last two weeks?"

Three nods.

"No questions? Problems? Anything we need to go over one more time?"

"Don't worry about us," Kieran said.

Crawl said, "Good. And even if the kid or the aunt screams loud enough that the doc hears them from way down at the house, all it'll do is heighten the effect, you know? Make him all the more desperate. So don't try to stop them if they scream."

Michael said, "We'll take her screaming."

Brenna said, "She probably will be."

"And take her without hurting her," Kieran said.

Michael smiled. "Oh, hell, no."

"Make sure we don't hurt her."

Michael said, still grinning, "We wouldn't do that, would we, Bren?"

Brenna said, "No need. And the aunt will be screaming all the way back to the house, so you guys will hear her coming."

"Just make sure about grabbing her keys," Crawl said. "Make sure when she goes back to the house, she's walking. Don't let her follow you out of there." Then he thought for a second and added, "Is the girl gonna be throwin' up?"

Brenna said, "Throwing up?"

"Morning sickness. When do they start throwin' up?"

"Sherri puked at about three or four weeks, I think," Michael said.

"I don't clean it up if she's puking," Crawl said, looking at Brenna.

Kieran's gaze rose from the photo of the girl to settle critically on Crawl. "Seven and a half million dollars on the table, probably a life sentence if we're caught, and what? We're going to sit here and worry about who cleans the floor?"

Michael raised his hand and rose, grinning broadly, from the table. "I agree with the young man from Belfast," he boomed.

Suddenly, laughing, he hurried across the room.

Crawl, seeing where his brother was going, smiled and pulled his chair closer to the table.

Michael picked up the two green backpacks that he had placed near the door and said, walking back with the packs held high, "Let's talk toys, instead."

Slowly, without sitting down, he bent over the table, opened the first of the two backpacks and carefully unwrapped a stainless steel Heckler & Koch 9mm compact automatic handgun. "Insurance," he whispered. "More than we'll ever need, but ..." He picked up the weapon and held it in his open palm. "It's the only way to shop."

He placed the gun on the table and unwrapped another, this time a black H&K .40 caliber.

Kieran glanced uneasily at Brenna.

She was smiling even wider than Michael.

The third weapon was another black H&K .40 caliber. The last, another stainless steel 9mm.

"I want one of the silver ones," Brenna said as soon as the fourth weapon touched the table.

"Beautiful," Crawl said, reaching for the first of the silver 9mm H&Ks.

Brenna picked up the second 9mm and weighed it in her hand. Her eyebrows arched, as if she were surprised to discover how heavy a gun really is. Another smile, this time nodding.

Kieran said, "I never knew you liked guns."

Brenna shrugged. "I never held one," she said quietly. "But I don't mind it."

Michael took a .40 caliber and snapped the bolt back hard, testing the action.

Brenna saw what Michael had done and tried it herself. The first time her fingers slipped off, and she giggled. The second time, she made it happen.

Kieran picked up the last of the weapons, the other black .40 caliber. He checked the weight. He slipped his finger around the trigger. He worked the safety several times with his thumb. He checked the action. He put the gun down.

He glanced at Brenna. He glanced at Crawl. He glanced once again at the photo of Marie Groves.

Under the table, his knee was bobbing fast.

It was nearly dusk. Crawl and Michael had gone to the river to visit and, they said, to talk over old times.

Maybe to make their own plans in secret was the way Brenna saw it, and she said so to Kieran after the brothers left.

"You're talking crazy," he told her. They were sitting at the table, side by side. He was pulled back farther from the table than Brenna, with his legs crossed. "What's gotten into you?"

"What do you mean, gotten into me?"

He shifted his weight and uncrossed his legs. "Nothing." He crossed his legs again, this time with the left leg on top. "But where's that come from, 'Maybe they're plotting something' down by the river?"

"I didn't say 'plotting something.'"

"What'd you say?"

She waited several seconds before answering, then chose her words carefully, speaking softly. "I just think we have to remember, this is all I'm saying, that there's seven and a half million, real, live, U.S. dollars in this." She began to peel the label off her empty bottle of stout. "I didn't mean plotting." She sucked in her lower lip, held it with her teeth for just a second, then released it and said, "I'm sorry."

"He'll always be my brother," Kieran said. "As close to one as I'll ever get, anyway."

"I said I'm sorry." She slid the bottle away and reached for her H&K. "Everything is planned really good, and we're all on top of it, and it's going to be fine." Picking the gun up, she slid the chamber open, then let it snap shut. Aiming it at her empty bottle, she pulled the trigger.

"I don't think we should load those," Kieran said, studying her.

"Oh, God, Kiero." She laughed and shook her head. "We're so past that question." She put down the gun, slid her chair nearer and leaned to slide her arm around his shoulder. "This guy has guns. He doesn't have any bodyguards watching his house, he must have guns. Everybody living in these mountains has to have guns."

"I didn't say he hasn't got guns."

"He's got the witch driving around in a car all by herself, driving all through the backcountry with a kid to protect, she's probably got one herself; one in the house, one in her car. At least. One for each of them in the car, how do we know?"

"I didn't say we shouldn't have the weapons. I just said I'm not sure about loading them."

"Michael's even talking about bears that eat us for lunch. We hadn't even figured on that."

"I just said I don't see why we have to load them. You really think we need that? You show it, that's all you have to do."

"Show it to a bear?" she said.

They stared at each other in silence for nearly a minute. Then she smiled warmly. Her hand started rubbing his shoulder.

"Tell me about the teenage Jesus," she said, murmuring softly. Her smile faded but didn't quite leave the corners of her lips. "What you and Crawl were talking about."

He exhaled in a soft laugh and shook his head. "That was nothing."

Her free hand moved to take hold of his wrist. She whispered, "Hey," very softly.

Kieran tightened his jaw for several seconds. Then he said, "This is all so damned weird, Bren. Don't you think it is?"

"Teenage Jesus."

He cleared his throat and shrugged. "Just something that popped into mind. Crawl and I were talking about it for about ten seconds back in Italy. I said, we do this, maybe a teenage Jesus would show up someday, come to find us, and he wouldn't be happy."

Brenna closed her eyes and laughed out loud. "I'm sorry," she said, suddenly forcing herself to stop. Then she giggled again and lowered her head. "But that's really funny, Kiero."

He laughed too, but just with a breath, briefly. "That's what Crawl thought."

She shook her giggle away and said, "I'm sorry. Really."

"I wasn't serious about it. But you know? It says things, about when he comes again."

"Jesus or Crawl?" She laughed again.

"Don't laugh, Bren, c'mon. You said nobody ever took you much to church, but it talks about trumpets going off and time slamming to a stop and all, you know what I mean? I'm just saying, it might be a shaky thing to be screwing around with."

Brenna said, "The weird part I see coming is, if the doctor does pull it off, she'll deliver a freak baby. Probably D.O.A. That blood is older than dirt."

"Does DNA get old? How do you know about that?"

"Hell, love, I don't know if it gets old." She shook her head with irritation and rose to cross the room and open the door. "It has to grow old. Isn't it alive?" She stood in the doorway, very still, looking out at the gold and orange beginning of the sunset, the sun just starting to slip into the tops of the mountains. "I do know it's not going to be Jesus, though, Kiero. Give the doctor credit for being a raging genius, but it's still not going to be Jesus. You don't have to be Saint Peter to know that the thing about Jesus that made him whatever he is wasn't in his DNA. Even if she makes it to delivery, which she won't, that's what she's going to get: a baby that won't be the Jesus that lived before any more than I am, or you are, or Crawl. So . . . let's just grow the hell up."

Kieran stared at her, waiting for her to turn and face him.

"There's only two big parts to this," she said, raising her voice but still not turning around. "And neither of them is really hard. One, we stop an old lady and a teenage kid. And two, we borrow the kid for about twenty-four hours. Probably not even that."

"I know," Kieran said. He rose to his feet. "I know it'll be okay." He moved toward her. "I'm not going to stay awake worrying about teenage Jesus, Bren."

"So what are you worried about?" she said, turning, at last, to face him. "You're thinking something."

He stopped. His fingertips slipped into the pockets of his jeans. She said, "Just tell me what you're thinking."

He nodded. "Okay. I'm thinking I'm surprised at how much you're enjoying this. I'm surprised at how much you enjoy having that gun in your hand. I'm thinking this started out to be not a big thing, now it's kidnapping, and you don't seem real bothered with that. Nobody does. Everybody's enjoying it as though we're still back talking about knocking off something that's barely a crime."

"Enjoying what?" she asked, narrowing her eyes, raising her voice. "Enjoying finally getting the chance of ten million lifetimes? Enjoying getting a chance that gives us as good a lock as anybody will ever have on an easy two and a half million U.S. dollars?" Her hands swept the air in frustration. "Enjoying getting that money for us, for you and me? Money for our future? Money to let you help your mother? Get her a beautiful place to live? Get her well again? Money to say, 'You never have to worry about anything again,' for God's sake! Is that what I shouldn't be enjoying?"

"No," he said. "I can see all that. We're just thinking about different things now, you and me. Maybe that's it. You're thinking about the money and slapping the chamber of that gun open like it was a toy. I'm thinking about kidnapping a pregnant teenager in the U.S. at gunpoint and stealing millions of dollars. It's all changed so much, and somebody should take it serious, so I am."

"Stealing from who? Stealing from a thief who's richer than God, the kind of person who'd do that to a sixteen-year-old kid? Not just a kid, but his own niece? Hell, Kieran, what if he did that to your sister, Colleen? She was sixteen, wasn't she? So that's not hard to imagine. What if he made her pregnant from a test tube, would that clear it up for you, what kind of bastard he is? Him and her aunt, too, because they've got to be in it together."

Kieran's face was flushed. He didn't speak.

"Just remember, sixteen. Like Colleen, right?"

He still didn't speak.

She stared at him with her mouth slightly open for a long moment, then she nodded once, rubbed her eyes with her fingertips and said, very quietly, "What do you remember most in your whole life, Kiero? What's the strongest memory you have, from your whole life?"

He shrugged.

"Tell me."

Kieran inhaled, thought about it, shrugged again and said softly, "Things at home, I guess."

"Colleen dying? I know that was bad for you. Would that be the strongest for you?"

"What are you getting at?"

She inhaled another long breath, paused to think, then said, "I remember two things most of all. I remember the smell of snow melting on my winter coat and my rubber boots. I don't know why that's so strong with me, but I can smell that when I think about it, even standing here." She paused for nearly ten seconds. Her eyes turned dull. Her voice lowered to a heavy, dreamy cadence. "The thing I remember most, though, is finding my bed on the sidewalk. In Wexford. My bed outside on the sidewalk. That was in the wet snow, too. I think that's why I remember the smell so much. My bed, outside in the street and the snow. All my things."

She tilted her head, as though trying to see the snow again, somewhere over Kieran's shoulder. "I was eight years old." She shivered. "I came home from school. It was raining and snowing at the same time. Mostly snowing. There was my little bed. Out on the sidewalk. In front of our flat. Part of it sticking into the street. The headboard with flowers on it right out in the street. All my clothes on it, not

145

even in boxes." She bit her lower lip. Her eyes were moist. "My dolls, I had two dolls, they were on it. Everything I had. All of a sudden it's trash. Everything my mother owned too, put into the damned street. We're trash. My mother sitting on her kitchen chair, looking lost. She was lost. Sitting outside in the snow on her kitchen chair. She looked up—saw me—cried like hell."

She leaned against the frame of the open door. "My father had been gone for two years. My mother couldn't pay the bills."

Kieran closed his eyes, inhaled, opened his eyes slowly.

Brenna blinked and stood upright.

"God told the world to find a way to break my heart, Kiero. And yours, too. And the world has to do what God tells it. But we can step up this time and say no. This time, we have to step up and say no."

Kieran moved slowly toward her.

"I will not let this chance get away from us, Kiero." Two tears traced down her cheeks. "I will not be put into the street again. Not me, not any children I'll ever have, not fifty years from now, not ever. And this is the only chance I'll ever have to nail a guarantee on that. Nail it down and put it away, certain. This has to be it. No matter what."

Kieran reached for her hands.

She lowered her head. "No matter what," she whispered again.

He whispered, "It'll work out."

She raised her head. Her eyes, still moist, looked very soft. "I swear I won't shoot anybody," she said.

"I know you won't."

"I couldn't do that."

"I know that."

"And the girl," she murmured, drawing nearer, "I swear I'll take good care of her. That will be my part of it."

Kieran nodded.

"I'll make sure she gets the mother kind of treatment she deserves, okay? Even if she's sick."

"It's okay, Bren." His right arm circled her waist, urging her to press against him.

She said in a whisper, "I'll know how to be a good mother, if that's what she needs." Her hands slid under his arms and circled his back.

She drew her lips close to his. "I'll make a good mother, Kiero. I promise I will."

Kieran looked at her, loving her. He loved her flashing, green eyes. He loved her full lips and soft skin. He loved her deep red hair, how it curled in waves and wrapped past her shoulders and was haloed now by the fierce orange glow of the setting sun.

She looked like a woman on fire.

13

Crawl eased the blue Malibu past the dirt entrance road that led to the doctor's house at 6:30 P.M. He drove another three hundred yards up Ridge Road before he turned the car around and shut off the engine to wait. Kieran sat beside him. Neither of them had spoken for twenty minutes.

The sun, already sinking toward the horizon, was hidden behind a long bank of clouds inching toward them from across the lake.

Kieran pulled his automatic from under his untucked green-and-blue plaid shirt and stared at it.

They had made the pass-by early in the morning. They stayed on the state road; they didn't go down the entrance road to look at the house. The only other vehicle they saw was an old van with a sixty-something couple in it. They looked dark skinned, maybe they were Native American, and they were three miles from the house and heading the other way.

Other than Michael's pointing out the spot where they would take the girl and the entrance road leading to the doctor's house, and Brenna's making a few "if the kid is really Jesus" remarks, they didn't talk much. She said maybe they should all look and see if there were any angels hanging around. Might be a thousand or two of them, she said, coming down from the clouds. She said she would like that, and she chuckled about it.

Kieran had said, no, that was the last thing she wanted to see. Then he dropped it, and she did too.

Crawl glanced at him and asked, speaking casually, "How come your knee's not pumpin' up and down?"

"What?"

"Nothin'. Just, your knee's usually pumping up and down. Now it's not."

"So?"

"I said. Nothin'."

Those were the only words either of them spoke as they sat and watched the empty road and the sun glimpsing at them off and on from behind the dark clouds as it sank behind the lower Rocky Mountains.

They waited in silence, alone with their thoughts, until 7:05, when Crawl's two-way radio crackled with Michael's voice.

Crawl sat up straight and answered with a simple, "Talk."

Michael said, "They're on the way," and clicked off his connection without waiting for an answer.

"Okay," Crawl whispered to Kieran, inhaling deeply. "Let's do it right."

He started the engine and pressed the accelerator to the floor. The Malibu spun viciously to the left, kicking up a cloud of dust and pebbles, then lurched forward and swerved hard into the entrance road. As they approached the house, Crawl slammed on the brakes and cut the wheel sharply to the left, skidding to a stop in light gravel thirty feet from the doctor's front door.

"What's the hurry?" Kieran asked.

"I'm excited," Crawl said. His eyes were laughing. "What the hell's the difference?"

Inside the house, the doctor heard the roar of an engine as he passed the shaded floor-to-ceiling window at the top of the stairs. He looked out and saw the Malibu skid to a stop.

Crawl was the first one out of the car.

The doctor recognized him immediately. The blood drained from his face. He blinked and stared, his heart racing. He recognized Kieran, too, but didn't focus on him. He turned and dashed, whispering, into his bedroom, where he flung open the door of the mahogany wardrobe cabinet that stood in the corner a few feet from his bed. He unbuttoned his shirt, pulled it off and threw it onto the bed. From inside the cabinet, he withdrew a powder-gray bulletproof vest, state-of-the-art, just five-sixteenths of an inch thick, very lightweight, very strong. He also reached for the ten-round .40 caliber Smith & Wesson that was in a holster hanging on the inside of the cabinet over the middle of the door, where it was out of immediate sight.

The doorbell rang once.

He tossed the S&W on the bed and raced to put on the vest and slip his shirt over it. He was still whispering, willing his fingers not to miss a button.

149

There was a loud knock at the door, another ring of the doorbell.

The doctor yanked a tie from the cabinet and ran it under his collar. He tied it in six seconds, threw on a charcoal gray blazer, grabbed the automatic and rushed down the stairs.

More knocks on the door. This time, four heavy ones. Again, the doorbell rang. Once.

"I'm coming," the doctor called as he passed through the front hallway.

Moving as quickly and silently as he could, he placed the automatic behind a ten-volume set of books—*The Art of War: From Agincourt to Vietnam*—that stood propped among several dozen other books on top of a bookcase in the living room, halfway between the entrance hall and the archway to the dining room. The rest of the books on top of the case, as well as most that lined the first of three shelves, were also about military campaigns.

"Just a moment!"

He checked his shirt buttons, inhaled deeply, made sure the shirt was tucked in, and buttoned his blazer. After inhaling one more time, he opened the door.

Crawl was grinning. His hands were held out wide in a gesture of surprise, greeting and friendship all mixed into one. "Oh, my God!" he exclaimed. "Look who lives here, Kieran! Of all people!" He turned to Kieran briefly, amazement beaming from his face.

Kieran smiled back at him, nodding.

Crawl turned back to the doctor. "Isn't God good? We were just in the neighborhood and saw this place, and look who the hell we find. And here we are, the three of us, back together again."

The doctor stood as motionless as a painting. There was neither surprise nor greeting in his expression.

Brenna saw them coming from two hundred yards away. Her heart hammered, but it felt good. Everything would begin now: the girl, the money, a whole new life with Kieran, all the security she ever wanted, all coming toward her and kicking up dust in a white Lexus sedan. The Chevy pickup, with Michael pressed down in the front passenger seat, well out of sight, was at her side, its hood raised, the driver's door hanging partly open.

She began to wave her arms and move out into the road, blocking Leah's path, then forward toward the oncoming car. She waved again and pressed her right hand theatrically against her chest as she smiled with a sigh of relief.

Her automatic, tucked into her belt in the small of her back, pressed against her as she walked.

She was glad to feel it there. Glad it was all happening, but anxious to get it over with. Her heart slammed in her chest even harder than before.

She could clearly see now that it was just the girl and the aunt; the aunt driving, the girl in the passenger seat beside her.

Everything perfect.

Less than fifty yards now.

She walked toward them, being careful to keep the open lane in the road blocked.

Thirty yards. Twenty yards. The Lexus, going very slowly, pulled over to the side and stopped a few yards behind Michael's truck.

Brenna smiled at the girl and the old lady. Her hair blew free in the rising wind. The smell of the lake was in the air. A bird screeched in the trees behind her. She was surprised at the wave of exhilaration she felt. It was so immense that she almost felt sick with it. She was feeling more excitement and more danger than she had ever felt before. The wave was elating and terrifying her at the same time.

Leah had slipped the car into neutral and lowered her driver's window four inches, no more.

Brenna said through the open window, with a smile and a distinct Irish lilt, "I thank you so much for stopping, ma'am."

Marie leaned forward to see the stranger with the Irish accent a little more clearly, her dark eyes smiling.

"It's no trouble," Leah said. "Is it something you'll need roadside assistance with? We can call for help just a few miles from here."

"Well, let me tell you what I'm doin' out here, then you decide," Brenna said cheerfully, leaning down to speak more directly into the open window.

Leah started to ask, "And what would that be?", but the sentence died in her throat. She had noticed movement from the corner of her eye. She turned and saw Michael getting out of the driver's side of the pickup, grinning. She breathed a startled, "Oh," and dropped her hand onto the gearshift.

Furious that Michael hadn't stayed hidden longer and had panicked the woman, Brenna jerked her automatic from the back of her belt and thrust its barrel awkwardly through the open window. "Turn off the engine or I'll shoot the girl!"

Marie grabbed Leah by the upper arm.

Leah sucked in her breath and froze. Even her lips were pale.

Michael snapped at Brenna, "What the hell are you doing?"

At the same time, Leah spoke to Brenna, too, demanding in a thick and frightened voice, "What do you people want?"

Brenna leaned forward, struggling to hide her sense of panic. She said in a voice that sounded forced and uneven, "Well, we didn't come out here to hurt the girl's new baby, now, did we?"

Leah's mouth opened, but no sound came out. Her eyes were suddenly wild with rage

Brenna realized she had made a terrible mistake. She stood straight, yanking the weapon from the window.

Michael charged across the front of the Lexus. "Damn it, girl!" He pulled out his automatic and, in a single sweep of his arm, pointed it directly at Marie in the front seat. "Out of the car, you!"

With a sudden guttural sound, Leah dropped the gearshift into drive and slammed the accelerator to the floor.

Brenna screamed.

Marie screamed.

Michael opened his mouth without making a sound. He froze for a single fateful second as a cry rose from his mouth and he pulled the trigger. The car's front bumper snapped him backward. The grille drove hard into his chest, crushing his back into the rear of the pickup truck.

His single bullet had entered Leah's forehead just above the right eye a split second before the air bag exploded into her ashen face.

The doctor hadn't said a word. Not, "What are you doing here?" or "What do you want?" or "How did you find me?" Nothing.

So Crawl did the talking. But not without producing his automatic and holding it casually at his side.

"Actually, we knew you lived here. We can't fool a clever man like you, can we?" The weapon waved clear directions for the doctor to back into the house.

Crawl and Kieran followed him inside.

Kieran closed the door behind them.

"The thing is, we need some money," Kieran said.

Crawl said, "Five hundred dollars."

He and Kieran both laughed.

"Cash," Kieran said.

Another laugh.

"And if we don't get it, we're going to burn your tapes."

No more laughter.

The doctor, still without expression, took a step backward, moving toward the entrance to the living room. His arms hung straight at his sides.

Crawl waved his H&K like a metronome. "Too late," he said. "Now we want more than five hundred dollars."

The doctor retreated farther into the room.

Crawl lowered the gun, pointing the muzzle at the doctor's waist, and moved with him.

Kieran stayed at his side.

The doctor said, "What is it you really want?" His voice was low and even. He took another step back. "When you leave, what, exactly, do you want to have with you?"

He was staring at Crawl, not at Kieran.

"We want seven and a half million of your dollars," Crawl said evenly. "Not cash this time. This time, U.S. dollars transferred to the accounts we'll give you. We want no police involvement. We want to disappear with your seven and a half million and never see you again. And we want you to know you'll never see us again."

"Is that all?" the doctor whispered.

"Okay," Crawl said, nodding. He stopped moving. "You don't like that, we'll settle for something else. Maybe come back to that later."

With that, he raised his automatic, pointed it toward the large gilded mirror hanging over the fireplace in the living room, swung it around slowly to face the doctor, then slowly lowered it and began to circle the doctor, walking between him and the bookcase. "How about, instead, we start with mama and the baby Jesus?" he said. "And we take them out of that nice white car right about now."

The doctor's eyes rounded with a threatening fire.

And in that moment, with Crawl smiling and Kieran looking deadly serious and the doctor's eyes boring into Crawl without blinking, the sound of a single gunshot cracked through the woods outside like a blast at the end of the world.

Crawl exclaimed, "What the hell?" He raised his gun instinctively, pointing it at the doctor's chest. He said loudly, practically shouting, "Kieran! Sit him down! If he moves, blow off his kneecaps."

Kieran jumped to follow orders. His heart was pounding. He yelled, "Sit down there!" and waved his weapon in the doctor's face, forcing him toward the couch in the living room.

Crawl left running to get back to the car.

Brenna was screaming.

Marie jerked off her seat belt and groped to get away from the deflated air bag.

Brenna shouted hysterically, "Back it up! Back it up! Oh, God!"

But Marie was already out of the car, crying and screaming and suddenly running as fast as she could up the road toward the house.

Brenna screamed at her to stop, then raised her gun, aimed it over Marie's head, and fired three times, quickly.

But Marie didn't stop.

Crawl heard Brenna's three shots as he pulled away from the house. He muttered and bit down hard, then exploded into a shout, "Damn it to hell! What are you doing?"

He wheeled the car onto the entrance road, pounding on the steering wheel as he went. His automatic was on the seat beside him. He started to grab it, but didn't. Instead he just pounded the steering wheel again and screamed in sudden fury at whatever had happened and whoever had caused it, "Damn it! Damn it! Damn it! What are you doing?"

The doctor sat on the edge of the couch, studying Kieran. His mind flitted from one possible point of attack to another. And attack would be needed. They knew about Marie and the baby, they knew about the car, which was due back home at that very time. Shots meant that others were here, not just these two. And not even Crawl or Kieran knew at what, or at whom, the shots had been fired.

He could see Kieran was scared. That might be useful. It might also be a hindrance. Scared young men did stupid things. But it was a start. Kieran was scared. And now he was alone.

154

He thought about the young Irishman's father, dying young. Did that absence bind Kieran closer to his friend Crawl, making it harder for the doctor to turn one against the other? Or could it be the wedge, with him now becoming a father figure to Kieran; someone older, accepting him at last?

He didn't know as much as he wished he knew about the boy's mother. But he knew about the old wounds and the newfound religion. What could he do to pry an opening into Kieran using memories of the mother?

A gray satellite phone stood on a glass-topped table next to a leather chair by the fireplace, its thick antenna sticking up like an arm signaling for attention. Kieran walked around the couch to grab it.

The doctor stared after him, his mind racing furiously.

Better yet—much better—there was the sister, the dead Colleen. She may be buried, but surely she was there to resurrect if needed. Love or guilt. It didn't really matter which of the two would be his most powerful weapon, did it? With the dead sister, the doctor had both to work with.

Kieran's automatic swayed at his side. He tossed the satellite phone onto a green chair that stood against the wall behind him. "You won't be using that," he said.

The doctor rubbed his scar with the thumb of his left hand. Four shots. And God only knew what was happening now, with the more violent of the two already joining whoever else was down the road.

No, he decided. He would not take the time for cat-and-mouse, for love or guilt, for twisting memories of a broken family. The Smith & Wesson was waiting for him in the bookcase just ten feet to his left, already propped up for easy taking, the safety off, ready to fire.

Brenna cried, "Oh, God! Is this really happening?"

She dropped the gun in the road and stood, paralyzed, watching Marie get farther and farther away, then staring at Michael like a child staring at roadkill. She felt overcome with the horror of things she had never seen before as a question pounded in her head: "Is this really happening?"

Michael's eyes were open. He was staring back at her, blinking. Blood leaked out of the left corner of his mouth. Sounds were leaking out with it, helpless, gasping sounds coming in shallow breaths.

Brenna felt her whole body shudder. She willed herself to think, move, do something.

Realizing the Lexus was stalled but still pressing against Michael, she raced to open the door, instinctively wanting to start it again and drop it into reverse, but the driver's door was locked. She cried, "Damn! Damn! Damn!" and, for the first time, even as she cursed the locked door and this whole day and the whole of her life, she looked at Leah behind the deflated air bag. The back of her head was a wad of blood. There was blood on the headrest, blood on the back of the seat, blood on the old woman's delicate white sweater.

Brenna breathed deeply and tried to steady herself. She heard herself whimper, "How did this happen?" and forced herself to move on shaky legs to the front passenger door of the car, which Marie had left open. She was trying not to look at the woman who was dead. She heard herself sobbing. She tried not to look at Michael, either, who was staring at the darkened sky and dying, his face barely visible to her, just six feet in front of the car's windshield.

Then she realized: she didn't have to back up the woman's car to help Michael. All she had to do was to pull the Chevy pickup forward. She burst into fresh tears and forced herself to try to think more clearly. She was alone now, with what was left of Michael. And the woman was really dead and the girl was really gone. She had to do the smart things, now more than ever.

Oh, Jesus!

Walking away from the car. Walking now toward the truck.

Keep breathing, she thought. Deep breaths. Don't look at the lady. Don't look at Michael. Don't faint.

Listening. Hearing Michael's breathing but still not looking at him. Thinking, thank God he's alive. Focusing on walking all the way around the front of the truck to the open driver's door on the other side. Thinking, Michael's not dead yet.

The old lady's dead. Michael's dying, for sure.

Just not dead yet.

He would be, though, by the time Crawl got there.

She felt what little strength was left in her legs drain away like water. She thought, oh, God, Crawl will kill me, him and Michael being so close. He'll go crazy. He'll kill me, for sure.

But Crawl wouldn't know she had started it by saying something to the lady about the baby. How could he know that?

156

Unless he caught the girl and the girl told him.

She was still crying, but softly now, and breathing in more regular breaths. She started the Chevy's engine and pulled the truck ahead, moving it slowly away from Michael's body. She hoped he wasn't stuck to the rear bumper and being pulled along with her, tearing open his wounds, maybe, or turning a broken neck.

Maybe he had just died anyway. She couldn't hear his breathing anymore, not from inside the truck. But how could all this have happened? How could all of this awfulness have actually happened?

She was sure she was going to be sick.

She turned off the pickup's engine and closed her eyes. Her head sunk to her chest. Her hands went limp on the steering wheel.

What was she doing here? Why was this happening so far from home?

With her head still lowered, she grabbed her hair with both fists and screamed a scream that was high and long and pounding with pain.

14

Crawl nearly ran Marie down. He spun onto Ridge Road and she was there, running right toward him, not watching where she was going, panicked and crying and out of breath.

He slammed on the brakes with a new and overwhelming rage at whatever had totally screwed up the easiest job in the world; an old lady and a kid, and here she was, the kid running loose and four shots going off at God-knew-what.

Marie screamed and tried to pivot and run in the opposite direction as Crawl jumped out of the car, but she slipped in the gravel and went down. Crawl, even with his limp, had her by the arm before she could get up.

"What do you want?" she shouted. "What do you want?"

Crawl said, "Get in the car!" He jerked her hard to her feet. "And if you screw with me, I'll break your neck."

Marie cried out, "Leave me alone!" and swung at Crawl, catching him squarely in the cheek with her fist.

Crawl staggered, then swung back at her, cracking her across the face with his open left hand hard enough to buckle her knees. He reached into the car, grabbed the automatic from the front seat, thrust the barrel hard between her upper lip and her nose and said, "Get in the car right now or I'll hurt you, girl." His cheek was already flushed by her blow. "If you try and run, I'll shoot your legs. Then I'll drag you into the car, anyway."

Marie looked past the cold steel and nodded. As she let him force her into the passenger seat, she said, for the third time, more weakly than before, "What do you want?"

Crawl slammed the door and walked quickly around to the driver's side. He looked down the road before he got in, trying to see Michael and his truck, but all he could see was empty road and a wall of trees and the curve that began a hundred yards down the road.

"Why are you doing this?" Marie asked as Crawl tucked the automatic between his legs and spun the tires in the gravel, roaring toward the curve in the road. When he didn't answer, she steeled herself and announced, "He killed my aunt."

Crawl's foot went limp on the accelerator. He stared at her.

She began to cry, then said, "And she killed him."

Crawl's mouth dropped open. His eyes flooded with disbelief. With raging panic his hands tightened on the steering wheel and his foot drove the accelerator to the floor.

The doctor said thoughtfully, "Do you know what war is, son?"

"I know what war is."

The doctor leaned forward. His long hands wrapped over his knees. "War," he said, "is the purposeful pursuit of disintegration."

Kieran said, "I'm thinking I've been closer to it than you have."

The doctor let ten seconds pass, during which he stared at Kieran without blinking. Then he said, speaking softly, "Of course you have. That's what you came here for, isn't it?"

Kieran's eyes narrowed. He didn't answer.

Ever so slowly, the doctor rose to his feet. "Here," he said, "let me show you what a very brilliant man named Fendholt said about war. And about you and me." He turned and moved toward the bookcase. "His book is called *The Delicate Art of War.*"

"Back down!" Kieran said sharply. He raised his automatic and took two quick steps backward, bumping into the chair holding the phone.

The doctor didn't even turn to look at him. He said a quiet, "Nonsense, son. You're in this description. You'll be surprised," and kept moving.

"Get back!"

Four more feet.

"It's just a book, son. And if you kill me, you get nothing, do you?"

The air exploded.

The doctor flinched and froze.

A small black hole showed in the wall just above the bookcase.

"You know I hit what I aim at," Kieran said coldly from behind the doctor. "And I'm not your son. If you turn and look, you'll see I'm aiming at your right thigh, five inches above your knee. If you take one more step forward, or one step either to your right or left, I'll blow your bone into a thousand pieces. You'll still transfer our money. You'll just be hurting really bad when you do it."

The doctor didn't move.

"Step back now. Only step backward. That's all. You're on the floor if you don't move straight backward, so help me God."

The doctor took a single small step backward with his right leg and turned slowly around.

Kieran stood next to the green chair, ten feet away. He was braced. His gun hand was extended straight toward the doctor's leg. His left hand gripped the heel of his gun hand. His gaze was locked on the doctor's thigh, not on his eyes.

"So help you, *God*?" the doctor said incredulously.

He moved slowly back to the couch and, just as slowly, sat down.

Kieran shifted his automatic to his left hand. "Bad people in your house ..." he said in a soft voice. "Shots going off outside ..." He walked to the bookcase, keeping his eyes on the doctor. "One of the bad guys telling you we're ready to kidnap your niece if we have to ..." He began to sweep the books off the top shelf of the case, one handful at a time. "Ready to take her and her freak baby with five lungs and no stomach, too ..." The books tumbled in a slow cadence to the hardwood floor. "And you want to show me a book about war?"

The Delicate Art of War and two other books tumbled to the floor. Kieran stared at the exposed Smith & Wesson.

The doctor watched, still sitting erect, looking impassive.

"I don't think so," Kieran said softly.

He picked up the weapon, engaged its safety with a flick of his thumb and pressed it behind his back, into his belt. Then he remarked calmly, "You're a liar and a thief and a violent man, Dr. Cleary."

The doctor's dark eyes flashed. "And you," he said slowly, in a deadly whisper, "are a twenty-two-year-old man who helped kill his own sister and who is now at war with almighty God."

Crawl was doing eighty-five on the straight section of the road, kicking up clouds of dust and gravel. He saw Michael's pickup with the hood up, saw Brenna climb out the driver's door. She didn't wave at him, Crawl noticed, and there was no sign of Michael. His heart pounded. There was no aunt, either. There was just Brenna with her back pressed against the side of the truck and her fists clenched against her cheeks. An echo of the niece saying, "She killed him!" rang in his head.

He felt his stomach twist into a knot and heard himself shouting in a silent rage to God, or to fate, or to whatever it was that made sure everything he did turned totally bad: "Is this you again, getting back at me one more time, letting them kill Michael now like they killed my father, saying everything was my fault?"

He careened to a stop beside Brenna, who turned with sagging shoulders to the side as though she wanted to hide.

Her expression said she wanted to be anywhere but here.

Grabbing the keys, Crawl tumbled wild-eyed out of the car. "Where's Michael?" He looked past the trembling redhead to the bullet hole in the windshield of the white Lexus and the woman sagged over the wheel behind a spiderweb of glass.

Then he saw Michael and he screamed: no words, just a high-pitch sound, like that of an animal dying.

Brenna whispered, "Crawl?" as though his name were a painful question. Then she was silent again.

Crawl dropped to his knees beside his brother, who was lying in the road with his face turned up and his eyes still open and his breath still coming in terrible whispers. "What happened?" he screamed. He touched his brother's face with the fingertips of both hands. "What did you do?"

"I didn't do anything, I swear to God." Brenna was crying hard. "He just stepped in front of her car, and she went crazy and ran into him, and he shot her as the car hit him. I don't know why she did it. And I don't know why he didn't move. Honest to God, though, she just went crazy. I didn't do anything wrong, and neither did he. I just told her I was having car trouble, and she started to open her door to get out, and the girl started to get out, and then she saw his gun, maybe, I don't know. He was out of the pickup, and she saw him and freaked out. She said, 'Who's that?', and she slammed her door again and locked it and just plowed into him. And he shot at her without getting out of the way. He just froze, Crawl, honest to God."

She noticed motion to her left and wheeled to see the passenger door of Crawl's car opening and Marie suddenly jumping out and running fast, not back toward the house but into the woods. Brenna shouted, "Stop!" and sprang after the girl.

Crawl barely paid attention. He talked to Michael, breathing like a man who had just run for miles, saying, "You're all right, brother, I swear to God." "We'll be at the doctor's in just a minute. He knows what to do." "Michael, I didn't want this. It isn't my fault, you know that."

He got to his feet and opened the truck's tailgate, moving fast. He was sweating. "The doctor was an internist first, before everything else," he said. "You told us that, Michael. You did everything really good." On his knees again, he slipped his arm under his brother's neck and shoulder, then he moaned loudly and lifted. "He'll save you. He's got all the stuff he needs right at his house, remember?"

Straining with the weight, he lifted Michael to the lowered tailgate.

Then, climbing up into the bed, he pulled his brother gently forward, away from the tailgate. He took off the black shirt that hung open over his white T-shirt and slipped it under Michael's head, bunching it into a pillow.

Jumping back down to the road, he slammed the tailgate shut and turned to see Brenna pulling the teenager across the roadside ditch and back to the truck, her strong fist knotted in the girl's short black hair.

Crawl said, "I'm taking her and Michael to the house. You get in with the old lady and drive her car into the marsh down the road, back toward the house, on this side. Take it way back in, as far as it can go."

Brenna's eyes widened but she didn't object.

The wind began to swirl, blowing up small clouds of dust. Crawl winced in the dust and rubbed his left eye with his fingertips. Then he grabbed Marie by the arm and pushed her toward the cab of the truck. "Run again and I'll kill you."

She hunched her head against the gusting wind and climbed into the pickup.

Crawl said to Brenna, "Get it behind some trees if you can. Far enough, no one will see it from the road." He tossed her the keys to the Malibu. "Then come back and drive this one back to the house." Checking on Marie, he stepped closer to Brenna. He hovered just an inch from her left ear. "And bury Michael's gun. Don't just throw it away. Bury it where no one will find it. Wipe it down first. And the car. No fingerprints. They'll hang you if you leave any."

"I know. I know."

162

Crawl looked closely at Michael one more time, whispered an angry, "God Almighty," and jumped into the driver's seat beside Marie, who was pressed tight against the passenger-side door, watching him. Then he started the pickup and pulled away, but at a slow, even pace.

Whatever else happened, he didn't want to jar the broken body of the one person left in all the world who really mattered to him.

Kieran stared at the doctor. He felt his nostrils flare and his face flush. He pointed the barrel of his H&K at the doctor's chest.

"You also have a temper you'll want to control," the doctor said.

Kieran didn't move.

The doctor inhaled and leaned forward. "Kieran," he said, "I want you to know that I'm going to make it incredibly right and easy for you to have everything you've ever dreamed of. More than you've ever dreamed of. More than you could ever have imagined."

Kieran didn't move.

The doctor rose to his feet in slow motion. His eyes glistened with a dark, new fire. "I'm asking you to understand what is happening in that young girl out there. I'm asking you to understand what is happening on this sacred ground." He inched closer. "I want you to understand that what we are bringing about in this place is the most longed-for event in all of human history." He took another slow step. His hands opened and spread, palms out, like a curtain. "Listen with all your mind now. Listen with all your heart and soul. What is happening, and what I am here and now inviting you to become a full partner to, with wealth beyond your highest hopes and a glory which will be yours for all eternity, is the ultimate and final fusion of science and spirituality." He paused. His voice dropped to a triumphant whisper. "Kieran," he said. "What we are bringing about, in fact what is already upon us, is the Second Coming of Jesus Christ!"

"Who are you people?" Marie had pressed herself against the door of the speeding truck, as far from Crawl as she could squeeze. Her arms were crossed. She had stopped crying and was insisting to herself that she not start again. All she would show would be anger, not fear.

"Just hope my brother doesn't die," Crawl said without looking at her. "You'll find out more than you ever wanted to know if he dies."

"What the hell does that mean? He killed my aunt!"

Crawl nodded slightly as he said in a menacing tone, "You're going to have to watch your language from now on, too, darlin'. The baby and all that."

"What are you talking about?"

Crawl grinned humorlessly. "I thought you didn't know."

"About what? What baby?"

"I'll tell you what baby. Your uncle won't tell you because all he wants to do is use you. But I'll tell you."

Kieran stepped backward. He felt his heart speed up.

The doctor's scar twisted slowly as he smiled a hard and unexpected smile. "I know you've heard about Jesus coming again, haven't you? Did you ever think you could be a part of making it happen?"

"I know it doesn't say it'll happen in an upstairs lab."

"No. It actually says on the clouds. Seen suddenly by everyone, from east to west, like a flash of lightning."

"Frankenstein," Kieran said coldly. "That's closer to what's going on here."

"The Bible uses so much figurative language." The doctor tilted his head. "But you see, what actually happens is that God works through us. It was God that caused the sciences of DNA and cloning to develop in me, wasn't it? And that happened for a reason. Can you see that? All of that special knowledge I've acquired, that's all in God's plan. That's why it's happened."

Kieran slid to the side. He didn't lower his gun, he didn't divert his stare. He said, "God's plan is for you to give us seven and a half million dollars and we go away and never look back. That's what I know about God's plan."

The doctor moved again. Two small, slow steps toward Kieran. "Think with me what it will mean to a world gone mad," he said. "All the killing you've seen, stopped. All the hunger, stopped. All the breathtaking, entirely unnecessary pain, all of it stopped."

"You gonna tell him what to do? How to do it?"

"Alive again, here in the flesh, bringing us, finally, all the peace we've always wanted but have never, never, never gotten to fully experience!"

"People runnin' things will just kill him all over again," Kieran said. "How's that for a theory?"

"I want you to listen to me, now, please," the doctor said, speaking even more softly.

"And I want you to show me your lab. Show me where you decided to be God for awhile. Show me where you thought all this up, and show me your computer, too, where you'll be transferring my money."

"You want the money, you can have the money. You can have all seven and a half million dollars, all to yourself. I swear it's true. Just help me!"

"But you're a liar," Kieran said, quietly but firmly. "A liar. And a thief. And a son of a bitch. Did the girl know what you were doing to her?"

"I'm not lying to you about what I can give you. I swear it on my soul. And I would not risk my soul for anything, you must know that."

"So I get all seven and a half million dollars, and then I just walk away?"

"I trust you because I know so much about you. But your friend out there, Crawl, and whoever else is out there with him right now, no, him I will not trust. But you can join me, Kieran. Join us. Just help us to be free from them. You're concerned about the girl, help me keep the girl free from them."

"And how would I do that?"

"Let me arm myself. When they come back, disarm them with me. You don't have to hurt them, just leave them with me. We'll bind them, then I'll transfer your money. You keep your weapon. You can stay until the money settles and transfer it again, yourself, in private, so it's entirely your own. I know you must have arranged to do that. Then you can leave, breathtakingly wealthy and free as the wind. More than that, you'll leave profoundly right with God. You'll live your whole life knowing that, and God will know it too."

"And you'll kill them after I leave?"

The doctor blinked.

Kieran raised his weapon again, pointing it first at the doctor's waist, then at his chest. "I know you will," he said. "And more, I know I'd be dead as soon as they are. We both know that."

The doctor shook his head. His eyes blazed. "You're wrong! How can you think I'd lie and kill at the risk of my soul?"

"And after we're all out of the way," Kieran said, "will you make a dozen or so more of Jesus? Maybe a few extra to keep the grounds up around your house, say the miracle words for you, keep the place painted, keep your grass cut? Or will you go for a whole committee full of Jesuses, send them to run the UN, maybe? Or, hell, you've got enough DNA, why not make a whole city full? Jesus runnin' the hardware store. Jesus runnin' the auto repair. Half a dozen Jesuses runnin' the healing salon down on the corner."

He paused. He inhaled, still staring at the doctor. "Yeah, I do know somethin' about the Bible," he said. "You think you're sailin' into the last book, don't you, where all the glory is going to come down? But you're back at Square One. You're back at, 'Hey, let me play God!' Makin' new people, for God's sake, all by yourself. Makin' Jesus, for God's sake!"

The doctor's lips were sealed tight. His nostrils were flared. His eyes were narrowed to slits. But his rage still showed through.

"You're back in the Garden," Kieran said, suddenly speaking calmly, and suddenly feeling exhausted. "You just set if off again, is what you've done." He studied the doctor for a full ten seconds in silence. Then he said, slowly and sadly, barely above a whisper, "Booooom."

Crawl said to Marie, "Have you ever heard, in that pretty school of yours, about something called the Shroud of Turin?"

Marie tilted her head. She could feel her stomach tightening. She didn't answer.

"You know what it is, the shroud? You know whose blood is supposed to be on it?"

Her arms tightened across her chest.

"You know what microbiologists can do with DNA these days, don't you? Hell, you live with one of the best. So can you imagine what one of the best, who knows DNA really well, might try to do if he got hold of some DNA from the blood of the Shroud of Turin? Especially if he had an egg and a healthy young woman for an incubator."

Five seconds went by before Marie, suddenly pale, whispered, barely moving her lips, "I don't know what you're talking about."

"But you know about cloning. And you know how they do it, don't you? Taking some DNA, oh, from some blood or something, and then putting that DNA into an egg and the egg into a mother. You ever heard about Dolly the sheep? Well, the next step is to try it with humans."

Marie's mouth hung open. A wave of nausea swept through her. "You're a murderer," she said. "You'll never get away with this."

Even with the sun setting, Crawl could see that the color had drained from her face. He grinned. "Let me put it this way, young lady. Have you missed any school lately?"

Marie's body seemed to collapse in on itself. Another five seconds passed in silence before she breathed a weak, "What do you want with me?"

"Not me, girl," he said. "It's what your lovin' uncle wants with you. Or maybe I should say, from you. And you really weren't in on it, were you?"

Marie didn't say anything. She was having trouble breathing.

Tears threatened, but again she stifled them, determined not to break.

"Weren't you just out of school for a few days, just a short time back?" Crawl asked. "Were you sick? Is that what they told you? The day you said, 'Hey, how'd it get so late?' Or, 'How'd it get to be Wednesday', or whatever it was? You sayin' to your dear aunt, who was in on the whole thing, 'What happened to Wednesday?' Your uncle standin' there saying, 'Well, you were really sick there, weren't you? I'm sure glad I got you well again.' Any of that sound familiar?"

Tears rose and trailed down Marie's cheeks. She thought about the afternoons that had passed without her even realizing it because of what her uncle had called her "flu" and her "necessary sleep". She thought about her uncle's almost getting a Nobel Prize, he knew so much about DNA. And she thought about these men and the woman with them. They sounded as though they might be from Ireland, but why were they here, unless they were after something? Unless they knew something about her and her uncle, and about Leah?

Then, with a rising terror that sucked the air from her lungs, she thought about her uncle being right next to her ear and whispering what he had never said before, and in a way he had never spoken to her before, when she was sick and he had just given her milk that tasted like peaches: "I love you more than anything in the world."

What had he done to her?

Crawl noticed the tears. He noticed her mouth hanging wide open. He noticed the color all gone from her pretty white face, and the deadness taking over her eyes. He grinned again, but only with his mouth.

The entrance road to the house came into view on their right.

Dark clouds had covered the setting sun, moving fast, east to west. The trees were losing their long shadows in the falling darkness.

Marie's mouth closed, and she swallowed hard. She whispered, "I don't believe you."

"You're dear old Uncle John's sixteen-year-old Virgin Mary," Crawl said softly as he eased the pickup into the entrance road to the house. "We broke into the shroud with him and got the DNA for him, that's how we know."

"I don't believe you."

She tightened her arms around her waist, squeezing hard against the nausea that rose and fell and the dizziness that rose and fell with it.

Crawl turned and glared at her. "Yes, you do."

The house appeared through the trees, large and silent and gray in the low light.

Marie was shaking her head in slight, slow movements. A moan escaped. She turned her face and pressed it against the glass of the window.

"Problem is, they don't really know whose blood is on that shroud," Crawl said, glancing back to check on Michael, who hadn't moved.

Marie forced herself not to listen. She thought, instead, about Terry.

"Could be some monkey-faced killer, is the problem," he said, practically growling.

She wondered what Terry would say if any of it would turn out to be true. She wondered if he would want to help her or if he would want to run in the opposite direction, as if she had some horrible, contagious disease.

"Cause they don't really know, do they?" Crawl said. "Just seeing what'll happen. Let's try Marie, why don't we? See if we can get us a Jesus."

As he approached the house he hammered suddenly on the horn with the heel of his fist; five short blasts and then three long ones, held down until he pulled sharply to the left, braked hard, and backed

the truck toward the house, positioning the tailgate just ten feet outside the front door.

"Move quick!"

He killed the engine, pocketing the keys, and jumped out.

Marie stared after him with dead red eyes.

15

The doctor came out of the house first, moving quickly.

Crawl was at the truck's tailgate, grasping at the handle with one hand and stuffing his automatic into his belt with the other. He yelled, "Help me!"

But the doctor saw Marie in the passenger seat and ignored Crawl's panic. He started to rush toward his niece, but stopped as he saw Michael's body in the back of the pickup, his legs twisted like a rag doll's, his blood pooling in the slim, metal gutters of the truck bed.

Kieran was out of the house, automatic in hand.

Crawl slammed open the tailgate.

Kieran staggered as if he'd been hit in the gut. He uttered a breathless, "Oh, my God."

The doctor blinked against the sight of Michael, then turned with wide and wild eyes to Marie, who still had not opened her door.

Kieran moved to the tailgate, his empty hand out like a sleepwalker's. He breathed it twice more: "My God. My God."

"Help me!" Crawl shouted. He reached for Michael's arm and tried to pull him toward the tailgate. "Get him to where we can grab him!"

Kieran gasped, "What happened?" as he squeezed his weapon into his belt. Then he looked around wildly, "Where's Brenna?"

"She's coming," Crawl said. He inched Michael's large frame forward.

Kieran reached for Michael's other arm and pulled. He looked frantic. "Is she okay? Was she shot?"

"She's coming. Take his legs. Get his weight on the tailgate."

The doctor had opened Marie's door, but the girl had not turned to greet him. She just sat there, still and staring.

The doctor laid his hand on her shoulder. "Are you all right, Marie?"

"How can she be all right?" Crawl shouted. "She's pregnant. You expect her to be all right?"

The doctor's eyes bulged.

"She knows all about it," Crawl shouted even louder. He was wrestling Michael's hip closer to the tailgate. His hands were covered with blood. "She knows all about it!"

Marie shook her head slowly. Her wide eyes filled with tears. She pressed her palms to her ears. A muted squeal escaped her pale lips.

The doctor held his breath. He didn't move. His hand hovered over Marie's shoulder without touching it. In a strained whisper, he spoke her name.

Marie turned slowly and stepped out of the truck, moving like a robot. She looked at her uncle as if he were covered with blood.

"Help us carry him!" Crawl shouted.

Michael's hip was on the open tailgate. His left arm was hanging toward the ground.

The doctor rose to attention like a startled deer. He spun to face Crawl. "Where's my sister?" he demanded. Then, loudly and quickly, to Marie: "Where's Leah, Marie? What's happened to her?"

Kieran let go of Michael and pulled his automatic from his belt. He stepped back from the truck, watching the doctor.

It was Marie who answered the doctor's question. She said in a voice that sounded as dead as her aunt, "Leah was killed, Uncle John."

Kieran wheeled to face Crawl. "What about Brenna? Tell me what happened!"

The doctor's right hand released the open door of the truck. He moved toward Crawl and Kieran.

"I told you, she'll be here!" Crawl yelled at Kieran. "So ask me again and I'll blow your face off. My brother is dying, Kieran, don't you see this?"

He turned to the doctor. "My brother dies, your niece dies!" His voice shimmered with rising panic. "And her baby dies, too! So get over here and help me with him. Now!"

The wind gusted hard, filling the gathering darkness with clouds of dust.

Kieran backed up another step. He kept his gun leveled at the doctor. He was shaking his head, muttering, "This is unbelievable. This is unbelievable."

The doctor set his jaw and slid his arms under Michael's knees.

Crawl, pulling to lift Michael's shoulders, said to Kieran, "Keep the girl in sight. She runs, this whole thing's for nothing. She's already tried it, so stay with her no matter what."

But Marie did not run. Her expression looked very much like that of the man being pulled from the open tailgate of the pickup.

Kieran stood beside her. "Nobody will hurt you, girl. I promise. Nobody wanted this."

Marie turned to him with a blank look. She whispered, "You go to hell."

Kieran grasped her arm lightly and guided her toward the front door.

Crawl and the doctor were right behind them, carrying Michael by his shoulders and knees as his head bobbed like a heavy branch in the wind.

"You drop him," Crawl said to the doctor, "and I swear it, your sister won't be the only dead one in your family."

The doctor shot Crawl a steely glance but said nothing.

Kieran swung open the front door of the house. He flipped the light switch inside the door and guided the girl through the front hallway, then pulled her aside to let the men pass with Michael.

As Crawl struggled past him toward the living room, Kieran asked him again, this time in a groan, "How did all this happen, Crawl?"

"I don't know," Crawl said bitterly, without looking up. "I wasn't there."

Michael had bled six drops on the polished oak of the doctor's entrance hall. He bled more, both from his mouth and his nose, as his head sagged sideways into the cushion of the beige couch in the living room. But he was still breathing.

"Fix him," Crawl said to the doctor, partly commanding, partly asking. Anything to keep Michael alive.

The doctor said, "Elevate his feet," and Kieran lifted Michael's ankles onto the opposite arm of the couch.

Marie walked to a leather chair and lowered herself to the edge of the seat. No longer dazed, she was staring at her uncle, who had gone down on one knee to open the shirt of the man who had killed his sister.

"He's still bleeding," the doctor said.

"He's still alive," Crawl countered.

"It's internal."

"You can fix him."

"He has broken ribs. He sounds like he may have a collapsed lung."

172

"Somebody collapsed it for him."

The doctor looked up. "Leah hit him with her car?"

"Just fix him. You were an internist. You've done surgery."

"This man needs a hospital. What can I do here?"

"He's not 'this man'. He's my brother, Michael."

"He's a badly injured man who needs a hospital."

Kieran said to Crawl, "He has a lab. It's upstairs. An office, too, where the computer is. I put the phones in there, but he may have one I couldn't find."

"He may be bleeding from his stomach," the doctor said. "In his chest cavity, his lungs, around his heart. He needs a hospital. Not a mountain clinic, the hospital in Santa Fe."

Crawl said, "If he's bleeding inside, he hasn't got time to get to a hospital. You know that better than I do."

"I can't even take an X-ray."

Crawl said, "You're very close to having a dead niece, I swear to God."

"And you're very close to letting your brother die. You could meet the ambulance halfway, between here and Santa Fe. You could be twenty miles closer to them by now, they, twenty miles closer to your brother."

"You can stop the bleeding," Crawl said, raising his voice. "Do it, you son of a bitch."

Kieran stepped forward. He said to the doctor, speaking loudly, with an urgency of his own, "How much can you do?"

The doctor looked at Marie. His niece's eyes were closed. He thought for a second. He said in a flat voice, "I can equalize his lungs. If it's pericardial, I may be able to draw blood from around his heart. A catheter to his stomach, if that's bleeding. Let gravity drain it. I don't know."

Crawl said, flatly, "Michael can't die, Kieran."

Kieran handed Crawl his gun and thrust one arm under Michael's shoulder. His other arm went under Michael's knees. "He does cloning here," he said, standing up with Michael in his arms. "He's got his own lab. He can stop Michael's bleeding here."

The doctor looked again at Marie. Her eyes were still closed. He said, "Marie?"

Kieran was moving Michael to the stairs.

"Marie," the doctor said again.

She still didn't open her eyes.

Crawl said to Kieran, but loudly enough so all could hear, "If Michael dies, Kieran, don't you get in my way."

Brenna hated the last half hour more than she had hated anything she could remember in her whole life. She hated the blood, the stupidity; how everything suddenly went to pieces with the biggest chance she would ever get—all going to hell with no sense to it at all. She hated the violence of it, too. She hated being terrified, being in a foreign country, having to get into the car next to the dead woman, having to push her puffy body to the side and sitting in her bloody seat.

She hated it so much she talked out loud to the old lady all the way to the swampy area of the woods. She told her, nearly shouting, that it must have been her fault that the old man wanted the DNA in the first place. Told her she was glad she was dead, that none of this would have happened if it wasn't for her. Asked her why she wasn't happy just to be rich and to live in America in a big house with her smart brother and her pretty little niece. But no. She had to give her brother crazy ideas about raising Jesus and then to harass him until he went along with her.

She said all of that and more.

She never said she was sorry.

When she arrived back at the house she was red-eyed, bloodied and out of breath, her hands and arms soiled from digging to hide the gun.

She rushed into the house just as Kieran was approaching the stairs with Michael limp and bloody in his arms. The tall man, the one she knew must be the doctor, stopped to stare at her with dark, glaring eyes.

He was wishing her dead and she knew it.

She looked away, first at the girl, who was in front of Crawl and who seemed drugged, then at Crawl with an automatic hanging from each arm as if they weighed fifty pounds.

She moved closer to Kieran, not knowing what else to do, and touched Michael's arm. "Oh," she whispered, "he's so bloody. Will he make it?"

"He's alive," Kieran said.

"Thank God."

Then she saw Crawl staring at her, and the look in his eyes took her breath away. He looked so different from the man they had downed many stouts with and had laughed with and had come to America with on a great adventure for seven and a half million U.S. dollars, which would fall into their laps without anyone getting hurt.

He looked as though he hated her. But why? Her heart raced. Did Crawl know that she had set off the whole bloody episode? Did the girl tell him that when Crawl had her alone on the way back to the house?

She felt like screaming again or running or both.

Kieran started up the stairs, moving away from her. The doctor followed him.

Crawl moved toward her.

She wondered with an overwhelming sense of helplessness if her expression was confirming what she was sure he had heard. She struggled to breathe normally, swallowing hard, mindful of her eyes and her lips, holding them in what felt like a relaxed position, trying to keep them slightly open, not tense.

"You stay down here with the girl," Crawl said quietly.

Brenna breathed more easily.

"Keep her in the other room, out of our way."

She nodded and closed her mouth. Her mind groped desperately for something to say that would turn his attention away from her.

Incredibly, she heard herself say, "Are you going to get him to transfer the money now, from upstairs?"

It was her own voice and her own question, but the sheer stupidity of it startled her. It was why they had come to this terrible place where everything had gone wrong, but even as the words came out of her mouth, she realized that, with Michael maybe fatally injured and Crawl tied so closely to him, she had made another terrible mistake.

She said weakly, before Crawl could respond, "When Michael's okay, I mean. You know what I mean."

Crawl nodded and looked her up and down, as if figuring out the answer took an enormous amount of thought. "In due time," he muttered.

Brenna nodded back at him as she edged away and moved toward Marie.

She saw Kieran with Michael, both of them motionless at the top of the stairs, Kieran watching her and Crawl with sad eyes.

He seemed to have climbed a thousand miles away from her.

16

Blood bubbled on Michael's lips as he labored on the white-sheeted table in the doctor's upstairs lab, trying not to leave his brother and wife and son forever.

The doctor cut away his shirt. There was a bloody tear in his chest, on the left side and low, and deep bruises had already formed across his abdomen. His skin looked as thin as toilet tissue.

Crawl stood at the foot of the table, staring.

Kieran, standing at his side, muttered, "At least there's breath."

It meant nothing to point it out. He just wanted it to be said.

The doctor, looking grim, gathered a stethoscope, a blood pressure monitor and a stainless steel instrument case, which he placed next to Michael's head. Then he brought out several hypodermic needles, including one that was very large, plus two small bottles and a small stack of white towels.

"Tell us what you're doing," Crawl said.

The doctor slipped the stethoscope on and pressed its black circle against Michael's neck, chest and abdomen. "I'll try to equalize his lung," the doctor said with neither inflection nor emotion. "It's punctured." He picked up the largest of the hypodermic needles and inserted it deep into Michael's chest, on the left side, between the third and fourth rib.

Crawl started to pace, his eyes locked on Michael.

Kieran said, very quietly, "Easy, Crawl."

Crawl looked at him and muttered in a hard voice, "He's gonna kill him, Kieran. He'll kill Michael to get even for his sister."

The doctor said without looking up, "If you care about him as much as you want us to believe, you'll let me call an ambulance."

"He dies, the girl dies," Crawl repeated in a sharp, low voice. "And the clone baby, too."

"Maybe we should let him call the ambulance," Kieran said.

"All an ambulance gets us is the police. If Michael dies, just don't get in my way," Crawl said again.

Kieran fell silent. He watched the needle in the doctor's hand and noticed the glisten of sweat on his brow. The doctor, not knowing what to do. Something new for him, Kieran felt sure. He was thinking, though, Kieran was sure of that. All the time the doctor was working on Michael, the man was getting ready for something, like a cornered bear.

Kieran wondered if they were watching Michael's life drain away or if he really had any chance at all. And if he did die, it wouldn't be only his life that was lost, but the plans they had made together, the money, and, in fact, their lives too, his and Brenna's.

For the first time, he felt fear grip at him like a claw. It was all going to end badly, and they wouldn't even be at home in Ireland when it happened.

Michael dies, the girl dies, Crawl said. But who was he to make that decision? If Michael dies, don't get in his way, he said. Twice now. But who was he to tell Kieran that, when his and Brenna's lives were on the line?

Deeper memories surged back. Belfast and home, the smell of cold rain on cold streets, school lunches of biscuits and sausage eaten on hardwood green benches, his mother singing her gospel songs with his sister, Colleen, who died before any of them and who really did look a lot like the girl Marie.

He moved suddenly, jerking his head up and inhaling deeply.

The doctor had finished aspirating the lung. "I'll see if his stomach is bleeding," he said flatly, eyeing both of them for several seconds. "I'll try to drain it with a catheter. The ambulance could have been halfway here by now. You'd be meeting it already, back on the highway to Santa Fe."

Michael, still with them, moaned lightly.

Crawl said something to Kieran from what seemed like a distance, but Kieran wasn't paying attention. He wondered if Michael felt pain while he was dying in front of their eyes, and, if he did, if it was deep and terrible or something as distant and as light as his moan.

And he thought again about the black-haired teenager, not much younger than Colleen was when she died, who was sitting downstairs assaulted and scared on the couch with Michael's blood on it. The only one of them that hadn't done anything wrong. The one with God-only-knew-what growing in her belly and having to come out.

Crawl had moved to Michael's side, across the table from the doctor.

At least he still had his weapon, Kieran told himself. He and Brenna both.

The doctor had gathered several feet of thin, clear plastic tubing. He was applying a lubricant to the end of the tube.

Kieran stepped abruptly forward and exclaimed, "Wait!"

Crawl stared at him blankly. So did the doctor.

"Get the tape!" Kieran said, suddenly animated with a surge of excitement. "Get the tape that touched the shroud, the tape with the blood on it!" He rushed to Crawl and grabbed him by the arm. "Crawl, we can try the tape on Michael!"

"Try the tape? What does that mean?"

"The blood. Remember what he said about touching the tape to his niece if she was dying, because if it really was the blood of Jesus, it could heal her?"

"But she wasn't dying," Crawl said. "He was lying and he's crazy. What are you talking about?"

Kieran waved his hand and shook his head. What were the right words? "I'm saying, it doesn't matter if he was lying about the girl having cancer, not if the blood is real. If it's the real blood of Jesus, it's worth a try, isn't it? What if it does have power? What if it would make him well?"

Crawl was incredulous. "Touch him with it?"

"Yes! Just touch it to him and let's see what happens."

"Touch Michael with his tape?" he said angrily, shaking his head. "I can't believe you're saying this."

Kieran swung around to face the doctor. "Get the tape!" he demanded. "It'll take you ten seconds."

Crawl's eyes had narrowed to slits. "You're serious," he said.

"Ten seconds, Crawl. Nobody's ever touched it to somebody who's been dying. We can try! Why isn't it worth a try?"

Crawl paused, blinked, then nodded firmly and said, "Okay. Ten seconds." He spun to the doctor. "You've got ten seconds. Get the tape!"

"I don't understand," the doctor said, looking puzzled.

"Get the tape!" Crawl turned suddenly, rushed to the counters and shelves on the other side of the room and began sweeping bottles and silver containers with instruments in them onto the floor as quickly as he could rifle through them. "Where do you have it?"

"I don't have it."

178

Kieran moved toward the doctor, his weapon held chest high. "You wouldn't lose something like that," he said. "Get the tape!"

The doctor shook his head. "After I was sure the implant was successful," he said, "I took the tape into the woods and buried it where I could never find it again."

Kieran grabbed him by the lapel of his sport coat with his free hand and pushed him against the wall. "This is not the time to be lying."

The doctor stared at him without expression. "You thought of it yourself, don't you remember? What happens if I make fifty clones, or a hundred? I deliberately confused my path so I couldn't do that. This is a work of God. I was afraid I'd make it my own work, be tempted to go back and do it again and again. I did the only thing I could think of to protect myself from that, and now I can't get it back. It's impossible."

Crawl's outburst had scattered instruments and materials across the floor. He shook his head suddenly and said to Kieran, "The hell with it. It's a joke, anyway." Then, he wheeled around again and shouted at the doctor, "Do the catheter. Now! Now! Now!"

Kieran's expression hardened, but just for an instant. "Start the catheter," he said. "But I'm going to try something better than the tape."

Crawl said, "Like what?"

"I'm going to get the girl."

The doctor's head came up and his eyes flashed.

"She doesn't know where he'd have the tape," Crawl said. "She didn't even know about it."

"Leave the girl alone," the doctor said, nearly growling.

"I don't mean so she can find the tape," Kieran said, animated again. "I mean, if it's really Jesus' DNA, then she's carrying his own clone inside of her, and that could mean she has powers you and I can't even imagine."

Marie didn't like the red-headed woman staring at her, not talking, sitting on the far arm of the couch with both feet on the cushion, her left boot on one side of the dying man's blood, her right on the other. The woman held her gun in her right hand, her arm hung over her knee. Her other arm rested along the back of the couch.

Marie sat as far away as she could, squeezed at the other end of the couch with her arms crossed. "Stop staring at me," she said at last.

"You didn't know about it, did you?" Brenna said. "Until today."

Marie stared at a copy of the *Smithsonian* magazine on the glass-topped table that was past Brenna and to her right.

Upstairs, Crawl's voice shouted something behind a closed door.

"Crawl told you about it, didn't he?" Brenna said.

On the cover of the magazine was a pink flower that looked like a cartoon character with its mouth open, revealing its round black teeth. It was, the headline on the cover said, a flower in American Samoa. Marie wished she was in Samoa. She wished she were anywhere in the world but here.

"He would," Brenna said. "That would be like him."

Marie's mind had not stopped bouncing back and forth between terrors. She was still trying to wrestle with the fact that her uncle, and her aunt too, had actually done this to her. She was feeling, she decided, what a rape victim must feel. Worse than that, what an incest victim must feel.

She felt so dirty and so ashamed, even though she knew that she hadn't wanted this, didn't invite it, didn't even know about it, hated it with everything inside of her. That was terrifying in itself. What if she would never be able to shake this feeling, not for the rest of her life? That possibility was even more frightening.

Brenna said, "So, when this is over, you can just get it aborted."

Marie didn't answer. She wouldn't have an abortion. Even if she did, she thought, who would she be aborting? And that brought her back to one of the deepest fears about the pregnancy. What if her uncle—who was a genius, she didn't doubt that—had really done it right, so that she really was carrying the clone of the man on the shroud? And what if the man on the shroud really was Jesus, as so many people believed? How could she live with aborting the clone of Jesus?

"It might not even be growing, you know?" Brenna said. "Could be it's dead already. Who knows the way clones might go?"

Marie responded softly, without meeting Brenna's eyes, "I don't need advice from a murderer."

"I'm not a murderer."

"You're a murderer."

"Nobody meant for that to happen and you know it."

"You're a murderer."

"Nobody here is a murderer."

"You are. And they are too."

"Well, you go to hell, little girl."

Marie pulled her knees up to her chin and wrapped her arms around her legs.

It would be easier if it died. But she couldn't be the one to kill it.

Whatever happened, though, she would not stay with her uncle. It would all come out to other people, she was sure of that, but even if it didn't, she couldn't ever live with him again. And if she didn't live with him, where would she go, especially if everybody knew about the pregnancy and was watching her to see what she would deliver?

Terry came to mind again, but she was afraid to think about him now. Later. Not now.

She felt like a freak show, with the curtain ready to go up.

Nightmares on top of nightmares.

She felt sick and lowered her face to her knees.

Why did she think these people would even let her live, with her knowing about Aunt Leah? Her and Uncle John, both. They knew the killers' faces, and now they even knew their first names. And her uncle must know more than that. They would be able to pick them out for the police, for sure.

She raised her eyes. "You killed Leah," she said, "and you're going to kill us too."

"No, we're not," Brenna said. But she moved her legs uncomfortably and shifted the weapon from her right hand to her left, and her eyes didn't seem as certain as her words.

Suddenly Marie raised her chin high. Her eyes widened with alarm. She exclaimed, "Oh, God," and leapt from the couch to bolt for the hallway on the west end of the room.

Brenna jumped to her feet and charged after her, shouting, "Where are you going?"

"I'm throwing up."

"Stop! I'm going with you!"

But Marie had already slammed and locked the bathroom door.

"Crawl," Kieran said, still refusing to give it up, "if you were lying someplace dying, and Mary, the real mother of the real Jesus in the Bible, was alive and right there with you, and she still had Jesus growing in her belly, and she wanted to pray to God to make you well, wouldn't you at least let her try it?"

"*Pray* for me?"

181

"For you, or for Michael, yes. It's the same DNA in the girl as on the tapes, only there's more of it every minute by ten billion times. Isn't that better than a piece of tape?"

But before Crawl could respond, they heard Brenna kicking at the bathroom door downstairs and screaming, "Crawl! Kieran! She's in the bathroom and there's a window in there!"

And then, two shots, fired quickly.

Crawl shouted at Kieran to stay with Michael and rushed past him as fast as he could; jerking from his limp like a marionette.

"She just got up and ran," Brenna shouted as Crawl started down the stairs. Her chrome-plated automatic was flapping like a flag. "She just ran!"

"Go out the back. Along the lake."

"I shot the lock but she was already gone."

Crawl charged for the front door. First he shouted, "Go!" Then he said, "Wait. There're flashlights in the truck and the car. Come with me."

It was raining lightly, but the wind was strong as Crawl ran out of the house, strong enough to bend the tops of the trees and power thick clouds fast across the face of the moon. He squinted and ran for the truck. Brenna was right behind him.

Suddenly, there she was: the girl, all ready to be taken.

Crawl saw her first. She was in the pickup, her head silhouetted in the rear window. He didn't believe his eyes at first, but it was Marie, all right. She had been ducking down as if she were looking for the keys that were still in Crawl's pocket, but now she was up again in full view and her door was flying open.

He closed the ten yards that separated them, reaching her just as her left foot hit the ground.

Marie heard him before she saw him. She turned her head and cried out sharply, and she lunged back into the truck, kicking at him in the open door. He tried to grab her ankle, but she was kicking too fast and too hard. She had hurtled across the bench seat, and, still kicking, groped for the passenger-door handle, screaming, "Help me!"

But Brenna was there on the passenger side, right in front of her and cursing as she yanked open the passenger door.

Marie screamed and twisted backward again, but Brenna grabbed her by the hair with her left hand and pulled hard.

Marie cried, "Let me go!" and pounded at Brenna with both fists as she tumbled out of the pickup.

Brenna pulled Marie's hair straight down in front of her, forcing the girl's head down, then she jammed her right arm, with her gun still in hand, across the back of the girl's neck and leapt on her, letting her weight drive her to the ground.

Marie kept shouting, "Let me go! Let me go!"

Crawl reached them and grabbed Marie's wrist with his left hand, twisting it. "Get off her," he snapped at Brenna. "Get her on her feet."

Together, they forced Marie to her feet, but she yelled and kicked Crawl hard in his lame leg just above the ankle, and then, just as hard, kicked him in his knee, sending him falling back into Brenna with a vicious cry.

Marie twisted and jerked her hand as hard as she could, tearing herself free.

Brenna reached for her, but Marie was too quick, swinging around the tailgate, nearly falling, then racing into the darkness of the road that led away from the house.

Brenna flew around the tailgate in pursuit.

"This is faster than you, girl," Crawl shouted, and he fired once into the air.

The power of the explosion instinctively slowed Marie. For just a second, she threw her hands up to cover her head, then she glanced back to see Brenna charging after her and broke again into a dead run. She screamed involuntarily—a short, quick scream—and then the only sounds she heard were her own pounding feet and her own pounding breath.

Crawl fired a second time, and then a third.

The doctor had already positioned Michael on his left side in anticipation of the stomach catheter. Now he stood facing Kieran and his automatic with the catheter tube in his hand.

He was rigid.

Kieran said, "Get the catheter in." He waved the automatic once and added, in a bitter whisper aimed at no one, or at everyone and everything, himself included, "Son of a bitch."

The doctor turned to Michael and, grim faced, inserted the catheter into the dying man's stomach.

183

"Your friend gave his intentions away," he said, eyeing Kieran and speaking quietly. "He told you I'd kill to avenge my sister, but he was really saying, that's the way he thinks. Because that's what he intends to do. He's going to kill Marie, and me too, to avenge his brother."

Kieran said, "You don't believe it's really Jesus either, do you? Why the hell did you do this to her if you don't even believe it yourself?"

Gravity was doing its work. Both the catheter tube and the bottom of the silver pan were pooling dark red.

"You can save an innocent girl, Kieran. A pregnant sixteen-year-old girl who hasn't hurt anyone. Does that remind you of anyone?"

Crawl's first shot boomed from the yard outside.

The doctor flinched, but recovered.

Kieran stared at him coldly.

The doctor slowly twisted the cap from a small brown bottle of antiseptic solution. He began to rub Michael's ribs with the rust-colored liquid. He said, "The next world war—you can keep it from ever happening, Kieran! By one act of courage on your part, spears will turn into plowshares. The lion will lie next to the lamb. The next plagues, averted. No one's father getting killed. No one's sister dying alone and in misery. No one losing their lives to alcohol or drugs, ever again." He looked fiercely at Kieran. "And in addition to heaven on earth for everyone, for you, personally, seven and a half million dollars and a singular chance for your atonement before God and before your own heart and soul."

Kieran was holding his breath.

The doctor sensed it. "You can have it all. Salvation, falling like rain."

Kieran shook the words off. "You're a liar going in, you're a liar now. If you really believed it was Jesus, you would have let the blood save Michael."

The doctor shook his head. "No," he said. "If I really believed it was Jesus, I would rather die, and see my niece die, too, than put his precious blood into the hands of someone as corrupt as Crawl Connell."

He put down the swab and picked up his scalpel.

Crawl's second shot sounded, then his third.

The doctor pressed his eyes shut and held them closed tightly for several seconds. He was perspiring. He opened his eyes and murmured, "I have to make the incision now. I have to try to close off any ruptured vessels around the broken ribs."

"God, man," Kieran said softly, stepping forward. "Are you saying you do have the tapes, after all?"

"No. I buried them in the woods and can never find them again."

"You're lying about this, too."

The doctor raised his eyes. "I'm not lying when I say you can bring salvation to the entire world. I'm not lying when I say you can have the money and I'll let you go and never pursue you again. I'm not lying when I say you can take the red-haired girl with you if you want her, that the only one you have to leave is Crawl."

"But he doesn't want the bloody tapes!" Kieran shouted. "What the hell would he want them for? He doesn't even care about the money anymore. I know him. All he wants now is to get his brother back!"

"You don't understand him at all," the doctor said coldly. "All he wants now is not to have to live with the knowledge that he's killed his brother the same way he was responsible for killing his father."

Kieran stared, taking in the doctor's words. "And what do you want?" he asked bitterly. "Is it really peace on earth? Or is it being Dr. John Cleary, almighty creator of the Second Coming of Jesus? Setting off the bomb. Bringing down a kill zone."

With Crawl's second shot, Marie slowed. With the third, she stopped.

Her hands were clamped tightly around her ears. Her shoulders were hunched. Her legs were trembling. She began to cry quietly.

Brenna caught up to her, but she didn't take hold of her. And she didn't curse again. She didn't even speak to her. She just stopped beside her after a last slow stride, breathing hard, and then she began to circle her.

As Crawl came up behind them, she slid her arm around Marie's shoulders and said softly, like a mother, "Now why did you go and do that? We really aren't going to hurt you, love. We just want some of your uncle's money."

The front door banged. Crawl shouted from the foot of the stairs, "How is he?"

The doctor's head swiveled like an owl's.

"He's okay," Kieran called, drifting toward the doorway. "We're making progress. Did you get her?"

185

"We got her."

"Is she okay?"

"Don't worry about it. I'm just going to have a little heart-to-heart with her about her behavior. I'll be right up."

The doctor shouted, "Are you all right, Marie?" He moved toward the door, but Kieran waved his weapon, blocking his way.

"I'm not hurt," Marie answered.

"Don't worry about her," Crawl shouted. "You worry about my brother."

"So get the damned incision going," Kieran whispered loudly after another ten seconds of silence. "He'll be up in a minute."

The doctor stood iron faced and silent next to Michael, staring at Kieran.

Kieran snapped, "On with it!" He jerked his gun like a pointer, trying to direct the doctor's attention back to Michael.

Still no words, no movement.

Kieran stared, taken back by the look in the doctor's eyes, by the distance, by the deadness. His eyes looked as if they had turned to tar.

Like a hand slipping through a curtain, the terror reached for him slowly at first. Then, as his mouth opened weakly to speak again, it rushed at him. It rammed his chest and stole his breath even as a thin "Oh, Jesus" escaped his lips.

He moved around the table, his heart hammering. He pressed his index and middle fingers against Michael's neck and held them there for a full twenty seconds. Then he let them slip away. He felt sick. He said softly, in a stranger's voice, "Is he dead?"

Silence.

He looked at the doctor. "Is he dead?"

The doctor said, "No one could have saved him. Not here."

"So he's dead?"

"Yes. He's dead."

Kieran took a slow step backward. "And you can't do anything? You can't bring him back?"

The doctor still hadn't moved. He said in a voice like a recording, with no hint of human touch or emotion, "You know what will happen now, don't you? You know it will happen in cold blood and with cold pleasure. Evil within evil within evil."

17

Crawl was in a hurry to take it all in. He saw the mask on Michael's face and the rust-colored antiseptic smeared on his brother's ribs and the doctor holding his scalpel and Kieran standing nearby with his gun hanging at his side. He rushed to the foot of the table, saying, "How is he? What are you going to do?"

Kieran said, "He's going to close off any vessels bleeding around his ribs. He has to make an incision."

Crawl looked shaken. He leveled his gun at the doctor. "By God, you be careful what you cut, you hear me?"

"He sedated him," Kieran said. "To make sure he doesn't feel any pain."

Crawl turned to face Kieran and, as if with a sudden curiosity, he suddenly reached for Kieran's weapon. "Let me see that, just for a second," he said.

Kieran drew his hand away. It was instinct. "Why?"

Crawl shook his head with agitation. "Just let me see something."

He reached for the gun again, this time taking hold of it.

Kieran released his grip. "What do you want to see?"

Crawl stepped back and raised his own automatic, pointing it at Kieran's midsection. "Don't fight me on this, Kieran," he said. He slipped Kieran's automatic under his belt in the middle of his back, out of sight.

Kieran took a long step forward, reaching for Crawl. "What the hell are you doing?"

Crawl's automatic came up higher. "Do ... not ... fight me on this." When Kieran stopped, Crawl added, "Give me your other gun."

Kieran stared at the muzzle of the automatic. Then he nodded and handed over the gun in his belt. "Just tell me what the hell you're doing."

The doctor stiffened. "What have you done to my niece?"

Crawl swung his weapon slowly, aiming it at the doctor's chest. He said nothing.

The doctor glanced once at Kieran and moved backward.

"I had to take Brenna's gun too," Crawl said to Kieran. "I don't trust her. You shouldn't either. All she's done is fire the thing every chance she gets, and that was the third time the girl got away from her. The first two times, back on the road. I got her the first time; she was nearly all the way into the woods before we got her back the second time. Honest to God, three times now."

"What's that got to do with me?"

"Well," Crawl said, "I can't have you going soft, with her begging you, all teary-eyed, 'Oh, please, Kieran, let me have your weapon. He took mine,' and you goin', 'Well, sure you can. Don't want to see you cry, now, do we?' That's how you'd go. I can't risk it, is all it is. It's nothin' to worry about."

They stared at each other across the gulf created first by Crawl's obvious lie, second, by the fact Crawl didn't even care enough about Kieran to try to make up a believable story.

"Too many things have already gone wrong," Crawl said. "I can't take any chances."

Kieran thought for a moment, then he turned and walked slowly to the door. His heart was hammering.

"Where are you going?" Crawl asked sharply.

Kieran turned to face him. "I don't have a gun, Crawl," he said. "I can't watch the doctor without a gun, can I?"

He turned again toward the door.

"So where are you going?" Crawl demanded.

Kieran stopped again, but this time he didn't bother turning around. "First, to talk with Brenna," he said. "I haven't talked with her since all this started coming apart. I want to know what happened on that road back there."

"You don't have to talk with her."

"We didn't get the girl up here to pray with Michael yet, either, to see if she has any special powers because of the DNA in her." He was in the doorway. He turned back to Crawl. "I'm going to get her up here. We lose nothing. Michael might gain a lot. She's able to try it, right?"

Crawl thought for several seconds, then nodded. "I tied her up with duct tape from the truck. You'll have to cut her loose."

"Duct tape?"

"Three times she's run now. Make sure she doesn't run on you."

Kieran found Marie bound with duct tape to a ladder-back chair just inside the archway leading from the living room to the dining room. The tape that covered her mouth was wound all the way around her head. Her hair and clothing were damp from the rain.

Brenna, sitting in the chair behind the couch, jumped to her feet as Kieran rushed into the room.

"Come with me," he whispered sharply. "Gotta find the kitchen."

"What is it?" She stayed behind him with long strides.

Marie turned her head and rolled her eyes to watch.

"He's going to kill her, Bren."

"What?"

"He's going to kill both of them. Michael's up there dead, but Crawl doesn't know it yet."

"Michael's dead?" Brenna asked with a shrill whisper.

In the kitchen, Kieran started rifling through drawers. "And Crawl will find out any second."

Brenna's gaze bounced to a half-dozen different spots. "Well, what does that mean about getting our money?"

"Bren, when he finds out, he's going to kill this girl, that's what it means. We've got to help her."

"He's still getting the money, though, isn't he?"

Kieran paused, looking at her, squinting in disbelief. "He might if he tortures her, is that what you mean? But it's not about the money now. Are you listening to me?" He had found the knife drawer he was looking for. He chose a thin boning knife with a serrated blade. When he turned again, he gripped Brenna's shoulder. "It was over when the aunt died. Crawl knew it. We should have known it too."

"He's not going to have to torture anybody," she said, pulling away from him, whispering faster. "What are you talking about? You're just doing one of your things again, getting all crazy and not letting me be part of whatever the hell it is you're thinking."

"The reason the doctor wouldn't identify us was that we'd put him in prison for the shroud if he turned us in. But that changed when the aunt died. He can't hide that. He won't try and hide that. He's going to the police if he gets the chance, that's all he can do. But Crawl won't let him identify us as his sister's killers, isn't that obvious?"

"No, that's not true," she said, clutching at his arm. "What good will identifying us do for him?"

He shook his head and moved past her, the knife in his hand.

She lunged after him, grabbing his arm, holding it hard, forcing him to stop. "It won't bring his sister back, will it? He'll tell them someone else must have killed her, but he won't tell them it's us."

"There's no time for this, Bren. If he doesn't kill them to keep them quiet, it'll be to get even for Michael. Didn't you hear what I said? Michael is dead."

"So what is the knife for? You're going to let her go?"

Kieran reached out to touch her cheek with his fingertips. "Listen to me," he said. "You remember me saying about Crawl getting his dad killed?"

"This is crazy," she said, pushing his hand away. "Who cares about any of that?"

"It's his brother now, Bren. Don't you understand what's happening?"

Brenna's eyes were round and dazed and frightened. She was shaking her head. "It can't be over, Kiero. It can't be."

Kieran pulled away. He rushed to Marie's side. "Now the girl will die, too," he said. "Please understand. We have to save her."

Brenna's lips twisted. She began to cry. "But it's two and a half million dollars! It's more than that now, isn't it? Michael can't take any."

Kieran was on one knee, cutting through the tape at Marie's ankles.

"What's all this been for, then?" Brenna sobbed. She was crying hard. She said it again, this time loudly. "What's all this been for then? It can't be for nothing!"

The tape was off Marie's ankles. She raised one foot and leaned her face toward Kieran, making sounds, raising her chin.

Brenna said, "We can talk him out of killing anybody, you and me together. But let's do it after we get the money. Please, Kiero." She grabbed his arm as he reached for the tape around Marie's mouth, trying to hold him still. "You're not in this alone!" she said. Her voice was angry and rising again to a fever pitch. "Damn you, you're not in this alone!"

Kieran jerked his arm free. "He took my gun." He slipped the knife under the tape in back of Marie's left ear, serrated edge out. "Otherwise we could face him. Took mine and yours both. He even took the doctor's, the one I found."

Brenna backed away. Her fists were clenched.

Kieran whispered to Marie, "Quiet, now," and pulled away the tape that was wrapped around her head and across her mouth.

Marie nodded twice as she opened her mouth wide and sucked in air with a gasp.

From upstairs, a loud shout from Crawl: "Kieran!"

Kieran's heart jumped. Glancing around quickly to check the stairs, he called out, "I'm coming! We'll be right there!"

Kieran was sweating.

"There's no chance she doesn't die, Bren," he said. "I can't let that happen and you can't, either, and you know it. She doesn't deserve it."

Marie whispered a quick, "Thank you."

Brenna exploded in a muted cry, "He's not going to do that unless you take her and run, then he might. You're just making everything worse!"

Kieran cut through the tape holding Marie's upper arms. He muttered, "This is taking too long."

"He's going to come down," Brenna insisted. She was wild-eyed. "He'll catch us and kill us both."

Kieran spun to look at the stairs again, a quick and fearful check, but still no one coming. "No," he said. "He won't leave Michael alone with the doctor. Not as long as he thinks he's alive."

Marie's arms were free. Kieran tore at the last tape as she struggled to stand; a double wrap around her waist.

Marie said in a whisper, "We can run to the house down the beach. Use their phone. There's no key in the truck." She sounded out of breath.

"I won't let you do this!" Brenna said. She took several steps backward, toward the stairs.

Marie started to move, looking terrified, waving her hand, like a flag, urging Kieran to follow her. "We can get there quicker than him, the way he limps."

Kieran let his knife fall to the floor, but he didn't move. He stared at Brenna, who was crying, her fists clenched tight and her shoulders hunched like a fighter's.

She said, "You're throwing away two and a half million dollars, and you don't have to. I won't let you do this to me!"

Kieran's eyes filled with tears. "Please come with me."

"You're making this up because you're afraid she's got God in there."

"Bren, please." He reached out his hand.

"She's got *nothing* in there. She's got nobody."

"She's got me, Bren. I have to do this."

Brenna's eyes blazed. She twisted her lips and hissed with outrage, "She's not your bloody sister!"

Kieran looked as though he had been struck. "Scissors and guns and money," he said, "and blood and more blood. Who the hell are you?"

Brenna stared at him for nearly five silent seconds, then she turned to bolt up the stairs, taking them two at a time. "Crawl!" she screamed. "He's taking the girl!"

The doctor had used as much time as he could.

With Crawl studying his every movement and muttering increasingly graphic threats, he had swabbed Michael's side for the second time, examined the scalpel and pretended to find it insufficient, searched for and found another, and carefully administered another few drops of the anesthetic into the mask covering Michael's mouth and nose.

Then, with no more credible ideas for eating up time, he wiped away the perspiration that was building on his forehead, gripped the scalpel hard, placed it against Michael's side, and began in terrible slow motion to cut through Michael's flesh.

Crawl watched with his head tilted, not blinking, barely breathing.

In the middle of the first incision, after the doctor had cut no more than three inches side-to-side, Crawl's eyes narrowed.

The doctor wiped away more perspiration.

Crawl stretched his neck and tilted his head even more. He began inching closer to Michael, moving up the table on the side opposite the doctor.

The doctor's heart raced. He was painfully aware that very little of Michael's blood was oozing to the surface where the skin had just been cut. Just a few drops. Not a flow. He pressed a pad of gauze over the incision and held it there, determined not to move it.

Every second might help.

He risked a glance at Crawl. He saw his eyes widen, his mouth twist, and watched him lay his gun hand on Michael's chest, then reach to press the middle and index fingertips of his other hand into his brother's neck.

Crawl began to groan at the same moment that Brenna bounded up the stairs shouting, "Crawl! He's taking the girl!"

The doctor sprang with a cry of his own. In an instant, his left hand locked on the wrist of Crawl's gun hand, pressing it tightly against Michael's chest, while he drove the scalpel like a sword through the back of the hand.

Crawl screamed just as Brenna rushed in, freezing her in the doorway.

His fingers sprang open in an involuntary thrust for escape, loosening his hold on the gun. With his left hand, he tore the scalpel from his right.

The doctor swept the gun off the table and onto the floor. Then he dove for it.

Crawl had fallen back, against the wall. He shouted, "Get it!" to Brenna, but she was paralyzed with fear.

The doctor had Crawl's gun. He twisted to his feet and swung the weapon around in a half circle like the hammer of God, pointing it toward the man who had invaded his home.

But Crawl had already pulled the automatic he'd taken from Kieran out from the back of his belt. He pointed Kieran's weapon at the doctor's heart and pulled the trigger.

The force of the bullet knocked the doctor's body back a full two yards. The gun swung helplessly on his index finger and tumbled to the floor. His left hand went slowly to his chest like a man making a pledge. His head, which had snapped forward with the explosion, rolled to his left shoulder.

His eyes were closed before he hit the floor.

Kieran realized that they were starting to slow down. It was hard to run in the sand and patches of mud at the water's edge, especially with the rain, as light as it was, now coming at them nearly sideways in the wind and growing cold enough to sting.

To their left, baby whitecaps pushed the black water toward the shore in choppy waves. To their right, the sand gave way to rocks made slippery by the rain.

They weren't even halfway there and he was already out of breath.

Marie ran beside him, closer to the water's edge, running in short, steady strides where the sand was soaked and a little more firm.

Kieran could hear her breathing hard.

"You doing okay?" he asked, out of breath himself.

"Taking the road would have added ... another three-quarters of a mile," she said between breaths. "At least."

The shore twisted to their right. They followed it in an arc that swung back to their left again after taking them a hundred yards back, to the edge of the woods.

They would call the state police when they reached the other house, Marie said.

"They might have already been called," Kieran said. "Guns going off. Wouldn't somebody wonder about that?"

"If somebody's close," Marie said. "Maybe. It's hard to pinpoint guns up here. Hear them from two miles away. All the time."

They ran on, trying to run faster but gradually slowing down, instead.

Kieran wondered what was happening to Brenna. He was wondering if she were wishing now that she had come with them, away from Crawl. He wished he had forced her, but how could he have done that? He even felt a sudden impulse to run back for her, but he shook it off. He had come only a half mile, it seemed, and he was already second-guessing himself.

The rain was falling faster and getting colder. He found himself thinking, in the sudden and overwhelming grip of the fear, that he would never be going home again, that the ghost he had carried for so many years was familiar with this kind of rain.

He thought of his mother. He thought about the way she smiled and the way she laughed, and he wanted so much to climb her stairs again, and knock on her door and watch her light up one more time over a tin of mints "like no other mints in the world, only better". He thought about how she would take it if she knew what he had just done. She would bring down the sweet thunder on him, absolutely. And along the way, she'd say that they were all as dumb as ducks if they thought it was the blood and the bones that made Jesus, Jesus. He wanted to feel her hand again resting softly on his hair. He wanted to hear her voice again reciting her favorite prayer and wrapping it around him like a blanket. He wanted God to bless him and keep him and shine his face on him and give him peace.

He thought about Brenna. He thought about Michael. He thought about Sherri and Michael's little boy, and about home, and about a bomb, and about a kill zone.

He thought, "God, I don't want to be here!"

He wanted to cry.

He had also, without realizing it, slowed down to a weak trot.

"What's the matter?" Marie called, turning around and slowing down in front of him.

"Nothing," he said, speeding up again. "Are you still okay?"

Maybe she nodded yes and maybe she didn't. He couldn't tell in the dark and the rain.

She said, panting, "You came all the way from Ireland ... to do this to my uncle and aunt and me?"

He couldn't believe it himself, hearing it put that way.

"We never meant to hurt you," he said. "Honest to God." Then, realizing how pathetic that sounded, he added, "It started out ... not to be like this. We'd take it back if we could. All of us. I know we would."

They ran without speaking for another hundred yards and more.

Rocks took over the beach, jagged pieces, most of them angled and uneven.

They held hands and worked their way across the rocks.

The rocks gave way to more sand, and high, prickly weeds.

"What will he do to my uncle?"

"He won't hurt him now," Kieran said, without believing it. "Not when he knows we're getting help."

Their footsteps had slowed to a leaden jog and their breath was coming in sharper gasps, but they could see the house they were searching for clearly now—white and tall and dark. A large pontoon boat bobbed slowly in the wind-driven water straight ahead, beyond the house.

Kieran said, "Still okay?"

"You mean besides being scared?"

"Don't be."

"Aren't you?"

"Not any more. It's all right now. I promise you."

From the darkness behind them, the muffled crack of Crawl's gunfire in the doctor's laboratory rolled down the lonely beach like the warning of a town crier.

Crawl placed his bleeding hand on his dead brother's chest.

Brenna walked toward him on legs that felt like glass ready to break.

Crawl's other hand pressed lightly on Michael's dark hair.

"He's dead, Bren," he said quietly.

He bent and kissed his brother's cheek, and then, with long moans, he began to sob.

Brenna took his right hand. "You're bleeding bad," she whispered.

She looked at the bandages and tapes and other supplies scattered around the counters and across the floor. "They've gone to the house down the beach. They'll be calling the police," she said, sounding incredibly tired. "I'll stop the bleeding." She started around the table, still in a daze. "I don't know," she said. "Maybe we can still just drive away. I don't know."

Crawl wiped his face with his left hand. He said very quietly, "Every damn thing goes wrong." He shook his head, staring at Michael, then looked at the doctor. "It's not my fault," he said, "but every damn thing . . ." He bit his lip, then muttered, "God, Michael," and he began to cry again.

"It's hard to see a man cry," Brenna whispered without emotion. She placed gauze bandages and tape on the table and took his wounded hand. "I've wondered why that is. I see a woman cry, I don't seem to care. I see a man cry, and it tears my heart. I don't know why that is." She was winding the bandage very slowly. "A man crying is a grievous thing." She paused and stared at Crawl. "I'm sorry about Michael."

Crawl looked at his hand. "He stuck me like a pig."

"No veins or arteries, though." Brenna bit a long piece of surgical gauze and tore it from its roll. She wound it slowly over the bandage.

"I'm going to go and get them," Crawl said. His eyes looked dead.

She struggled to think. "Why get them? It's over, isn't it?"

"We have fingerprints all over the house." His voice was mechanical and distant. "You stay and wipe them."

She stared at him. "Isn't it over now? Why do you have to go and get them?"

196

"Keep going," he said, jiggling his hand slowly.

"We can't get the money now."

"Finish me."

She rubbed the loose end of tape against his palm and reached again for the roll of bandage. Tears slid down her cheeks. "But we can't get any money now, can we?"

"Maybe not."

"All this. And no money." When he didn't answer, she looked at him and said, "Then no more hurt, okay? Don't hurt him, Crawl. And don't hurt the girl."

"He turned on me, Bren."

"Please. Make it stop now."

"A traitor, after all our time together."

"But what good will it do?"

"He's a traitor to you too," he said coldly.

"You're his only brother. And he's your only brother now." Her eyes filled with tears.

"He's not my brother. He never has been. And he's a killer. You didn't know that, did you?"

"He was just afraid it might really be Jesus."

"He killed his sister. He killed Colleen, and he killed her baby too."

Brenna froze. "No," she gasped. Her mouth fell open. She shook her head. "He couldn't have done that."

"He killed them. He says he set Willy Doyle on fire for getting Colleen pregnant, but most of all, it was just trying to smash somebody because of what he did to her himself. I know that much."

Brenna stared and said, "Don't, Crawl."

"Doyle was a motley faced hood. Hustled drugs. Sick all the time. Must've been fifteen years older than Colleen. Kieran goes nuts when he finds out Colleen's pregnant by him. Temper takes over. Knocked the hell out of her. Then he goes over and sets Willy Doyle on fire. Next thing she knows, she's lost the baby. It was Kieran that did it, so she runs off. Time they find her, four weeks later, she's dying of pneumonia down in Banbridge, where she's been trying to live in the streets. Middle of winter. Didn't even get her home. She died on the way."

Brenna's eyes were closed. She was shaking.

"So cry for Michael," Crawl said. "But he's the only one." Slowly, he moved to the table to kiss his brother again, this time on the forehead. "You're the one to cry for," he said to his brother quietly. Then he stood up again and pulled his lips tight.

"But Kieran's been like your own brother, even if he isn't blood," Brenna said, her lips quivering, her eyes filling with tears. "And I love him, Crawl."

"That's two good reasons he shouldn't have turned on us. That's why he's the last one should be a traitor to me and you, both. But he is."

She said, now in a soft whine, "He said you wanted to kill the girl. You don't want to kill the girl, do you?" She backed away from him.

Crawl turned. He looked at the doctor's body, at the way his arms were spread out wide, and the legs, long, like a spider's.

"Crawl?"

Turning again to Michael, very slowly, Crawl murmured, "I'm going now, Michael."

Brenna had backed into the corner of the room. She was pale and shaken and sobbing. "Please don't kill him, Crawl. And don't kill the girl, for God's sake. She doesn't deserve that."

Crawl looked at her with a quizzical expression. "It's not the girl, Bren. It's the baby."

Her lips twisted. She folded her hands over her heart.

"It's the baby I'll be killing," Crawl said. "The girl is just there."

Brenna slid slowly down the wall to a sitting position, her knees propped up in front of her. She moaned, "I don't understand."

Crawl looked around as if he had forgotten something. Moving like a sleepwalker, he crossed the room and retrieved his automatic from the floor near the doctor's right hand. "If he were to wake up, and you had to shoot him again, Bren," he said, "you'd do it like this."

He leveled his gun at the doctor's chest and fired twice.

Brenna slapped her hands to her ears and buried her face on her knees with a muffled scream.

He heard her wail softly from the corner.

She raised her eyes. "Please don't kill me," she whined.

He walked back to stand at her feet, looking down at her, the gun hanging at his side.

Sobbing, she pressed her eyes shut and buried her face in her hands.

"Oh, Christ, Brenna," he said. "Why didn't you stay home?"

18

It took Kieran and Marie another seven minutes to reach the house. Gasping for breath and soaked with rain they tried the door. It was locked.

Kieran pulled a cushion from the swing on the porch, pressed it against the window in the door and hammered it with his fist, smashing the glass.

Two more tiny explosions, badly muffled in the distance, sounded down the beach.

Marie's eyes widened with alarm. She put her hand on Kieran's arm and drew closer.

Kieran reached through the broken glass and unlocked the door. "Don't turn on the light," he said, still struggling to catch his breath. "Not if we don't have to. It'll just show Crawl for sure where we are."

Marie was already at the kitchen counter, trying to see the walls in the dark, feeling for wherever the phone might be. Her mind was still pounding with the last two shots they heard from back at her house. Was her uncle still alive? She doubted it. But maybe. She thought, whoever fired those last two shots was the one who was alive. Maybe it was her uncle, after all.

Even if it wasn't, Crawl couldn't cover the ground nearly as fast as she and Kieran had, not with his limp, so they still had time.

But her heart refused to slow down.

"Where do they keep the bloody phones?" Kieran demanded, flashing anger. "You've been in here before, haven't you?"

"They use satellite," she said. "They could be anywhere." She felt a light switch, a framed picture. She knocked over a blender on the kitchen counter, near the sink. "Try the drawers. Anybody with a boat and an outside generator has to have flashlights around."

"I give this three minutes," Kieran said. "Then we're turning on the lights."

They groped the kitchen counter, but as they found the drawers to the right and left of the sink, Marie spun suddenly and rushed to the door. "The boat!" she exclaimed. "They had their boat put in the water. They'll have flares on board."

Kieran said, "Good. But let's be quick!" and he joined her at the door.

Marie pressed her hand against his chest, holding him back. "I can get them," she said. "You keep looking through the drawers just in case." She ran outside. "I'll be right back."

There were fifty yards of lawn between the house and the boat, all of it sloping toward the water. To her right, the grass and shallow beach ended, giving way to shelves of gray rock that rose sharply into a thickly wooded mountainside with jagged cliffs overlooking the southern end of the lake.

The rain had nearly stopped. A thick slice of moon was emerging from behind its cover of clouds, making visibility easier. But the wind had not diminished. It drove off the lake hard, blowing straight into Marie's face and swallowing the words she spoke loudly and in cadence as her legs pumped and her breath came in sharp bursts. "And maybe keys. Get the keys. Find the keys. Take the boat."

She raced onto the dock, her footsteps pounding.

Reaching the pontoon boat, she swung open the aluminum-tubing gate and rushed to feel for a key in the empty ignition. Nothing. She tried to think clearly. There may not be a key on board, but if there was, where would it be?

She felt in the ashtray and over the awning by the wheel and in the beverage deck, then looked again, terrified, at the dark house, where nothing had changed. She tried around the base of the pilot's console and under the cushion of the pilot's chair, still talking out loud to herself, now saying breathlessly, "Where? Where? Find the keys. Did they hide the keys? Find the keys."

But she didn't find them, and she realized she was out of time.

Moving to the back of the boat, she flung open the panel doors under the rear seats and pulled out the emergency kit that was beside the spare five-gallon fuel drum. The kit held five flares. She grabbed two of them and rushed back onto the dock.

Then she stopped.

It took her just three seconds to think it through.

Laying the flares on the dock, she jumped back into the boat and dragged the spare fuel tank out from under the rear seat. She lifted it onto the seat, took off the cap, and wrestled the tank upside down. As fuel poured over the seats and onto the deck, she took the fuel line from the five-gallon tank that was tucked beside the pilot's console and tipped it over, making sure that it, too, settled on its top, not on its side.

Fuel covered the soles of her shoes and filled the air with fumes.

She climbed back onto the dock, tucked one of the flares into her belt like a knife and ripped the cap from the second one, striking the tip and the core together for ignition. It popped and spit a tongue of hissing orange into the air. She threw it onto the deck of the boat and turned in the same motion to pound back up the dock toward the grass.

The air thumped behind her and the lawn pulsed with orange from the fire that suddenly filled the deck of the boat.

She didn't look back. She focused on the door to the house, and on pulling the second flare from her belt. She slowed only once, and then only barely, halfway between the boat and the house, as she tore the cap from the second flare and ignited it. It would be their flashlight. It would help them find the phone. If there was a phone.

Kieran was already coming out the door as she leapt onto the porch.

He shouted, "What happened?"

"It'll bring the state police, or rangers, or somebody," she panted. "Everyone can see it from any of these mountains. The lake pin-points it. They'll call for help. They're panicked about fire up here. Did you find the phone?"

"No," Kieran said, stepping aside to avoid her flare as she rushed past him, back into the house. "But we might as well turn on the lights now. We can't tell Crawl where we are any clearer than we've just done."

Crawl drove the truck slowly, staying at the water's edge, showing no lights. He was steering with his left hand. His bandaged right hand lay limply in his lap. His eyes were half-closed but his mind was fiercely focused.

When he saw the boat ignite, he slowed instinctively, easing down to twenty miles an hour, wondering if Kieran and the girl had been caught in the explosion. He thought of one of the Bible stories he had heard as a child, the one about Moses seeing a pillar of fire in the desert and knowing from the fire which way he should go, and he smirked.

Then he saw the second flare pop to life in Marie's hand in the middle of the lawn and let out a low chuckle. He could see her plainly as she ran with it. She was glowing at the edges, even from three hundred yards away.

He brought the pickup back up to thirty miles an hour, then began to sing the same words over and over again, very slowly and methodically, in a deep, rolling cadence: "Run, Mary, run, Mary, run, Mary, run. Herod's gonna kill your baaaaby."

The house lights went on.

"Run, Mary, run, Mary, run, Mary, run. Herod's gonna kill your baaaaby."

Even with the lights, they couldn't find a phone.

They raced through the lower rooms and then the second story while Kieran said over and over again, "They took 'em. They took 'em." And finally, "We're out of here. No more time."

"We should head for the road, out the front door," Marie said. She was out of breath from racing through the rooms. The flare was still blazing in her hand.

"Get rid of that out back, then," Kieran said. "He'll see us a mile away if we take it with us."

Marie ran for the back door.

"Just toss it!" Kieran shouted. "Quick!"

And she did. She took three long strides onto the porch and threw the flame onto the grass.

Then her breath froze in her throat.

Crawl's truck was parked right next to the porch, twenty feet to her left.

It had been pulled up and parked, and the engine was already off, and the door was hanging open. The truck was empty.

She inhaled a sudden burst of air. For three excruciating seconds she stood too frightened to move. Then she wheeled suddenly to look behind her, and the air she had inhaled exploded in a sharp, high cry.

Crawl's right hand was wrapped in bandages and blotched with red. His gun was in his left hand, already raised and pointing at her waist from less than four feet away.

"That's a good scream," he said with a grim whisper. "That'll bring him."

Taking a step backward, she shouted out the beginning of a warning, but she got no farther than, "Look out—" before Kieran charged through the door, drawn by her cry.

He saw Crawl and stopped, his hands in midair in front of his chest.

He and Crawl stared at each other for several seconds in dead silence. Then Crawl said, "I came to tell you the bad news. Our big brother is dead."

Kieran said softly, "We heard a shot."

"You didn't know that, did you?" Crawl said, speaking very slowly. "About Michael being dead? So I came to tell you. What's a brother for?"

"Is the doctor dead, too?"

Marie held her breath.

Crawl darted a glance at the fire in the boat, and at the flare burning in the grass ten yards away. "I was thinking of something important on the way here. I was thinking . . ." He stopped. "We should get that flare off the grass, don't you think?" He eyed them both, giving time for an answer but not expecting one. Then he said with a slight wave of his automatic, "Let's all three of us step out there on the lawn so I can pick it up. Burn a hole in the folk's grass this way."

He jiggled his gun again and moved them onto the lawn, near the flare.

"Just step back," he said. "I'll get this little beauty." He picked up the flare and faced them; fire in one hand, gun in the other, all of them glowing orange. "My hand got hurt," he said. "Did you notice that? But I can handle it."

"Where's Brenna?" Kieran asked.

"Brenna's watching the doctor, as far as I know."

"Are they both all right?"

The flare hissed in the wind.

"You know what we forgot to do in all the fuss, little brother?" Crawl asked. "This is what I was thinking about on the way here.

We forgot to have the mother of the Jesus baby, here, give her powers a try on Michael."

Marie took Kieran's arm and held on tight. "What do you mean?"

"I mean you didn't pray for him, darlin', that God would come down and heal him."

She stared, waiting.

"It was your hero's idea," Crawl said. "We were going to try it, but we didn't, did we? It got lost in all the commotion. He decided he wouldn't try it, after all."

Marie looked at Kieran.

Kieran kept his eyes on Crawl.

"Let's have her say the holy prayer," Crawl said. "Let's have her kiss Michael on the eyes and tell him she's sorry she killed him."

Kieran said, "Crawl."

"Let's have her tell that little bit of God in her belly to bring him back, right, Kieran?"

"I said make him better. I never said bring back the dead."

Crawl waved the flare from side to side. "But I've got a little problem if I want to test it now, don't I? Because here we are, all the way down the beach. Your choice, not mine. But I wouldn't want to have to drag her all the way back to the house just to find out what kind of power she has, would I? You see what I mean? We make that long trip back, and me with my hand hurting and all, and then we find out it doesn't work anyway, what good is that?"

Kieran said it again, this time with a growing edge of urgency, "Crawl."

"So I asked myself on the way over, how do I find out way down here by a burning boat on somebody else's yard if she's got that kind of power? Without going all the way back to the house, I mean."

Kieran felt Marie squeeze his arm tighter. He said in a loud whisper, "This gets you nothing, Crawl." Fresh raindrops hit his cheek and forehead and hair. He didn't feel them.

"So then I thought, hey. I've got an idea. And you can help, Kieran."

"It gets you nothing, Crawl."

Crawl squinted at Marie, then shifted his gaze back to Kieran. "Didn't anyone ever tell you, little brother? What's done is done. How the hell can you be Irish and not know a thing like that? It's the biggest hurt of all, Kieran: we can never go back."

And he fired.

Kieran's legs jerked as he stumbled backward, then locked like a mannequin's.

Marie jumped to the side instinctively, screaming, "Oh, God!"

Crawl fired again. And then a third time.

Kieran fell to the lawn in a sitting position, his hands resting limply in his lap.

Marie rushed to his side and dropped to her knees. She tried to hold him up, putting one hand behind his head, grabbing his sleeve near his shoulder with the other.

Kieran looked at the sixteen-year-old who was scared and not wanting to be pregnant. He saw her matted black hair and round dark eyes, and he saw she was crying.

He whispered, "I'm so sorry."

She groaned, "No."

He twisted his lips, trying to keep from crying. He said, very weakly, "I really did try " Then he closed his eyes and fell sideways to the lawn.

Marie moaned, "No," once more, and tried for a brief few seconds to lift Kieran's head. Then she withdrew her hand.

She turned to Crawl and knotted her fist and cried out, "Why are you doing this?"

"You should be glad," he said softly. "Guns going off in the middle of nowhere, people hear it, hikers and campers, maybe some rangers. They start asking where it came from. Maybe start circling around. Then you show them a fire they can see from any of those other mountains, put it right on the lake. First thing, you've got red lights and police radios going off everywhere. Wasn't that the plan, to mark the spot with the fire on the boat?"

"Tell me why!"

"Well, then," Crawl said grimly. "Now let's see what you can do."

Brenna was still on the floor of the doctor's laboratory where Crawl had left her; still sitting pressed against the wall, still pressing her raised knees into her chin. Her hands were still wrapped around her ankles. The house was silent. All she could hear was her own labored breathing as she tried to stop crying.

Then, suddenly, she heard something more.

She stiffened but she didn't raise her head. She barely breathed. Was it something close by?

She heard it again. A shuffling sound. Muted, but clearly something shuffling. This time, very near.

Her head bolted upright. Her expression froze in a mask of horror.

The doctor was hovering over her, alive, and staring at her with a dark and terrible expression.

She tried to plead, "No," but instead of a word, a high-pitched sound began to rise from her throat. She shut her eyes as tightly as she could, shielded them with her white-knuckled fists, opened her mouth wide and let the dreadful sound escape in a desperate, trembling scream.

Marie didn't move. She didn't know if she could move. Even Crawl saying "Now let's see what you can do" sounded like someone speaking from a hundred yards away.

Crawl dropped the flare to the lawn beside Kieran's head. "Put it in the ground close by," he told her. "It's our altar candle. Shed some light on the big event."

She forced herself to fight back more tears and pressed the flare's metal spike into the lawn twelve inches from Kieran's right cheek.

"Now pray for him," Crawl said.

Marie answered, very quietly, "You're insane."

"And you're pregnant," Crawl said. "And we aren't sure with what, are we? And Kieran's dead. And you're already on your knees. Pray for him."

She closed her eyes and sat back on her heels, her hands folded, one resting on the other just above her knees. She lowered her head.

"Put your hand on him," Crawl said. "Show some gratitude."

She rested her right hand on Kieran's chest, away from the blood.

Crawl said, "He tried to save your life, you know."

Marie lowered her head again.

"Pray out loud, so I can hear you."

Marie gathered her thoughts, then said in a voice barely above a whisper, "God, please don't let him die."

"He's already dead. You're praying to bring him back."

Crawl sank to one knee beside her, his gun still facing her.

She inhaled slowly, dropped her head again and said, "God, you love him more than anybody else ever will. And he tried to save me.

He died trying to save me." Orange tears trailed down her orange cheeks in the light of the flare. "So please don't let him be dead. You can do that. Please don't let him stay dead."

She grew silent.

Crawl was silent too. Then he inhaled and sighed and said casually, "Well, I guess—"

But Marie snapped, "Quiet!" She came up quickly, raising one knee off the ground. She was staring at Kieran. She exclaimed, "Oh, my God!"

Crawl looked at her, startled. Then he looked at Kieran.

Marie said, "Oh, my God!" again, louder, and this time in a high and excited voice. She reached to yank the flare from the ground. "Did his eyelids just flutter?" She moved the flare close to Kieran's face and bent down, squinting to get a better look. "Did his eyes start to open? Oh, my God!"

Crawl was right beside her.

Marie pivoted, and in a single, arcing sweep of her arm she drove the flare's tongue of fire with all the force she had into Crawl's gun hand, piercing and sizzling it in the same second.

Crawl screamed wildly and pulled his hand to his chest. The gun fell on Kieran's chest.

Marie leapt to her feet and raced toward the rocks that began to rise sharply a hundred yards from the house. She heard Crawl screaming curses behind her and realized she was making a moaning sound as she ran. She told herself to run faster, not to look back. Then, at the same instant she heard a shot behind her, she felt something burn the side of her right calf. She spun and tumbled to the ground.

As she struggled to her feet, she realized she had been shot in the leg, which meant she was no longer faster than Crawl. She might not even be as fast. And his next shot would drive her to the ground and she wouldn't get up.

But the next shot didn't come.

As she reached the first rising rocks she risked a quick look back just as Crawl threw his empty gun to the ground with a fiery curse and rushed to pick up the flare.

Marie stared, mesmerized, horrified, as if in a dream, until she saw him running after her with the flare in his wounded hand. Then she screamed and scrambled as fast as she could up the first shelves of wet rock.

Her leg burned, and the rain made the rocks slippery. They rose sharply in front of her, sloped and broken granite slabs with grass patches and tall weeds among the thickly gathering pines and aspens.

She climbed as fast as she could, but the pain was burning hotter in her leg, dragging her into slow motion. She tried to pick up speed by grabbing the trunks of the youngest trees and pulling at overhanging branches. Deep scratches opened in her palms and fingers.

Again, she looked over her shoulder. Again, she saw the flare bobbing toward her in the darkness, rising on the rocks behind her, now nearer than before.

She knew that she could never escape if she had to fight her way higher, wounded, through the heavy growth that rose like walls directly ahead of her, so she veered to her left, desperate to find the hiking trail that climbed the cliffs alongside the water.

Crawl shouted, "I can see you and I can hear you!" And he could. He was climbing after her. No longer cursing. Just breathing hard, in long hisses.

Marie found the hiking trail in the moonlight, but Crawl found it too, just two minutes later.

The terrible flare followed her, weaving and bobbing through the trees and the cold rain as the carefully cadenced words, so slowly droned and so dreadful, rose up behind her again. "Run, Mary, run, Mary, run, Mary, run. Herod's gonna kill your baaaby."

She heard herself making a sharp, moaning sound each time she stepped on her right foot, and she began to pray, begging God to make Crawl lose sight of her but knowing he wouldn't. Not now. The man who would kill her was already too close.

The deadly song drew closer. "Run, Mary, run, Mary, run, Mary, run . . ."

She turned her head quickly to look for the flare just one more time and almost screamed when she saw it. It was no more than twenty yards away, right behind her, moving faster, catching up.

She gasped a loud, "Oh, God, help me!"

"Herod's gonna kill your baaaby."

The black Mercedes slunk across the lawn like a cat. It showed no headlights and no brake lights, even when it stopped. It crunched softly into the young pines and junipers and rising rock that forced it to a stop ten feet into the brush at the base of the hiking trail, where its engine died.

The dome light lit when the door opened. It went out again when the door closed with a single muffled click.

Once again, the only light on the mountainside was the single orange flame that continued to rise with an uneven swagger high on the ledges where the wind blew and the tall trees swayed over dark and turning waters.

19

The trees to Marie's right and left glowed orange. New shadows cast by the swaying flare swung left and right across her path. She could hear the snapping of twigs and the scraping of Crawl's shoes on the rocks, and every word of the dreadful song, again and again.

She expected, at any second, to hear him breathing against the back of her neck.

And then the singing stopped.

Her heart hammered fiercely. She was too terrified to turn and look back.

The trail split in front of her. To the right, it led up and over the face of a steep, layered rock. To her left, it disappeared between two tall pines.

She turned left and drove herself to move, and move again, wondering with each step when the hiss of the flare and the bright orange of the fire and the man who was no longer singing would be upon her.

She lurched down the descending trail and through a short, curving corridor of pines and jagged red rock, and limped into the center of a long, flat clearing with an unprotected cliff overlooking the water breaking over the rocks nearly a hundred yards below. Then she stopped and turned with a sharp cry.

She wasn't on the trail any more. She had entered a scenic overlook that was walled in on three sides. The only way out was the same way she had come in.

She had recognized it too late. The pines that she had come through were already glowing orange.

Terror-stricken, she limped another fifteen yards backward toward the wet rock that walled her in at the farthest end of the clearing.

And then she saw his face.

She wanted to scream again, but she didn't. She pressed her back against the wall at the end of the clearing, not three feet from the cliff, and waited, helpless.

Crawl emerged into full view.

When he saw her captured in the glow of his flare, he stopped and grinned.

Marie raised her hand in front of her face and screamed into the wind, "Why are you doing this to me?"

Crawl repeated in a flat voice, "Why are you doing this to me?"

He was no longer smiling. He was moving closer.

"Why do you want to hurt me?"

"Why do you want to hurt me?"

She sank to the ground. She thought of her mother and father. She said, "I haven't done anything to you!"

"I haven't done anything to you."

Marie grubbed the thin trunk of the single young aspen growing out of a crevice in the rock near her foot. She knew it couldn't save her. She just wanted to hold on to something.

Crawl laughed abruptly, joylessly, and then, just as abruptly, he stopped laughing.

But he didn't stop moving closer.

Marie sank to her knees. Her free hand closed in a fist over her belly and she rocked back on her heels.

He was standing over her, the flare hissing very near, so near she felt its heat.

She looked past the hissing orange tongue and said to him in a soft and hopeless whisper, "What do you want?"

"You don't have the power to give me what I want," he said. "Remember?"

Suddenly Marie's eyes opened wider. She tilted her head, staring past Crawl, then raised her hand high and screamed, "Help me! Quick!"

Crawl spun.

What he saw was an impossible sight: a specter glowing hellish orange in the fire of the flare. The doctor was alive and walking, coming toward him, his shoulders rounded, his head hanging forward, his white hair blowing in the wind, his coat flapping open. In his trembling hand, pointed unsteadily at Crawl's face and moving steadily closer, was a silver-plated Smith & Wesson automatic.

Crawl struggled for breath. He stumbled backward into the wall next to Marie. His eyes bulged with fear and disbelief.

"Move away from her," the doctor growled bitterly.

"Did she pray for you?" Crawl said, struggling for breath. Then he called it loudly: "Did she pray for you?"

The doctor struggled to angle his gun skyward, and, straining, fired once into the air. The explosion seemed to rock the small enclosure. The weapon lowered again to point at Crawl. "I said, move away from her."

Crawl, still staring and breathless, ignored him. He spun to Marie. His words were desperate. "Did you pray for him? Can you really do it? Is that how you brought him back?"

The doctor took several more uneven strides forward. "For the last time, move away from her."

Crawl, still stunned, said to Marie, "My God, you can do it!" He looked from the girl to the doctor and back again. Then, before the doctor could react, he rushed at Marie, flinging his arm around her neck, holding the deadly fire just six inches from her chin.

Marie cringed instinctively, but the furious candle left her nowhere to go.

"Throw the gun over the edge," Crawl demanded.

The doctor started forward but stopped. He tried to steady the gun. He started to say something then stopped. His mouth was open. His eyes were narrowed to slits.

"You won't shoot for two reasons," Crawl shouted into the wind. "First, you'll probably hit her, your hand waving around like that. But more certain, I'll burn a hole in her throat as big as your fist if you hit me. I don't care who she is or what she can do. So help me God, it'll happen."

The doctor spit the words out like a curse: "Your dead friend said that to me. So help him, God." He worked to hold the gun steady.

"It's time to play our favorite game again," Crawl said loudly. "I count to three. At three she gets another open throat. If you shoot me after that, I won't care. I'll want you to." He stared for a moment at the man he had shot in the heart, then cried out, "One."

He moved the flare a half inch closer to Marie's neck.

She winced from the heat and pressed backward.

As the doctor's gaze met Marie's, the fury drained from his eyes. He said, suddenly sounding desperately sad and tired, "I wanted to make up for the death of your parents. I wanted to make you the house of God."

"I already was the house of God," Marie said, crying hard. "And you were, too."

The doctor blinked twice, his mouth half-opened, his eyes half-closed.

"She won't be around to bring anybody else back from the dead," Crawl yelled. "Or to bring the baby home to you. 'Cause in about a minute from now, the baby will be dead. Two!"

Only the doctor's gaze moved, sliding darkly from Marie to Crawl.

"Throw it over the edge. Do one thing right in all of this. Because now I'm saying . . . Three!"

"Don't," the doctor said. It wasn't even a shout. It sounded with no anger and no alarm. Just a single hollow word. Then, with an awkward jerk of his arm, he tossed his Smith & Wesson over the edge of the cliff.

Crawl relaxed his grip on Marie's shoulder. "Listen to me, both of you," he said. He eased his arm away from the girl, taking care not to point the flare at her. He focused on the doctor. "I wouldn't have hurt her, I swear to God. Even if you shot me. Not now." He shifted his weight and moved backward, inching away from the girl. "I just had to stop you. I don't know how this is happening here, but if she's the one that brought you back, if she can do that, then Michael can come back too." He looked at Marie and pleaded, "Can't he? And Kieran. He'll be okay too, won't he? I didn't want that." His voice climbed with a rising excitement. "But he already is, probably. You prayed for him direct. You touched him and everything. It just takes a little while, right?"

Marie stared, transfixed, then she leaned away from him, pressing her back into the wall of rock.

Crawl tossed the flare into the corner of the clearing behind him, wincing with pain as he opened his hand to let it go. "See?" he said. "I'm not going to hurt either of you."

The doctor slid his right foot forward and shifted his weight, very slowly.

"I didn't want any of this killing," Crawl said, looking down at Marie. "None of us wanted this. It just took over. It wasn't my fault."

The doctor took another step toward the flare. Then another.

Crawl grinned weakly at Marie. "But maybe we *do* get to go back," he said. He laughed suddenly, and tears rose in his eyes. He shook his head and said weakly, "My God, girl."

Marie glanced past him. Her uncle was bending down to pick up the flare.

Crawl watched her expression change and spun in time to see the doctor advancing with raging eyes, the flare held high.

"Leave her alone!" the doctor thundered, and he swung the flare like a sword.

Crawl leapt to his side, ducking and grabbing the doctor's wrist with his burned hand. He cried out in pain but held on as the doctor tried to pull away. Locked together and twisting, they slammed against the wall of rock, then swung back into the center of the clearing.

Crawl was shouting, "You don't have to do this! You don't have to do this!" His bandaged hand reached for the doctor's throat.

The doctor swung at Crawl with his left fist. Crawl twisted and pulled backward. The blow glanced off his cheek, but its momentum propelled them both toward the edge of the cliff.

Crawl held the doctor's flare hand at arm's length with one hand. His other hand found the doctor's chest and pressed into it. He grabbed at his shirt, trying to push him back. He yelled again: "You don't have to . . ." But before he finished the sentence, his eyes bulged and the words died in his throat.

He grabbed the doctor's shirt in his bleeding fist and pushed, twisting his hand viciously against the doctor's chest, this time with enough force to drive them both several feet backward, away from the cliff. In a blind rage, he spun the doctor to the ground and fell on top of him. Tearing the flare from the doctor's grip with both hands, he sent the fire rolling back toward the cliff. The doctor twisted with ebbing strength, trying and failing to work himself free. Crawl stared at the doctor's chest for the briefest of moments, and then he tore open the doctor's shirt with both hands and pressed his open palms into the doctor's bulletproof vest.

Stunned, he rose to his feet. Then he let out a cry, turned to Marie and lunged.

But the doctor clutched him tightly around his lame leg. With a cry of his own, he twisted as Crawl tried to pull away and rolled with all the strength he had left toward the edge of the cliff, spinning Crawl to the ground and taking him with him.

The flare sputtered and died, stealing the last of the terrible orange light.

Crawl tried to stop the doctor's momentum, groping frantically for a handhold in the rock. He cried out, cursing and shouting pain-filled sounds without words.

The doctor shouted just as loudly as Crawl, "Leave her alone! Leave her alone!"

The fingers of Crawl's burned hand slipped into a sharp crevice just as he and the doctor rolled over the edge of the cliff.

Marie screamed and scrambled toward them on her hands and knees.

A horrifying pain exploded in Crawl's hand and shot through his left arm and shoulder, but he held on, even with the weight of the doctor clinging to his legs and swinging like a pendulum and still kicking, trying to tear Crawl from the rock.

Crawl closed his eyes and yelled a long, tortured, "Ahhh!"

And then, with a single sharp moan, the doctor stopped struggling and slipped away into the rocks and the black water below.

Only Marie, who had reached the edge of the cliff, was still screaming.

Crawl's one-handed grip was secure enough to hold him, but it wouldn't be for long. He gasped and swung his right hand up and over the edge of the cliff, trying to find another handhold. "Help me!" he said as he rubbed his bleeding palm over the rock; but the rock was weather beaten and smooth, and he couldn't find a hold.

Marie rose to her feet, watching him in the dim moonlight. She said nothing, didn't reach to take his hand. She simply hovered over him, silhouetted against the dark sky like a gargoyle. The rain, which had picked up again, peppered her face. The wind blew her hair wildly and flapped the sleeves of her shirt.

"You can't let me die, girl," Crawl shouted breathlessly. "If you let me fall, it's the same as murder."

"I'm not strong enough to pull you up," she said fiercely. "My leg is bleeding. I'm shot."

"Just guide my hand, over here, just to get a good hold." He was gasping. "I can do the rest. I just can't pull myself up. Not with one hand. You burned my hand, girl!" When she didn't move, he screamed at the top of his lungs, "You're carryin' Jesus in your belly! You can't just murder me! For Christ's sake, girl, help me!"

She closed her eyes hard and opened them crying. Her head turned from side to side, slowly. She sank to her knees, wincing with pain and grabbing at her wounded leg. "I don't know what to do!" she cried out as much to herself, or to her mother and father, or to God, as to Crawl.

"Pull me up," Crawl said sharply. "Even a few inches. Just guide me to a handhold. I'm slipping away here. Please!"

"Everybody you've touched is dead."

"You'll be no better than me if you don't help me up," Crawl said. Then, calling her by her name for the first time, he lowered his voice and pleaded, "Marie, don't let me do that to you, girl."

She hesitated for several more seconds. Then she braced herself, planting the foot of her good leg just a dozen inches from the edge of the cliff, and she stretched to grab Crawl's free wrist with both hands. Then she leaned back and pulled as hard as she dared.

But her foot broke loose with explosive force, hurling both her feet past the edge of the cliff as she screamed and dropped hard on her back.

Crawl cried out with pain and swayed backward, but held on. He grasped for Marie's feet with his free hand as she twisted and rolled backward, out of reach.

"Help me!" he said again, this time frantic with fear, waving his free hand in short bursts, begging her with his eyes and his voice and his fingers to grab hold. "You can do it, Marie."

She found his wrist again and held tight as she planted her foot one more time, this time recklessly close to the edge.

Suddenly a light swept over her from behind.

It was a clear light, not a flare, and there were the sounds of shuffling feet, and a voice behind the light was shouting, "Here!"

"Help us!" she cried. "Help!"

But Crawl spoke, too, as the flashlights bounced and two men in uniform rushed to help Marie. "No. I can't do that, Marie," he said, and she could feel him pulling back, trying to free his wrist from her grip.

She grabbed tighter and shouted to him, "They're here. Hang on."

She heard men's voices giving hard orders beside her about the edge of the cliff and the man's arm.

Two lights swept in quick circles. Both of them found Crawl.

"You have to let me go now, Marie," he said, keeping his eyes on her face between the two hard lights.

A pair of strong hands grabbed Marie's shoulders. A man in a state police uniform said, "We'll get him," and reached to grab Crawl by the arm, just above Marie's grip.

Crawl shouted, "Marie!"

She wailed, "What can I do?"

They looked at each other for a brief moment in the beams of the flashlights, sadness to sadness, as Crawl twisted his wrist and Marie opened her grip.

He said, "Say a prayer for Crawl." Then he twisted again, this time hard enough to break the tenuous hold of a New Mexico state trooper, and pushed himself away from the cliff.

The police cruiser met an ambulance from Santa Fe fifteen miles northeast of the city. They transferred Marie from the cruiser to the ambulance in the entrance drive of a Sunoco station on U.S. 60. The ambulance took her the rest of the way with lights flashing but no sirens. She had lost blood and was being observed for possible shock, but the bullet had passed cleanly through the edge of her calf muscle. Her wound was not considered life threatening.

The state police officer who joined her in the ambulance had four weeks to go before his retirement. He was a father of five, with sun-baked skin, gray hair and mustache, and smiling eyes. He knew her name before she told him. "We found your uncle's car at the foot of the incline," he told her, "and we've already been to your house."

"They told me that," she said. "And you found the other man? That was shot, on the grass?"

He nodded and placed his strong hand on hers, on the edge of the stretcher. "You really don't have to talk about it now, Marie, unless you want to. We have it all, I think. And we can talk with you later."

"I know. They said the redheaded woman was still at the house. And she's okay?"

He nodded again. "She was still there, just sitting there in the rain, crying, next to a truck."

"She didn't have the keys. Nowhere to go."

"She was not in good shape. In shock, to some degree, but she was lucid. We think she pretty much told us the whole thing."

Marie said, "About Aunt Leah, too." It was not a question.

"Everything, we think. Up until the time you left, anyway. So we know about your uncle and saw the one she called Crawl. And, as I said, we found the fellow named Kieran."

She closed her eyes and rested. She could feel the ambulance curving to the right. "He saved my life," she said. "Kieran."

"We know."

"He said when he first saw me, no one would hurt me."

"And that will go well for him."

The siren sounded as they passed an area of lights, then it shut down again.

She cocked her head and stared. "What did you just say?"

"About what?"

"Something about, 'That will go well for Kieran?'"

"That he tried to save your life. They'll weigh that, I promise you."

She pulled herself up on her elbows. "Who'll weigh it?"

"The law. The court."

"He's dead, right?"

"Oh, no," the officer said. "He's probably at the hospital by now. We got him out right away, even before we heard the shot and came up looking for you."

Marie said, "This is Kieran? On the lawn, in back of the house with the fire?"

"The man on the lawn. Shot once in the midsection, but they told me he looked like he might make it. I'd guess he's still critical, but I think he's alive. It happens."

She was still shaking her head. "And this is Kieran? At the base of the hill where I was, only closer to the house? On the lawn?"

"Do you want me to check?"

"He was right in back of the house?"

"Yes. I can call and get his status."

"But he was shot three times."

"No, actually. Did the other one fire at him three times? He was hit just once."

She lowered herself down again without answering. She reviewed what she had seen and what she was hearing. Then she raised herself up again. "Would you call and get somebody who's actually with him? Get them to look at him, chest, stomach, all in front. I saw him shot three times from five feet away, I swear I did. And he was hit. Three times. Not once."

The officer shrugged his shoulders slightly, then nodded to the paramedic that was with them, seated up front, near the ambulance's cab. "Have him radio ahead," he said. "You heard what she saw. Ask them to check it out. Possible three bullet wounds. Front, close-range."

The paramedic said, "I'll do it," and got up to use the radio.

Marie settled down again on the thin pillow, but she didn't close her eyes.

It was eight minutes before the hospital emergency unit radioed back: "One bullet wound. And he's doing okay," the officer told Marie.

She rose to a sitting position, propping herself up with her arms straight behind her, her eyes wide and unblinking, her lips opened slightly, not moving.

"Lower left abdomen. And very lucky, actually. Nine millimeters is a good-sized weapon. He's received blood and he's stable. Still critical, but they're pretty sure they have him in a good place, medically."

Marie didn't answer.

"In my experience, when they say 'pretty sure', it means they're sure. They hedge for legal reasons."

She blinked several times as he was speaking, then lay back down on the pillow. She said, "Thank you," softly. Then she stared at the roof of the ambulance for a long time. Thinking about Kieran. Thinking about the doctor. Thinking about her mother and father.

Of all the things in the house, all she would take would be their picture; her mother and father holding her and smiling at her from their silver frame.

The siren whooped to life again, dying out after ten seconds.

"Are we close?" she asked. Her voice was dreamy, her gaze still locked on the roof over her head.

"Getting close. How are you feeling?"

"Tell them no weird drugs when I get there, okay?"

"I can do that. I doubt if you need anything too exotic."

"Seriously," she said.

"Okay. Seriously."

"Nothing that would hurt a baby. I think I may be pregnant."

"You're pregnant?"

She nodded. "I may be. A doctor told me I was."

He smiled at her and shrugged. "Well, a doctor should know."

"Yeah," she said softly, "a doctor should know."

She turned her head to stare out the window, but it was too dark to see anything but distant streetlights. The image of the cliff came back to her; the cliff, the wind, the trees, the orange heat of Crawl's flare, the sound of his terrible song which was inside of her now like a scar and would stay with her, she knew, for all of her life.

Why, she wondered, was he after her and the baby? Was it just revenge? His blaming her uncle for his brother's death so much that he didn't want anybody her uncle cared about to survive?

Or, she thought, maybe Crawl believed more than he admitted that the baby could be a healthy clone of Jesus. Maybe Jesus seemed to him, or God did, to be the biggest traitor of all, the way life played itself out sometimes. She had felt that herself, more than once.

Maybe killing her and the baby seemed like the only way Crawl could swing back.

She was too tired to figure all of that out, though. Crawl had asked her to say a prayer for him, and she would. For Crawl, for the others, for herself, too. God only knew what would happen to her now.

She turned to look again at the officer. He was smiling at her the way her own father was smiling at her in the photo.

She felt so tired.

She closed her eyes.

Her thoughts found Terry, and she wondered what he was doing as she was racing to a hospital after so many people had died. She hoped he would be able to smile at her too, someday. It wouldn't be right away, she knew that. What could he say when he heard about everything that had happened? What would anyone at school say?

She hoped he would still care.

She blinked twice to hold back fresh tears and whispered to the officer, "I think the doctor figured it might be a Christmas baby."

"Well, this is a good hospital," the officer said, smiling again. "They'll take care of you just fine. I promise."

The ambulance slowed. The siren wailed again. This time it stayed on. They turned left around another corner, then turned once more, this time to the right.

The officer peered out the window. "We're here," he said calmly. "ER. I'll see you inside, and then let you get some rest. We'll tell them about the pregnancy, too. Then I'll come back tomorrow and we can talk some more. Is that okay with you?"

"We can talk with Kieran, too," she said quietly. "He'll be well enough to talk with me, right?"

"I'm sure we'll both be talking to him," the officer said. "That should be interesting."

"Yeah, it will." She paused, then said it again. "Yeah. That'll be really interesting."

"Do you have a name picked out for your Christmas baby?"

"I'll know it when the time comes."

"We always do."

The paramedic stepped forward, releasing the clamps holding Marie's stretcher in place, front and rear, as the ambulance slowed to a stop.

"I think it might be a boy," she said.

The officer squeezed her hand. "Well," he said, "I'm sure he'll be something really special."

She squeezed his hand in return, and even shook it lightly, nodding once as the doors of the ambulance swung open. For the first time in a long time, her pale lips showed the beginning of a smile.